THE
CARDINAL
RULE

Also by CE Murphy

The Austen Chronicles
Magic & Manners * Sorcery & Society (forthcoming)

The Heartstrike Chronicles
Atlantis Fallen * Prometheus Bound (forthcoming)
Avalon Rising (forthcoming)

The Walker Papers
Urban Shaman * Winter Moon * Thunderbird Falls
Coyote Dreams * Walking Dead * Demon Hunts
Spirit Dances * Raven Calls * No Dominion
Mountain Echoes * Shaman Rises

The Old Races Universe
Heart of Stone * House of Cards * Hands of Flame
Baba Yaga's Daughter * Year of Miracles * Kiss of Angels

The Worldwalker Duology
Truthseeker * Wayfinder

The Inheritors' Cycle
The Queen's Bastard * The Pretender's Crown

Stone's Throe
A Pulp Adventure

Take A Chance
A Graphic Novel

Roses in Amber
A Beauty and the Beast story

Bewitching Benedict
A Regency Romance

& writing as Murphy Lawless
Raven Heart

THE
CARDINAL
RULE

C.E. MURPHY

a miz kit production

MKP

TITLE
ISBN-13: 978-1-61317-161-5

Cover: Indigo Chick Designs / indigochickdesign.com

The Cardinal Rule was, and remains,
for my grandmother,
Edith Lee Murphy

One

The problem with being a spy was that when it was as breathlessly exciting as the movies made it look, something had gone horribly wrong.

Alisha planted a hand on a hip-height rock wall, vaulted it, and came down hard on a round stone on its far side. Her foot—bare; she'd kicked off her three-inch leather heels the instant she knew she'd been made—slipped. Her ankle twisted and she fell so fast she had no time to think through the tuck and roll. A bullet sang over her head, slicing the air with a supersonic whine. Even in the midst of flight syndrome, she heard that unique sound, and sent a silent thanks toward the stone that had saved her life.

She was back on her feet before she'd really finished falling, running low to the ground. Her ankle throbbed with protest, not broken but objecting to the weight of speed. Alisha ignored the thrums of pain, focusing instead on the sounds around her. From behind were voices, angry men wielding the guns whose bullets winged over her head. The wind shrieked as loudly as the bullets, battering her crouched run. She put her fingers to the ground when she needed the balance, but let the wind buffet her back and forth. Submitting to the strength of its random gusts helped break any patterns in her escape that the gunmen might pick out of the predawn morning.

One other sound, even more critical than shouting men and bullets, thudded at bones behind her ears: the sound of the surf, smashing against cliff faces only sixty yards away. Sixty yards; fifty; forty. She might make it, if flinging herself off a hundred-foot cliff was considered making it.

Another bullet shrieked over her head. Alisha stumbled, forcing herself into another roll. Her ankle protested again as she pushed through to her feet, coming up at an angle from her previous trajectory. Her jacket and skirt were a dark, warm brown that set off her golden skin tones, but in the predawn grayness, all that mattered was that she didn't stand out against the dark like a beacon. A voice lifted in frustration behind her and she huffed a breath of relief. She had thirty yards to go, and they'd lost her. More bullets whined, but they were off to the right, following the path she'd been on, rather than her new one.

The Scottish countryside was not meant to be

raced over in darkness. Unkempt knots of earth appeared without warning, lumps that felt as hard as tree roots against bare toes. Rough-edged stones scraped her feet, though those, at least, didn't hurt too much. Calluses built from years of yoga, practiced barefoot, provided a lot of protection for the soles of her feet. Panicked, early-morning getaways weren't why she practiced the ancient art, but for the moment, Alisha was grateful for any tiny advantage she had.

The ground fell away into divots that sent her tripping and scrambling like a bull in a china shop but it didn't matter, so long as she stayed relatively quiet. The wind would hinder her pursuers as much as it knocked her about, throwing the sounds of her passage in directions she hadn't taken.

Ten yards. The next thirty feet were the critical ones. To make the jump she needed momentum. She couldn't afford to remain crouched, not with the thunderous waves below, ready to grab her and dash her against the cliffs. Alisha straightened up into a full-out run, legs flashing with speed and urgency. Pain sizzled up the big nerve along the outside of her right ankle, the damage from the twist more obvious now that she demanded everything from the injured joint.

"There!" Triumph in the voice behind her. Alisha didn't dare take the time to look over her shoulder, not with twenty—fifteen—feet to go. Eyes lifted, hands straight with sprinter's concentration, she kicked on a burst of speed, trusting adrenaline to get her through the sharpness in her ankle that meant the sprain was worsening with every step. More shots rang out, the deadly chime of air itself protesting the way it was being torn asunder.

Ten feet. Five feet. She gathered herself, thighs bunched, gaze focused far out at sea, far past the body-shattering stones at the foot of the cliffs. *Now,* she thought, and gave her whole being over to the leap from the cliff's edge.

Alisha flew.

For a few seconds it was freedom, pure and glorious. Nothing in the world but herself and the cool early morning air. The wind screamed and cut away any sounds of pursuit, swallowing the howl of bullets chasing after her. It was as honest a moment as Alisha could remember, no one and nothing, not even gravity, holding sway over her. Perfection. Absolute acceptance of the world around her, of who she was, of the choices she'd made to get there freed her from all worry for a few glorious seconds.

Then adrenalized glee set in and she hit reality in a dive, fingers laced together over her head, arms bent just enough that her elbows wouldn't lock and shatter with the impact. The water was cold, breathtaking: for the first seconds it took all Alisha's effort to not inhale with the shock of it. But that would spell her doom, and the data she carried would never make it back to her handler. She struck out blindly, kicking deeper into the water, instead of toward the surface. It would confound her hunters if she didn't come up for air, and down deeper, she might slip between the currents that smashed water against the cliffs.

Her lungs burned as she kicked, panic setting into the hind part of her brain, the need to breathe almost irresistible. Alisha kept one hand extended in front of her, still kicking as hard as she could, and fumbled in her skirt's waistband with the other. There were two discrete pouches there. One held what memory told her looked suspiciously like a wrapped condom. Alisha curled her fingers around that one and brought it to her face, shoving it firmly into her mouth. She kept her mouth closed tightly over it until she'd fit it between her lips and her teeth, like a kid with an orange peel stuck in her mouth. It felt as ungainly and awkward, but it would save her life.

It took an act of pure faith to exhale the last air in her lungs out in a salt-tainted burst of saliva. This time, like every time, there was one frozen moment of sheer animal terror as she dragged a breath in through the cleared pores of the filter, a moment when she expected the technology to fail and for water to flood her lungs.

This time, as it had every time, the breather worked. Damp, salt-flavored air rasped into her lungs. Alisha swallowed a gasp of relief and kicked forward through the freezing water, panic fading into confidence of survival.

With the diminishing of fear came memory. The breather—or one like it—had gotten her into the spy business in the first place. The breather, and Marsa Alam, a village on the Red Sea.

She'd noticed a slight man with an American accent wandering the beach almost daily. He looked dapper, but was far too old—at least in his forties!—for the nineteen-year-old Alisha to be interested in. They'd nodded politely at one another, and to her relief he hadn't seemed to be interested in conversation beyond exchanged hellos. She was there for the scuba diving, not making friends with expatriate Americans.

It was her last day in Marsa Alam when he approached her, diffidently, carrying two of the breathers. "They work like this," he'd said, and showed her how the ungainly little package blossomed into a piece of Bond-like technology. "Try it," he'd offered, and even a decade later, Alisha had to fight off a grin that always threatened laughter when she remembered that moment. He might as well have added, "The first hit is free."

When she'd surfaced two hours later, a little dizzy—the breather, he told her, only provided enough air for about sixty percent lung capacity—she'd wanted to know where on earth she could get one of her own.

"Langley," he said, very mildly, watching Alisha with careful, honest consideration.

And that was it. They'd had her at hello.

Alisha broke the surface when she was no longer struggling for every inch of distance against the current. Her limbs had gone numb, cold water sucking away her body's warmth and threatening her life. Her suit, the jacket long since abandoned and the silk shirt so plastered to her body it might as well have been skin, had no thermal capabilities. She owned clothes that *did*, but they were hanging safely in her closet at home. They were for missions in Russia, or the Andes, not for unexpected deep-water diving off north-coastal Scotland. There were breathers tucked into the waistbands of most of her clothes, or she wouldn't have even had that. She hadn't expected anything to go wrong.

Not that anyone ever did. Alisha spat the breather out and lay on her back in the sea, gasping for deeper breaths. The water, calm after the wind-wracked night, spattered gold and white in the early dawn, and she was grateful that she'd taken that cliff dive at mid-summer. Any other time of year, and it would have killed her through hypothermia. She'd been lucky. Stupid, and lucky.

She lifted her wrist out of the water, sunlight glinting off her watch and picking out the individual silver links that made up the bracelet-like band. It looked delicate and expensive in the morning light, which was half-true: Alisha had seen its like crushed by a bulldozer and come out barely scratched. She pressed a fingernail into a subtle indentation on its outer edge, sinking six inches back into the water before she was able to drop her hand and stabilize herself.

"Cardinal requires extraction." Frustrating words, implying failure, but there would be time for recriminations later. "Coordinates as follows." She read off the GPS coordinates at the bottom of the watch face and closed her eyes with a tired sigh, waiting for the men in black to swoop down and scoop her up.

The helicopter that dragged her out of the water only minutes later was a Seahawk, the same kind that had brought a vomiting Jack Ryan out to the U.S.S. *Dallas*. Alisha lay in a puddle of seawater on its metal floor, eyes half shut against the morning sun, and wondered just how many moments of her life mapped to the spy movies she'd watched growing up. "Not this one, at least." She sat up with a groan, putting the heel of her hand over one eye.

"Not this one at least, what?"

"I don't get sick like Ryan does."

Brief silence—as much silence as could be had in a helicopter—reigned before she heard Greg chuckle. "*The Hunt for Red October.* I'm occasionally astounded that we're able to communicate at all."

Alisha managed a half smile. "You know me too well." Sometimes she thought it was true. The man sitting across from her had brought her in to the CIA ten years earlier. Slight, beginning to bald through his brown curls, with bright eyes behind wire-rimmed glasses, Gregory Parker hadn't changed significantly since he'd first approached her on the beach. Alisha slid her hand away from her eyes to study him. A little more gray in the hair, perhaps, and deeper lines around his mouth, but by and large, he was unchanged.

"I know you well enough to know you don't get sick," he agreed. Polite banter; they had a whole helicopter ride to discuss what had gone wrong with the mission. Alisha was grateful for the respite, however brief, while she warmed up and dried off.

"I get sick." Her argument lacked conviction even to her own ears. "Every time I visit my sister's kids. No mere mortal could stand up to the array of germs those three carry." She shivered and reached behind her head to wring her hair out. Greg leaned forward with a blanket and she wrapped it around her shoulders, lowering her head to her knees. "Thanks."

"You're welcome. Are you all right?"

She nodded, as small a movement as she could make. Despite the noise of the chopper, she could all but hear his eyebrows lifting in disbelief. "Stoicism doesn't become you, Ali."

"Sure it does. Spies are supposed to be stoic." She lifted her head again, tugging the blanket around her shoulders as the ocean fell farther away beneath the helicopter. Greg sat back again, putting his fingertips on a folder beside him on the seat. Alisha followed the gesture with her gaze, then tilted her head back to thunk it against the wall separating her from the pilots. "All right. I'm ready." She wasn't certain it was true. She was still cold and numb, but there was an aura of impatience to Greg's actions, and she couldn't avoid the conversation in the long term.

"What went wrong?"

"Everything. Almost everything." She loosened her grip on the blanket and squirmed her fingers into her waistband again, digging into the second pouch sewn there. A moment later she fished out a tightly-sealed USB stick, holding it up between her fingertips. "I did get the data. I hope a little salt water won't hurt it."

"Even if it did, Erika should be able to clear it up."

"I wish you'd call her Q."

"Ali," Greg said, exasperated. She breathed laughter and, safely wrapped in the blanket, started squirming out of the remains of her wet clothes. Sitting naked beneath the dry wool would be warmer than staying in the wet scraps of silk, but she wouldn't have to: as she wriggled the skirt off Greg leaned across the cabin, popped open a compartment, pulling out black jeans and a black turtleneck sweater. He put them on the seat by Alisha's shoulder and sat back, tapping a finger against the folder by his thigh. "What," he repeated, "went wrong?"

Alisha stood up and pulled the jeans on, swallowing a sigh of relief. They were warm and snug against her legs, which were colder than she'd realized until that moment. The warmth gave her the fortitude she needed to say, "Reichart was there."

Greg's eyelashes fluttered. Alisha hid a wince; for him, the faint change of expression was the equivalent of saying, "Oh, Christ."

Frank Reichart. An Agency problem child, or he would have been, if he'd worked for the Company. He was a freelancer, a mercenary, and he came through with often brilliant intel, well worth the prices he was paid. But he would work for anyone, as long as they met his price. Dark-haired, dark-eyed, dangerous— Alisha shivered, hoping Greg would pass it off to the cold water and wet blouse she still wore.

She was fooling herself. Greg knew her, and knew that despite everything, Alisha found a man like Reichart to be attractive.

Attractive enough that she'd almost married him, once upon a time.

Alisha set her jaw, then lifted her chin in a show of defiance as much against herself as her handler. The relationship with Reichart was long over, and there was no danger of her going back. "He recognized me. I was on my way out, or I wouldn't have gotten anything at all." She sat down across from Greg, moving her feet away from the cold puddle she'd left on the floor. There was no reason for false modesty; the ruins of her blouse, plastered against her chest, didn't hide anything, so she pulled the buttons open and tugged the sticking silk off, drying her shoulders before she reached for the sweater Greg had provided. She used brisk, efficient movements, as if doing so would prevent Greg from saying anything else.

It didn't, of course. Greg exhaled, then pursed his lips. "He ratted you out."

"That suggests we're on the same side." Alisha pulled the sweater over her head, stifling another groan as the warmth enveloped her. She pulled her hair out of the sweater's neck, then made a face and shucked her wet bra from beneath the sweater. Bouncing was better than wet underwires soaking through the wool. "Reichart's not on anybody's side but his own."

"And how do you feel about that?" Greg asked neutrally. Alisha didn't bother to stifle the groan that time, leaning forward with her elbows on her knees and clawing her hair over her shoulder so she could twist it dry. Water fell in a steady dribble, though the tawny blonde curls, dark with water, didn't become noticeably lighter as the water petered out into drops against helicopter's metal floor.

"Good," she said to the puddle. "I feel good about it. It helps me sleep at night." She looked up, eyebrows lifted in challenge. "You're my handler, Greg, not my shrink. Don't worry, all right? I can handle Reichart."

"Does he know why you were there?"

Alisha gave him a flat look. "Yes. We had a nice cup of tea and some lovely raspberry scones and I told him all about the mission before he called the guards and they chased me over a cliff. But don't worry. I don't think I gave away any *really* important matters of national security."

Greg lifted his hands in apology. Alisha held him with her frown a few seconds longer, then shook her head, picking up the blanket again to rub it over her hair. "I downloaded a lot of data, Greg. They'll know what servers I hit, but there's a lot of information there, and I wasn't picky about what I collected. I may have been compromised, but I don't think the mission data was. I haven't spoken to him in years. Nor do I intend to."

Greg nodded a distracted apology, ex- amining the USB stick Alisha had handed him. It showed no visible damage, but Alisha had never tried drowning one before. Greg shrug- ged after a moment, then pulled a laptop out of a compartment above his head, turning it on. Alisha fumbled for the seat belt as she let her head fall against the back of the seat. "What's next? Home for debriefing?"

"Only if the data is corrupted." Greg fit the USB into the port and took a breath, holding it as he waited to see if it read, or if it its seal had been compromised."

"All right." Alisha closed her eyes, letting herself drift. The endless racket of helicopter blades was oddly soothing, as if the noise somehow signified safety she couldn't find in other places. *You've spent too much time in choppers, Leesh,* she told herself, but the admonishment didn't stop her from settling into a half-aware state of sleep. Flashes of Reichart's startled expression when he'd spotted her darted through her memory, too-clear imprints in her mind. The man had magnificent cheekbones and a mouth full enough to be feminine. Eminently kissable, that mouth. And his hair was longer. Just a little, but it looked good on him.

Even half-asleep, Alisha severed that line of thought as efficiently as a surgeon might cut through muscle, removing its emotional content. Frank Reichart was, at the most, nothing more than a job to her. Once that had been different, but not now. And if she needed a reminder of why, a Reichart-instigated compromise followed by a cliff dive did the trick nicely. Alisha let the memory go.

Compartmentalization: she'd been taught to put her emotions in one tidy package, locked away where they couldn't interfere with the job; the job and what needed to be done in another neat analytical package, far away from sentiment and passion.

Alisha loathed it. Slicing up emotion, tucking it away from the guts and punches of her daily life, of the job, felt like denying her own humanity. Not that she would ever admit that to Greg, or any of the Agency psychoanalysts. Maintaining emotional distance from her job and the people she encountered was critical, in their eyes.

So she'd found a way around it.

She called the illegal journals she wrote out in messy cursive on hand-made paper her Strongbox Chronicles. She used fountain pens that blotched and stained her fingers when she wrote, as if the old-fashioned pens and the tediously made paper grounded her, made everything more real, than smoother, more modern tools would. Those pages held her fears and her frustrations, the things that had gone wrong and right with each mission, full of the passion that drove her to do the job she did. They were a dangerous luxury; any one of them, found by the wrong person, could compromise not just Alisha, but sometimes dozens of other agents and assets.

So she never wrote them until the mission was over, usually taking one long night to scrawl out all the emotion that an official report couldn't afford to have. In the morning, when the notes were finished, she would find a bank and open a safety deposit box under her current alias. She'd left dozens of chronicles around the world that way, never going back for them. They felt like leaving traces of the truth behind, a promise to herself that her clandestine life had left at least one mark that someday might be discovered and understood.

Counter to the point of being a spy, perhaps, but she did it anyway.

Greg drew in a sharp breath, audible beneath the sound of the chopper blades. Alisha roused herself from introspective thoughts, coming fully awake with concern. "Greg?"

"You won't be going back to Langley."

Which meant the new mission was important, and immediate. Alisha sat back, shoulders relaxing. The opportunity for action, the chance to not have to think, was always better than hours spent cooped up on a plane replaying the last mission. Alisha doubted everyone found the prospect of imminent danger to be relaxing, but for her a new mission was always a chance to shed the skin of daily life. It was as freeing as the jump off the cliff, in its own way. "What's the job?"

"You're going into a Kazakhstani base to cozy up to an American scientist."

Alisha felt a little core of excitement build in her stomach, spreading out through her body to warm her in a way the dry clothes couldn't. "What's my cover?"

"You're a potential buyer for the project he's working on. Your name is Elisa Moon. The details are in the mission brief." He handed her the folder he'd kept at his side.

Alisha flipped it open, glancing at Greg before looking at the file. "And what's his name?"

"Brandon." Greg fell silent a moment before inhaling deeply. "Brandon Parker."

Alisha's chin came up, a sharp action that betrayed her surprise. "Your *son*?"

Two

Greg's mouth thinned as he looked away. Alisha closed the briefing folder and sat a few moments, looking out the window as she absorbed Greg's news. The early morning sunlight had lost dawn's soft edge and glared across the ocean below, making sharp lines of the few clouds on the horizon, like a child's sketch. Brandon himself had been an artist; she'd seen an old, solitary drawing of him on Greg's desk, a picture of a light-eyed young man with an air of impatient intelligence about him. The drawing was labeled at the bottom: *B., self-portrait at 19,* with the scrawl of his signature beside it. Alisha had often wondered how idealized the drawing was: in it, Brandon Parker was extremely attractive, features more angular than his father's, even if he was still a little baby-faced. There was less babyish about his broad-shouldered swimmer's build. She might have drawn herself that way, as if seen through a fun-house mirror that showed only the most flattering reflections.

"I thought you were estranged," she said carefully. "You told me a long time ago that you and he didn't speak."

Greg had said more than that, though it seemed neither appropriate nor necessary to remind him of that. He'd called Brandon arrogant and self-centered, with no eye for the bigger picture. Naturally, Alisha had broken a rule or two and checked the CIA's files on Brandon Parker.

The aura of intelligence given by his portrait barely touched on the man's potential, according to his file. He understood mathematics as instinctively as breathing. At nine—with the comparatively pathetic equipment available to him twenty years earlier—he'd hacked into his own father's CIA file and discovered the truth about what his dad did for a living. The Agency had chosen to develop the boy's skills, and he'd been groomed since childhood to become a spy.

But Brandon Parker had other ideas about what to do with his life. Not long after Alisha had been recruited—well before there was a chance she might ever meet him—Brandon had...defected.

Defect had an ugly enough ring to it that Alisha shied away from the word, even in her own thoughts. He hadn't *defected*, really. He hadn't gone to work for another intelligence agency. Like Reichart, he'd become a free-lancer, working for the highest bidder. When Alisha had read his file, it suggested his latest employer was having him work on a new computer chip—a piece of technology that literally encoded atoms, teleporting data from one place to another in an instantaneous transport. Called quantum computing, it had sounded like science fiction to her, until a news report mentioned the breakthrough technology and the anticipated price it would go for. If Brandon Parker was bringing in even a cut of the deal, he was a very wealthy man.

But that had been years ago. Parker's trail had gone cold. His latest project, if there was one, was so secret that no one had been able to find him or his sponsors.

Until, it appeared, now. Alisha leaned forward, touching Greg's forearm as the copter banked and brought the hazy British coast into view. "Greg?"

Greg exhaled and let emotion go: when he turned back to Alisha, his expression was the familiar careworn smile that she'd come to know over her career in the Agency. The smile that masked whatever went on beneath, and always had. "You're right, we don't speak. I haven't talked to him in years. Long enough that I doubt he knows about you. He never had much interest in my work, even when we were both involved in the Agency. His focus was always the laboratory. It's imperative, Ali, that he doesn't know you're working for me."

"It's imperative," she pointed out dryly, "that nobody knows I'm CIA. Even on my worst day,

I don't think I'd just happen to let it slip that Gregory Parker happened to be my handler. I mean, really, Greg. It would lack subtlety. But if you're concerned about it, why send me?"

Greg's expression tightened minutely. "You were recommended."

The tone sparked Alisha's curiosity, but left no room for further questioning. She studied her handler for a moment, then nodded. "All right. What's he working on?"

"A piece of new military technology. We think it's a rudimentary artificial intelligence, probably an AI that could potentially be sent into battle in lieu of human beings."

"We have the Talon robots already." Alisha pressed her lips together. "But those are remote control battle machines. I didn't think real AI was more than theoretically possible." She waved his response off before he spoke. "But that's why you say rudimentary, I assume."

Greg closed his computer most of the way, tapping a finger twice on its surface. "Our own military developers haven't gotten all that far with AIs, despite having extensive development budgets. Brandon is brilliant, but we think we're fairly safe in assuming his project isn't too much more sophisticated than our own."

Alisha twisted her hair again. Another line of water dribbled out of thick curls. Unmatting them later would take forever. "I thought his trail had gone cold. Where did we get the intel on this project?"

"My orders came from above." Which meant that the source was sufficiently confidential that not even he knew who'd brought it in. Alisha was accustomed to not always knowing who or what prompted her missions. It was part of the job, which didn't make it rankle any less. She wondered if Greg, privy to a higher level of security, found it as frustrating to be in the dark as she often did. There was no sign of it in his voice, but then, there wouldn't be.

"We went into the observatory to corroborate the information Director Boyer had been given." Greg opened the screen again, turning the computer to face Alisha. Satellite photos filled the screen, zooming in on pictures of a military complex. Greg keyed forward, flipping through more pictures. Individuals became visible, faces Alisha didn't recognize, until Greg pulled up a third screen.

Brandon Parker had aged from a college-polished youth into a more rugged outdoorsman. Stubble graced his chin and his cheekbones were gaunter, but he'd filled out, and the drab, loose-fitting paramilitary colors he wore couldn't disguise the strength in the lines of his body. Alisha studied the photos a few moments before glancing up at Greg.

"I thought the St. Abbs observatory took pictures of outer space, not surveillance photos on the planet's surface."

Greg made a face. "It's been an MI-6 installation since it was opened in 1972. They do a lot of real astronomy to keep their cover, of course, but...."

Alisha shook her head, amused, but her smile faded almost instantly. "I thought MI-6 was on our side, Greg. Why didn't we just ask for the photos?"

Greg's good humor fled as well. "Because the British government still has obligations to the European Union that may not be in our best interests. My superiors—*our* superiors," he emphasized, "would prefer it if we were able to contain Brandon and his latest project without any outside interference."

"I don't like it."

A faint, sardonic smile twitched Greg's lips. "That doesn't matter."

Alisha spread her hands. "I know. I'd just rather have it out in the open than let it fester." She shrugged, letting her concerns pass from her with the motion. It *didn't* matter; she would do her job and do it well, but dillydallying around the truth did no one any good.

"I appreciate your candor."

"Do you?" Alisha asked. He'd said the words before and she'd accepted them at face value, but curiosity suddenly caught her and she watched his expression for the answer.

It came with a wash of surprise that lit Greg's blue eyes to pale gray. "Actually, yes, I do. I'd rather work with an agent who put her opinions on the line than kept them hidden. If you've got a bad feeling about something, I'd be irresponsible to not listen." He paused. "*Do* you have a bad feeling about this?"

"No." Alisha spoke without taking a moment to think, then shook her head. There was no itch along her spine, no flat taste of copper at the back of her throat that told her something was genuinely wrong with the situation. A trained espionage agent wasn't supposed to rely on hunches and gut feelings, only cold hard facts. She had never believed it, and doubted most of her superiors did either. Intuition was as much part of the job as carrying a gun. "I just don't like going behind MI-6's back. I appreciate the whys, I just don't like it. It's fine."

"Good. The base is in Kazakhstan. You'll be going in as a potential buyer for the combat drones." Greg turned his gaze to the view below the helicopter, which was fast leaving ocean behind in favor of coastal towns and European forests. "Your objective, Alisha..."

"I know it's in here, if you'd prefer me to go over the mission myself." Alisha put her hand over the briefing folder, her heart aching for her handler. Sending in an agent he'd trained, one with whom he had an almost filial relationship, after his actual son couldn't be easy. The conflict set her stomach to churning, and it wasn't even hers to live with.

"It's better if I tell you. That way if there are any questions you won't feel awkward about approaching me with them."

"Greg, you've been my handler for almost ten years. I wouldn't feel awkward." Even as she said it, Alisha wondered if it was true. She'd never felt such sympathy for Greg's plight before.

"Thank you." He looked back at her with the fond, patient smile again. "Your mission objectives are as follows. First, you're to obtain the prototype drone schematics we believe they have in development. Second, destroy any research that you can't take with you. Third, obtain the drone itself if it's moved into an operational phase. And fourth..." Now Greg hesitated. Alisha pressed her lips together and waited, unwilling to push him. Greg put his chin to his chest briefly, then lifted his gaze again. "Fourth, determine if Brandon Parker is a clear and present danger to the security of the United States, and report back to not only me, but Director Boyer on your assessment."

Alisha felt her eyebrows shoot up again, surprise surging through her with unexpected strength. "Director Boyer, sir?" Only surprise or anger brought out the formality of calling Greg 'sir', and he knew it. She bit down on a smile that confessed to being aware of the tell, and he returned a similar expression that showed his tension clearly.

"The operation is Boyer's. Given my proximity to the situation, I recommended that I not be the first or only person you were to report to on this topic."

"*You* recommended, sir?" She'd done it again. Alisha ducked her head, humorously horrified at herself, and looked up unable to contain her laughter. It helped take some of the urgency away from the conversation, helped remove a little of the difficulty from the topic. "That was—"

"It was covering my own ass, Agent Mac-Aleer," Greg said bluntly. "I don't trust myself in this, and I'd rather make it clear to my superiors that the situation is better handled by someone else."

"Of course, having done that, you prove yourself all the more trustworthy," Alisha pointed out.

Greg turned his palms up. "I didn't say it didn't have its benefits."

Alisha nodded and turned her attention back to the heavy folder. She had a lot to learn about Brandon Parker, and her own cover story to familiarize herself with, and, if Greg's quiet urgency was any indicator, not a lot of time to do it in.

"Alisha."

She lifted her eyes, brows crinkled. "Yes?"

"There's one other thing." Gregory took a deep breath. "If, in your assessment, Brandon is a danger, and the situation warrants it..."

A chill that had nothing to do with her swim in the Atlantic spread over Alisha's body, lifting goose bumps beneath the sweater sleeves and making the tiny fine hairs on her cheeks stand up. "Yes?" Her voice remained steady and cool, the result of years of training, although the coldness she felt admitted she knew the next words Gregory Parker would say.

"If necessary, you have the authority to terminate Brandon Parker with extreme prejudice."

Alisha turned her face away, fully aware that her expression changed not at all. *Compartmentalization,* she mocked herself silently. *A very good show, Leesh. Fool them all.*

She'd only been given such authority twice before in her career, and the first had come to nothing. The second—

"You have the authority to terminate the subject with extreme prejudice." The words echoed in Alisha's mind, heartless and intense. *The subject. The subject* was a thing, not a person, not a living, breathing woman.

Not Cristina.

Alisha rejected all her training, forcefully, when it came to Cristina. Even now, she wouldn't allow herself to think of the woman who'd once been her partner as merely *the subject.* Lovely, fair-haired Cristina Lamken, who killed herself rather than face a life of imprisonment.

Or maybe, Alisha thought for the thousandth time, maybe Cristina had killed herself to save Alisha from having to do it.

They had been friends once, best friends, what seemed like a lifetime ago. Before Cristina, brave, intelligent Cristina, had proven herself a double agent. Her loyalties lay not with the CIA, but with the Russian FSB, the intelligence agency that had come into play after the KGB shattered with the rest of the Soviet Union.

Alisha could not forget, *would* not let herself forget, the fragile smile Cristina had given her, in the moment before she plunged off the Peruvian mountainside. There were a thousand things in that smile: determination, fear, regret, desperation. Maybe even apology. For what she was about to do, or just possibly, for what she had done.

The worst of it, though, had been the understanding in Cristina's eyes. There was no other way for it to end. They'd been partners and best friends, and they were, at the core of it, enemies. The last sight Alisha had of her closest confidante was down the barrel of a loaded .45, and Cristina's blue eyes were understanding. Cristina knew, as vividly as Alisha did, that it would have taken very little for the situation to be reversed. It could easily have been Alisha standing on the precarious lip of earth, three thousand feet of empty air only a stumble away. It could have been Cristina looking down the barrel of the gun, knowing she had to choose between her country and her friend.

Alisha had pulled the trigger an instant too late. Cristina was already falling, backward with her arms spread, a glorious fatal dive into the cold air. And the look in her eyes had been one of understanding. *It's all right,* it had said, *I*

*know. You have to do this. This is how it ends, for
people like us.*

Every day since then, Alisha had wondered
if she'd seen forgiveness in Cristina's eyes as
well.

If, had she been at the other end of the gun,
there would have been understanding in her
own eyes.

If there would have been forgiveness.

"Alisha?"

Alisha drew in a sharp breath, pulling
herself from the reverie of memory to look
back at Greg. Hard sunlight glinted off water
below, sending bright blinding streaks through
the helicopter's bay door. It was enough for an
excuse to brush away tears, but none had even
sprung to Alisha's eyes. There was still ragged
pain and betrayal in thoughts of Cristina, but it
had never come to tears. She had too much
anger, or not enough willingness to let go. "I'm
fine," she said aloud. "The mission's clear."

"Are you all right?" Greg's voice was gentle;
he knew as well as Alisha did that permission to
terminate would bring to mind one person only.

"Fine," Alisha repeated, and put on a brief,
edged smile. "It's all right, Greg. Sometimes
that's how it ends, for people like us."

"Sometimes," he agreed, then nodded at the
briefing he'd handed her. "We'll be landing
soon. Get to work, Cardinal. Memorize your
cover story. You're going in as soon as we can
arrange it."

Three

"Thank you! It was a wonderful flight!" Bellowed over the roar of helicopter engines and whipping blades, the thick liquid sounds of the Russian language sounded alien inside Alisha's mouth, as if she shouted garbled nonsense into the wind that swept down off the Ural mountains. The pilot she spoke to, however, offered a broad smile of understanding and cut her a little bow of thanks in return. Then he gestured, not bothering to out-shout the engines. Alisha followed the line of his pantomime to a group of men standing at the edge of the chopper pad.

Several were guards, hanging back a few steps from the man who led them. Alisha took them in briefly—five, all armed, none of them looking soft or approachable in fatigues and berets—and turned her attention to the sixth man.

Brandon Parker was different yet again from the recent photos she'd seen, his blond hair cropped in a near-military cut and the shadow of beard gone from his jaw. He wore khakis and a white T-shirt beneath a drab, olive green Army coat that snapped around his lips as the helicopter blades chopped the air. He leaned into the wind, hands in his pockets, then saw Alisha looking his way and raised a hand in greeting as he came forward. "Elisa Moon?"

As if she might be anyone else. Alisha nodded, taking a few steps away from the helicopter and yelling, "Brandon Parker?" back, no more needing a verification of his identity than he'd needed for her.

"At your service! Come on," he shouted. "This is no place for a conversation!" He lifted one hand and snapped his fingers twice, an imperious order to the guards. Two nodded in response, ducking forward toward the helicopter to unload the two small bags she'd brought with her. Alisha smiled her thanks at the closer guard. There was no harm in trying to make a few friends among the ranks, although the strong-jawed young man gave her no response other than a curt nod. Alisha shrugged mentally and followed the man who had greeted her.

"Welcome to Kazakhstan," he said the moment they were far enough from the chopper to be heard reasonably. "Sorry for all the military presence." He waved his hand at the guards, who fell in place around them as if it were natural.

"I have ID—" Alisha reached for her purse, stopped by Parker's explosive snort.

"You wouldn't be here at all if you weren't who you said you were."

"Of course not." Alisha pulled her wallet out anyway, offering it. Brandon flipped it open, gave it a cursory glance, then handed it back.

"I'm convinced." He put on a look of mock injury, offering his hand a second time. "Now will you shake my hand? Or shall I provide my own identification first?"

"That won't be necessary, Dr. Parker." Alisha took his hand, smiling back. The hand-shake: always a test. A test for _her_, not for the people she met.

"You're smart," Greg had said to her once, when she'd asked why he'd recruited her to the CIA. But smart had only been part of it, and he'd thrown that answer out almost before he said it. "You're _strong_."

Deceptively strong, Alisha would have said. She'd always had good upper body strength, able to out arm-wrestle her older sister since they were children. She'd discovered yoga as a teenager, and through that art had developed considerably more physical strength than women were expected to have. It gave her an advantage she loved to exploit.

So, for an instant, when Brandon Parker closed his fingers around hers, she was tempted to squeeze his hand until he under-stood how much strength she commanded. It was _always_ a temptation, although she never gave into it. There was no point in giving away one of her greatest advantages at the beginning of the game.

And Brandon's handshake gave her no reason to prove herself. It was firm and solid, expecting reasonable strength in response: not the fragile thing some men used, as if by her very femininity she might shatter from his touch. Alisha smiled again, never missing a beat. "It's a pleasure, Dr. Parker."

"The pleasure is mine, Ms. Moon. Although I must say, given your employers, you're not what we might have expected."

"You mean I'm young, an American and a woman."

Brandon's gaze flickered over her, appraising her both as a woman and a threat. Everything about her presentation played up the first and downplayed the second: she wore a professionally tailored skirt and low heels that set off the curve of her calf without being dangerous to run in. Her blouse was soft and melded against her skin as wind snapped and billowed around her. She'd deliberately foregone her suit jacket, to enhance a deceptive look of delicacy. Her hair was swept back in a chignon from which a few pincurls escaped, framing her temples. With her slender frame, she knew she looked breakable, as if the gusting wind could sweep her up and dash her against the mountainside. The only flaw in the projection was the bandage that wrapped her right ankle, providing support for the strained tendons there.

But Brandon Parker's assessment seemed to follow the lines it was supposed to, though his eyes lingered on the wrapped ankle. "A lovely woman. This way, please." He gestured toward a small convoy of older military vehicles, waiting at the far edge of the helicopter pad. "You don't look like someone who would be working for an Arabic consortium, Ms. Moon."

"That's very much the idea. If my employers wish to distance themselves from me, my very appearance and heritage provides them with plausible deniability." She climbed into the middle vehicle, an English-style jeep with the drive mechanism on the right. Brandon held the door for her and she leaned forward, watching him walk around the vehicle before she spoke again. "If I may...I didn't expect them to send their resident genius out to meet me. I spoke with a General Hashikov to make these arrangements, a Russian man—" She arched her eyebrows, genuine curiosity behind the question.

"Ah, yeah." Brandon pulled the jeep door closed behind him and thumped the driver's seat as indication they were ready to go. "Ukrainian, actually. His head spins if you say he's Russian. He runs the military side of the base. The cover for our development work, essentially."

"Ukrainian," Alisha murmured, nodding as if making note of the information. She already knew, of course, that Hashikov had been a young soldier when the USSR had fallen, and had climbed the ranks through the disaffected era that followed, carrying on his duty under a flag he had, perhaps, felt very little loyalty to; when opportunity to profit outside the military's chain of command, he'd turned his back on a life-long career with no evident regrets. Like many born under Soviet rule, Hashikov held his true nationality dear to his heart, and Alisha would never have called him Russian to his face. Still, offering Brandon Parker an opportunity to establish himself as a confidant was a good way to begin earning his trust. "I'll remember," Alisha said. "Thank you."

"No problem. I doubt you'll meet him, at least if he can avoid it. He doesn't like lay people."

"In that case, I'll be sure not to get laid."

Brandon shot her a startled look that dissolved into laughter. Alisha held up her hands, grinning. "Forgive me. That was entirely unprofessional, and I'm here representing some men with a great deal of power and money. I will," she said, schooling her features into solemnity, "behave myself. But if it's necessary I will speak with General Hashikov regarding your work and its military applications. With no offense meant, sir, you're a developer, and the general is a military man. As an interested buyer, it's imperative for me to have as broad and comprehensive an understanding of your work as is possible."

Cool steel crept into her voice by the end of her speech, all the laughter gone from her eyes.

She could see it in Brandon's expression as clearly as she could hear the tone modulations as she spoke. From sweet flirty thing to combatant inside a sentence, she congratulated herself. *Way to scare 'em, Leesh.*

Leesh. Only one person had ever called her by that nickname. Everyone at the Company called her *Ali*; everyone had always called her that, as long as she could remember. But Frank Reichart had ferreted out the nickname she had for herself: *Leesh,* the tough girl. Combat pilot, biker babe, the cool head in the face of danger. *Ali* was more fragile, the flirty woman who could convince men to lay a jacket over a puddle for her, a princess in a tower to protect. Alisha thought that was pushing compartmentalization far—*more* than far—enough, but it did help to be able to switch from one to another when the situation called for it. Almost everyone—even Greg, who should have known better—responded to soft flirtatious Ali, and Alisha wasn't above taking advantage of it. It made hard-core Leesh that much more effective, as proven by Brandon's brief flicker of a smile.

"I see now why you're the woman for the job, Ms. Moon. I imagine you're underestimated a lot."

"Hazard of the profession, Dr. Parker." *Ali,* Alisha thought. *Leesh.* It didn't matter which name she thought of herself as. Put them together and she got herself: Alisha MacAleer.

And she was the one who woke up with nightmares when things went wrong.

The drive up the mountainside to the base was horrifyingly dramatic. The road was a rough, one-lane gravel strip cut against the mountain. Alisha couldn't see the shoulder beneath the Jeep's body, only the thousand-foot drop down to the glacier-formed valley below. The mountain was close enough to touch on the left-hand side of the convoy as well, rough stone brambled with stubborn bushes determined to eke life out of a barren surface.

One good shove and there'd be nothing between her and the valley floor.

The memory of Cristina's eyes in the last moment of her life flashed through Alisha's mind. She shivered and wrapped her arms around herself, wishing it was cold enough to claim that as her excuse.

Perhaps it was. Brandon made a motion toward shrugging his suit jacket off, as if to give it to her. Alisha shook her head. "It's not the cold." She took a deep breath, glanced out the window, and lied, "I'm afraid of heights."

Brandon clucked his tongue. "I'd have put you on the left if I'd known that."

Alisha looked back at him to offer her thanks, and smiled suddenly, a real smile. Brandon's cheeks had paled, the pulse in his throat now suddenly higher. He honestly didn't like heights, and the noble offer alarmed him. "Thank you for the thought," Alisha murmured. "I'll be all right. In the meantime, are we free to speak about your project here?" She cut a glance toward the driver, then back to Brandon, her eyebrows lifted in question.

"We are. Please, feel free. I've got a demonstration set up once we arrive, but any questions you have now, of course." He spread his hands in invitation. Long fingers, Alisha noted; well-shaped nails, and strength in the quick way he used his hands. His CIA training would have taught him to make those hands a weapon. Alisha looked down at her own hands, all tapered fingernails and evident softness. Like Brandon, she was built to deceive. The question was, who would see beneath the surface fastest and best.

"In order for your so-called artificial intelligences to be most useful, they'll need to be both rapidly programmed and yet resistant to hacking." She chose her words carefully, focus tuned to the scientist beside her instead of a study of hands. Brandon let out a low laugh that said he knew she was challenging him by casting doubt on the AI aspect of his work.

"The process I've developed depends on a coding written in ordinary English, a series of if-then statements which allow a drone to assess terrain, likelihood of risk and the best way to proceed with that information." He shot Alisha a sideways look to see if she was following him, as much a test as the one she'd laid out.

"Programmers have been trying to successfully create plain English code for years. Decades."

"I succeeded." For the first time, his demeanor slid toward the egotistical, blunt tone blurring the line between utter confidence and arrogance. "More importantly, the program learns from its mistakes, and propagates what it's learned."

Alisha's shoulder blades pinched together, changing her whole posture as her eyebrows rose in surprise. "You're saying that one of these drones could conceivably teach another?"

"Exactly!" Arrogance evaporated into or smug delight. Brandon twisted in his seat to face her, hands spread in explanation. "As for the hacking aspect, the AI's wifi frequency changes randomly every few seconds on a logarithmic pattern established by a subset of the program. Every drone updates its frequency change at the same time, so there's no lag, but the cycle is too fast for anything shy of another AI to break into."

Alisha pursed her lips, more impressed than she wanted to be. "I'm impressed." If your prototype lives up to your pitch, Dr. Parker..."

If it lived up to his pitch, American military intelligence and development was desperately behind Brandon's curve. Moreover, he was obviously the clear and present danger that his father had feared he might be.

"It will. It's the culmination of years of work," Parker said rather grandiosely.

Alisha tilted her chin up, curiosity wrinkling her forehead. "I thought your previous projects involved quantum computing. Or—" she interrupted his indrawn breath before he had the chance to explain "—or does the prototype work on one of your quantum chips?"

A hint of a smile curved the near corner of Brandon's mouth. "What, after all, is the speed of thought? Is it faster than light? We make so many decisions so rapidly, every day, some physical, some psychological. How to keep from falling: an instinctive balance reaction, but a decision nonetheless. In order to create a truly viable combat intelligence, it needed to be able to think as quickly, for equally minute, yet vital tasks. I had to begin with the chip. All the brilliant programming in the world wouldn't matter if the chip couldn't handle the processing power necessary to make an artificial intelligence possible. I've been working on the theories since childhood."

Not according to his CIA records. Alisha bit her tongue on the comment, though curiosity flared in her. She'd taken Brandon's records at face value, but it was wholly possible he'd been working on projects so secret that his files were a cover story. She would have to look into it more closely.

Later, though. Right now, Brandon was still talking, and she brought her attention back to him as he said, "...uses infrared to determine whether a target is armed and should be dealt with using deadly methods, or if subdual is sufficient."

"Subdual?"

"It's rather amazing how badly incapacitated a human being can be by appropriate usage of sound waves. Okay." He straightened in his seat, gesturing ahead as the jeep went around a sharp curve that revealed a bleak fortress cut into the mountains. "Here we are, Ms. Moon. The heart of Project ACUTE."

Four

Alisha's eyebrows rose as a smile curved her lips. "'ACUTE'?"

"Artificial Combat Utility Experiment, capital U-T in utility. I can't decide if it implies the drones are soft and fuzzy and adorable, or all sharp angles."

"Which are they?" Alisha listened to his description with half an ear as the Jeep drew into the complex. Concrete walls with barbed wire fences atop them cut the road in half, bleak gates pulling open to allow passage. They swung shut behind the vehicles, ponderous creaking over the wail of mountainside winds. Alisha glanced over her shoulder to watch youthful men in uniform slam bars down across the inner wall of the gates. They came to attention again as soon as they'd finished, and Alisha turned her attention forward.

A valley spread out before them, empty fields that housed the buildings of the military base. "It doesn't look like a military base." As soon as the words were out, she shook her head. "It doesn't look like a place you'd expect to find one," she amended.

"No," Brandon agreed. "It's pretty, isn't it?"

Alisha tilted in her seat to squint at the mountaintops, sweeping above the complex to tips that looked sharp enough to slice a fingertip on. Gray and green scrubby spruce trees crept two-thirds of the way up the mountain-sides, petering out to bare rock, brown and gray under the blustery sky. Closer to the base itself, there were more deciduous trees, leaves so stirred by the wind Alisha imagined she could hear the hiss and bustle even over the Jeep's engine. The land itself spoke of strength and determination, mountains looming as if to remind the small creatures that peopled their feet that they were merely mortal, and looked on the face of eternity. "It's magnificent," Alisha murmured. "And what's that?" She nodded ahead, where a glint of silver against a partially constructed stone wall caught her eye.

"That," Brandon said, sounding anticipatory, "is our demonstration, Ms. Moon." He thumped the side of the driver's seat and the Jeep veered off its course to the main buildings, bouncing through fields that were deceptively smooth to the eye. Alisha heard Brandon's apology gritting through his teeth as she clung to the armrest in order to keep her seat.

"Pity this job doesn't cover dental," she muttered, not entirely intending to be overheard.

Brandon shot her a look of wry humor as the driver slowed the vehicle to a halt some fifty feet away from a solitary man standing in the field. "I'll make the rash assumption that the compensations are otherwise worthwhile, or you wouldn't be doing it."

Alisha laughed, enjoying Brandon Parker's company far too much. That made him dangerous, and made staying professional that much more vital.

But it would be better to bring him in rather than be forced to terminate him. Not just because he was Greg Parker's son, but because a man of his talent and intelligence could once again be an incredibly valuable asset to the CIA. If the attraction was mutual—and, she thought, with a tinge of old bitterness, cash dollars weren't quite as important to him as they'd been to Frank Reichart—there might be a way through this mission that would leave everyone satisfied.

Alisha clamped down on a smile and refused to allow herself to linger on the idea of satisfaction. "You would be correct." She nodded toward the man in the field. "And that would be... ?"

"Rafe Denison, my assistant. Couldn't do any of this without him." Brandon swung out of the vehicle, jogging around to be a little too late to open Alisha's door for her. She gave him a brief nod thanks regardless, inspecting first the rolling terrain, and then her low-heeled shoes.

"I noticed your ankle," Brandon said diplomatically as he offered an arm. Alisha considered the gesture momentarily before slipping her hand through his elbow.

"Thanks. I twisted it trying on heels at a shoe sale." She and gave him the best rueful smile she could summon up. Brandon laughed, and she thought, *don't get a lot of single women up here, do you?* without letting it anywhere near her expression. All the better for her if they didn't. No former CIA agent would be easy pickings, but if a little girlish idiocy smoothed the way, Alisha was happy to make use of it.

Rafe Denison was a small man, slender enough to look breakable, and had floppy hair, bright eyes, and somewhat unfortunate teeth. Alisha shook his hand, assessing his assertiveness as nearly non-existent. "It's a pleasure to meet you, Dr. Denison. I've read a lot about you."

"The pleasure is mine, Ms. Moon." He was as English as his teeth, voice cultured, though lit with curiosity. "Dare I ask what you've read?"

Alisha curled a brief smile. "You worked for World Electronics for seven years, the first two of which were during your final years of college. You were working on a graduate program, sponsored by WE, when you had what's politely referred to as a change of focus and left the company without warning." She lifted an eyebrow. "How am I doing so far?"

Rafe Denison's bright gaze held no surprise. "Very well. What do they call it in less polite company?"

"A complete fucking meltdown." Alisha chose the abrupt, harsh words deliberately, pulling no punches. Rafe's eyes narrowed very slightly before he nodded once in acknowledgment. "The company still mourns your loss, in fact," Alisha went on. "I understand you were doing breakthrough programming—"

Denison made a moue. "That's debatable."

"They said you were modest." Alisha brushed away her own comment as well as his with a flicker of her fingers. "Breakthrough programming work. Developing a software compression program that I don't fully understand," she admitted. "But I gather the idea was to render data storage to such small and manageable sizes that enormous programs could be carried on flash drives. But you left the WE umbrella and disappeared off the radar."

"For a variety of personal reasons," Denison said in an utterly aloof tone.

"Because of your brother." Alisha still spoke deliberately, watching the slim man. Denison's younger brother had died in Iraq, and he'd left World Electronics within weeks. His nostrils flexed, making a thin pinch of his nose and stiffening his upper lip. "I don't mean to bring up painful memories," Alisha murmured. Denison's face lost none of its tension, though he exhaled a disbelieving laugh.

"You fully mean to bring up painful memories, Ms. Moon. Yes, my brother's death is among the things that made me decide to change careers. He was only twenty, the baby of the family, as you Americans would say. I would do anything to prevent another family from suffering that kind of loss."

"Anything?"

Denison's face creased with bleak humor. "I believe I would do anything within my power, yes. Hence my involvement with Project ACUTE. I can hope the drones might lead to a lessening of human cost in senseless wars. I think my brother would have liked that."

This was another dangerous man. Alisha studied him, fitting him into the hierarchy of the AI development program. Dangerous, if he had the strength of his convictions, but naive, if he really believed that selling mechanical warriors to the highest bidder would prevent the wars that had cost his younger brother his life. Alisha wondered if he really did think their drones would make the world a safer place.

Not that it mattered. It was her job to make sure no one but the United States government had access to those blueprints and plans, or to their creator. Denison's work seemed to lie in the project's storage capacity. While astoundingly useful, it wasn't the critical part of the development, and she was fairly confident he couldn't replicate the drones themselves, not on his own.

She turned back to Brandon, whose expression lay between admiring and alarmed. "Should I ask what you know about me, Ms. Moon?"

"We're going to be working together for a few days," Alisha said with a smile. "You may as well call me Elisa. And only," she added, eyebrows lifted again, "if you want to know."

"I suppose you'd want to know what I knew about you then, huh?"

Alisha laughed, shaking her head. "A woman likes to pretend her life isn't an open book, Dr. Parker. Indulge me. Allow me to think you find me mysterious and charming."

"I can promise the second half of that, anyway."

Alisha lowered her eyelashes, glancing up again coquettishly. She murmured, "Join the club," and drew breath to turn her focus elsewhere when Brandon laughed.

"I wouldn't belong to any club that'd have me as a member."

"Oscar Wilde, right?"

"Probably," Brandon admitted, "but I got it from Groucho Marx." Alisha's heart tightened, a quick knot of pain that released as she managed a smile up at the scientist. "My father's favorite wisecracker," Brandon went on, with less good humor, and added more quietly, "One of the few things I have in common with him, I suppose. At any rate." His eyebrows went up and he brushed the comment away, gesturing to the distant, half-broken wall. Alisha turned to study it, squinting against the wind.

Dull silver glinted against the wall, light catching and breaking with the whipping wind and bursts of sunlight from between racing clouds. "Is that the prototype?"

"It is." Brandon slid his hands into his pockets, rocking his shoulders back, weight pivoting through his hips. Alisha, expression schooled, felt amusement bubble through her as she recognized his comfortable stance as that of a born lecturer. Brandon wasn't going to let the demonstration take place without a healthy lead-in. *Scientists and captive audiences,* she thought, wishing she'd decided to wear her suit jacket after all.

"Are you armed, Elisa?"

It wasn't the lecture she'd expected. Alisha shot Brandon a startled look. "No." The part of her that was the trained battle operative let go an internal growl at the admission. Never mind that it was considerably wiser to go in unarmed when it was likely she'd be searched. It still made the combatant in her uncomfortable.

"You're sure?" There was neither sarcasm nor doubt in Brandon's voice, just good-natured caution. Alisha looked down, as if caught in a lie.

"The thought occurred to me more than once, Dr. Parker, but I decided a show of good faith was more appropriate than coming in as if I were the enemy." She looked up again, eyebrows elevated a little. "I'm unarmed." Save for her own hand-to-hand skills, at least.

"All right, good. Come on, then. The drone will do a risk assessment on you—I explained that, right?" There was a note of hope in his voice, as if he suspected he had, but desperately wanted to give it again, just in case.

Alisha smiled. "I'm afraid so. Assessment whether to use deadly response or subdual, determined through infrared, right?"

Brandon's shoulders slumped perceptibly. "That's right," he said gloomily.

Alisha smiled even more broadly. "You can explain it again, if you really want to. I'll be very attentive."

"That's all right." He sounded as if he was doing his best Eeyore impression, before he flashed a smile of his own. "Thanks, though. There's plenty more to lecture about."

"Does the drone use any other nonlethal response systems?"

"I'm working on a foam spray—you're familiar with those?" Brandon gave her a cursory glance, clearly not expecting to have to explain himself.

Alisha nodded. "Immobilizing foam. Hardens almost instantly. It can suffocate a person very easily, if it gets in your face."

"Mmm. That's the reason I'm still working on it. The drone isn't very big—" He gestured to the prototype, more easily visible now. "Hobbit-sized." A wrinkle of dismay crossed his face, as if he'd let out his inner geek and was regretting it. Alisha, despite herself, laughed.

"Everyone knows how big hobbits are these days, Dr. Parker."

"Brandon. I know, but when a guy like me says something like that, a beautiful woman is going to think he's been a hopeless nerd since childhood."

"You have been," Rafe said idly.

Brandon shot him a look of exasperation. "But does it have to show? Anyway, in order to prevent people from suffocating the immobilizing foam can't cover their faces, and while the drone can assess an individual's—or a group's—height and mass easily enough, if the target is in rapid, unpredictable motion, it's proved difficult to launch the foam so that it both immobilizes the arms and yet doesn't suffocate the target."

Target. Alisha felt an unexpected pang of regret slide through her belly. Target, subject, objective; that was how their training had taught them to think about people. Not as individuals, but as missions to accomplish in one fashion or another. She wondered if it was easy for him, or if Brandon made himself hold on to his own humanity and refused to be wholly neutral about any given situation. She hoped so, but at the same time doubted it: the impulse to do so was a weakness by espionage standards, a secret that Alisha worked hard to hide.

And this was not the place to be considering that train of thought. Alisha returned her full attention to the scientist, shaking off her introspection. "Humans have the same problem, Dr —Brandon."

Brandon smiled at her. "Yes, of course. But my drones are supposed to be better than human."

"Like the hobbits," Alisha said, straight-faced.

"You're doomed," Rafe told Brandon, now cheerful.

Brandon groaned and turned his hands up in a helpless shrug. "Add that to your notes about me, Elisa. I work in remote mountains because I haven't got a chance in the world of proving myself other than as a complete geek. It makes talking to women very difficult." He sighed, over-exaggerating his misery.

Alisha laughed, shaking her head. "If you left the remote mountains, Brandon, you might find out that women are a little more forgiving of complete geeks than they used to be." She very much doubted Brandon Parker bought into his own story; the self-deprecation and laughter in his eyes suggested otherwise. Nor did his physique cater to expectations pre-sented by the word *geek,* and Alisha had no doubt Brandon was fully aware of that, too. "Your social aptitude aside, Dr. Parker..." Al-isha lifted her eyebrows and directed a look at the prototype.

"See?" Brandon said to Rafe. "I'm hopeless. Can't keep my eye on the ball."

Rafe gave a snort of derision that belied his cultured English voice. "The day you can't keep your eye on the ball is the day we're all driven out of here like so many sheep at the teeth of their master's dogs. You just changed balls for a minute there."

"That sounds obscene."

"I'm not the one flirting with the pretty woman." Rafe turned to Alisha. "We're normally somewhat more professional than this."

"I'll take your word for it. The drone, gentlemen?" Alisha let a trace of impatience color her tone, more than she actually felt. The two men straightened up like guilty children as she approached the wall and the prototype, circling the latter curiously.

It was not a friendly-looking thing, structured on a tripod of legs that, while rigid at the moment, were made up of jointed segments that looked as if they'd bend as easily as water. The body was circular, burnished silver distorting her reflection as she studied it. She could see fine lines of tight-fitting sections that made up the whole of the sphere, and reached out to touch it, holding the motion with a glance at Brandon. He inclined his head and she brushed her fingers over the material. It was cool and slightly rough, her fingertips more able to pick out the difference between the texture and the lines of the various sections than her eyes were. At a glance, the level of sophistication was astonishing, far exceeding the remote-controlled warrior-robots that had been used in Iraq.

"Did you read *The White Mountains* before or after designing this, Dr. Parker?"

"Actually, it was *The War of the Worlds* that ga—" He broke off, startled. Alisha looked over her shoulder at him, eyebrows lifted in amused challenge. He wet his lips, swallowed, and said, "I think I'm in love."

Alisha laughed out loud, crouching beside the drone. "I think you've been out-geeked." She ran her fingers over the prototype's lower half, shaking her head. "I see that there are sections that open—or so I assume—but I don't see how it can sense anything without compromising its own safety."

"Rafe?"

"Certainly," the Englishman said.

Beneath Alisha's fingers, the drone hummed to life. A glitter of red light passed over her palms, a whir sounding as the top half of the sphere circled to face her, as if it had turned to look at her, just as a human might." Another host of red light shimmered over her: sensory lasers emanating from the whole of the drone's globe, tiny pinpricks of light sparkling from just within the silver shell.

A nearly inaudible click sounded, precursor to a faint whine of power as two sections of the sphere opened and slid back to reveal far more powerful lasers nestled inside the drone's spherical body. The drone's legs ratcheted up, giving it a sudden height advantage over Alisha's crouched form. Her stomach cramped with nerves, the combat pilot part of her mind white with rage over having put herself in such a vulnerable position.

The only way out was forward. Through the drone's legs. She could grab one as she rolled through, perhaps unbalance the thing long enough to vault the wall behind it. That would offer some protection, might provide a weapon. There was no time for doubt, not even for a quick breath toward hyperventilation, nothing that might trigger the drone's attack mode. The muscles in her legs bunched, ready to propel her forward. Her taped ankle protested at the unexpected strain, suffering from pressure Alisha hoped didn't show in her posture. Three. Two—

Brandon said, "*Don't. Move.*"

Five

The effort of aborting her own leap forward before it began sent thin shards of pain through Alisha's thighs. She snarled without sound, trembling with contained energy. It swam inside her belly like too much caffeine, buzzing on the edge of illness. Her fingertips were cold, blood pumped into the vitals, all signs of adrenaline waiting to be used.

"The drone's assessing you as a risk," Brandon murmured. He sounded as if he was speaking to a frightened child, or maybe an unpredictable animal: calm and soothing, his voice pitched low. Alisha wasn't certain if the tone was meant for her or the drone; somehow the latter seemed more likely. As if the thing were alive.

But then, if it was as advanced an artificial intelligence as Brandon suggested it was....

She didn't give herself over to the luxury of a shiver. She wouldn't have in most cases, and with the drone looming over her she was even more reluctant to. Instead she spoke in as low a tone as Brandon had: "I am not carrying any weapons, Dr. Parker."

"I should have done a pat-down," Brandon said, though there was a dismissive note to his voice.

Yeah, Alisha thought, able to allow the rage she felt at least that much outlet. *I bet you'd have liked that.* Her lip curled, as much of that commentary as she dared afford. Parker murmured, "No, I believe you, Elisa. Just hold still for a minute. There's something wrong."

"No shit," Alisha said through her teeth. She turned her head slowly, until she could glimpse Brandon and Rafe over her shoulder. Rafe looked pale, sweat visible on his brow even from several feet away. They both studied a flat plastic sheet, about the size and depth of a laptop computer monitor.

"It's reversed the live target protocol," Brandon said after a moment. More color drained from Rafe's face; he must have been responsible for that protocol. Now Alisha knew whose ass to kick when she got out of this. A crick formed in her neck, stinging enough that she rotated her head back, stretching it cautiously before casting a glance up at the drone. Red dots danced in her vision, laser sightings on the small guns that were pointed at her.

She closed her eyes, not wanting to damage them by looking into the lasers, and a sense of absurd bloomed in her chest. AI laser damage was not a difficulty faced by most people in their day jobs. Holding on to that thread of absurdity, she said, "Are those actual blasters, Dr. Parker?

Laser weapons, rather than conventional?"

"Yes," Brandon said absently. "This isn't really a good time, Ms. Moon."

Alisha, dryly, said, "Of course it isn't." A few seconds went by, fear draining out of her as the sense of ridiculous grew.

"So," she said brightly, "what's its power source, anyway? I assume it's internal, but that thing can't be running on a Duracell."

"Ms. Moon." Rafe's voice was strained. "Please."

Alisha bared her teeth in a harsh grin. The drone above her adjusted its position with a click, perhaps not liking the aggression of bared teeth. She lifted her hands until they were even with her head and began to straighten, feeling the play of muscle in her leg slowly tightening and releasing. The drone ratcheted higher, until she was upright and it stood a few inches taller than her, silver sphere gleaming with warning.

"You," she said to it, "have a certain psychological advantage at first, but it doesn't last." The drone, somewhat to her relief, didn't respond, and then with a soft whine the guns retreated, settling back into place.

A cold burst of relief flooded through Alisha's body, starting in her core, sweeping out to her fingertips and toes, and leaving her goose-bumped in its wake. Hard on its heels came the heat of temper, making her even more aware of the chilly bumps that spread across her skin. All of her gallows humor at facing the drone fell fast to outrage now that the situation was resolved. Alisha spun toward the men, her jaw thrust out with anger. "A malfunction? Nearly falling to friendly fire does not inspire me with confidence, Dr. Parker."

"Nothing more than a reversed protocol," Brandon said hastily.

Alisha snapped, "The difference between live and hard targets seems to me a rather significant one, Dr. Parker," grateful for the chance to channel some of her fury immediately, rather than having to suppress it. Quicksilver emotions roiled through her body, her fists clenching in anger. "Dare I ask for a demonstration, or will your prototype see fit to mow us all down?"

Brandon had the grace to look embarrassed. Rafe, cringing, stepped forward. Brandon blocked him with his shoulder and a fractional shake of his head. "I take full responsibility for the error, Ms. Moon. The demonstration should go smoothly."

Rafe's shoulders stiffened as if chagrin threaded through his body, though in almost the same moment he lowered his eyes, gratitude or acceptance slinking into his posture. He knew he was being protected. Alisha was certain *she* wasn't meant to know, but it gave her an interesting insight into Parker's character. Certainly there were men who would step aside from the chain of command, allow an assistant to take the fall, but Brandon had chosen otherwise. Maybe the CIA had left a mark on him, after all.

"Shall we, then." The coolness of disappointment and anger still edged her voice, both of them quite real. The drone had frightened her; discovering that her fear had been set off by a malfunction was embarrassing to the point of infuriating. She'd expected the prototype to live up to Brandon's pitch. Expected, somehow, for him to prove himself one of the good guys after all, instead of a slightly inept mad scientist. She needed to assess him for his own skills and threat level, her own personal hopes and prejudices set aside. Although if the drone was going to prove this unpredictable, the security of the United States had less to worry about than she'd feared. Alisha flicked her fingers, an impatient gesture, and watched the two scientists all but hop to do her bidding.

With the bug worked out, Alisha had to admit the drone appeared to work flawlessly. Given a set of objectives—Alisha chose them, Brandon's hands darting over the tablet to program them in as he explained, "The drone's approach is autonomous. Once the mission is set, it chooses what it perceives as the best way to accomplish that. Its default programming always opts for non-lethal subdual, though in an outright combat situation it's fully capable of making the decision to defend itself."

"Second law of robotics." Alisha's anger faded, curiosity getting the better of her.

Brandon gave her a startled glance that blurred into a smile. "Third, actually."

"Mmm. My geek is slipping." Alisha dismissed the error, nodding at the tablet. "So it might opt to behave differently if I didn't specifically want it to scale the farther end of the wall, yes?"

"Exactly. We can run the objectives twice, once with your detailed instructions and a second time allowing the drone to behave in its autonomous and natural fashion."

"Natural." Alisha's eyebrows rose. "Is it possible for an artificial intelligence to be natural, Dr. Parker?"

"Philosophy's not my strong point, Ms. Moon. All right. Program complete." Brandon entered the command and Alisha put her shoulders back, watching the drone slip into action.

It looked like alien technology. The three-pronged metal feet were surprisingly quiet against the ground, even where it was rough. The ratcheting legs gave it a peculiarly smooth gait, its rounded body dipping and rising barely an inch or two as the drone flowed toward the far end of the wall. The stones there stood at least twice as tall as the drone did, even at its fullest height. Alisha had chosen that entrance point deliberately, curious to see just how well the machine was able to scale obstructions.

It fitted its clawed feet into breaks in the wall —Alisha could easily envision it using windows in a city to the same effect—and drew itself up, one leg after another, spider-like. A glance at Brandon's tablet showed scans being sent back, allowing the drone's human mentor to see what it saw. Its crown peeked over the top of the wall, light scattering to examine the area, searching for enemies. Then one foot snaked over, claws spread wide as it swung several inches back and forth. Brandon's screen flickered with images, first normal color, then—

"Ultrasound?" Alisha asked.

Brandon gave a pleased nod. "Searching for land mines, C4, anything set into the ground that could damage it. Infrared is most effective on warm bodies, obviously, so we needed to give it a variety of ways to recognize danger-ous objects."

"Very nice."

Brandon gave her a half sour glance that made her check an impulse to defend herself. If he was going to sell his drone to Alisha's fic-tional buyers, she needed to approve. None-the-less, after the years of work he'd put into it, having a complete stranger make cooing noises over his prototype had to be somewhere be-tween amusing and insulting.

"I'm glad you think so." His voice gave away nothing of the emotions Alisha thought he might feel, and humor pulled at her lips. There was nothing like an old-fashioned spy game to make her day. Everyone holding their cards close to the chest, everything kept under wraps, to see who ended up with the best hand.

I love this job. Even with the upset created by the prototype's malfunction, Alisha's smile grew into a grin, and lingered. The drone skittered across the field on the far side of the wall, still sending feedback to Brandon's screen. Rafe touched Alisha's shoulder, nodding toward the break in the wall.

"There's a platform just on the other side, where we'll be able to see everything more clearly. It's about to reach the more dangerous areas now."

"Excellent." Alisha climbed over the low stones, Rafe offering her a hand, and laughed, studying the platform. It was only five or six feet high, tall enough to see the entire field from. It was also tall enough to let the men look right up her skirt.

"I think I'll come up last," she said mildly. Rafe frowned, then blushed, his ears turning scarlet. Brandon, a few steps behind them, brushed by and climbed the ladder with absolutely no notice of the byplay at all. He even offered Alisha a hand as Rafe stepped out of the way, once on the platform.

"Thank you."

"Sure. Now," he said, nodding at the drone, "you set it to take the most straight-forward path to the west edge of the field. No avoidance of possible obstacles. This is what it's seeing." He handed her the tablet, tapping its screen. "Land mines, primarily. Not a friendly place to go walking in."

"Really," Alisha said dryly.

Brandon gave an absent nod, apparently not picking up on the sarcasm. "You'll want to watch out there. The first mine is coming up on its left—"

Without altering its fluid walk, the drone scooped a stone off the field bed and threw it several meters. It landed with military precision on the mine, nothing more than a blip on the screen before the explosion rattled the platform Alisha stood on. "It's always preferable to use what's handy rather than its weapons to activate unfriendly artifacts," Brandon yelled above the noise. "A random explosion might be a local animal getting in trouble," he added as the boom faded. "Whereas weapon fire is always pretty obvious."

"Although six land mines going off isn't likely to be a whole series of unfortunate animals," Alisha said a few moments later, as the drone worked its way through a string of bone-shaking detonations. Only once, on a concrete pad that had obviously been added to the field for just such demonstrations, was it obliged to resort to its own internal weapons systems to discharge a mine. Two bolts of red smashed from its guns, concussive force and heat exploding the mine with what Alisha thought of as violent satisfaction. "What about live targets?"

Brandon held up his hand as if to say, "Wait." The drone reached its first objective—

the west edge of the field—and turned north, running with liquid metal grace. "Over smooth terrain, it can reach twenty-five miles an hour," Brandon reported. "Eventually larger drones will be able to move much more quickly than that, but it's already a lot faster than a human."

A human-shaped target, complete with an AK-47 in silhouette, slid up from the ground. Alisha's stomach tightened, recognizing a threat. The drone reacted nearly as quickly as she did. Information flowed into the tablet, an assessment of danger that she struggled to keep an eye on while still watching the drone. The whisper-whine of laser fire sounded as she jerked her gaze back and forth, the "insurgent" on the field flattened by the force of the drone's blasts. As it hurried north, another dozen targets popped up, some wildlife, some human, one or two of them unarmed. One, no more than child-sized, "ran" forward on a mechanized slide. This time the drone reacted faster than Alisha could: her gut said "harmless," even as details about the "child's" bomb-laden coat poured across the tablet's screen.

Sonic waves deep enough to churn Alisha's belly, even though they weren't aimed at her, hammered the "child." Beside her, Brandon flexed his arms, an aborted signal of action and pride. "Errs on the side of caution," he said. "It's not perfect: if a suicide bomber is timed instead of self-destructing, I haven't yet figured out how to quickly and safely disable bombs, but even in the face of imminent danger when a target appears to be less than adult the drone will choose incapacitation over death. In the worst-case scenario a drone can be programmed to cover a suicide bomber's body with its own in an attempt to mitigate the damage to the general populace."

"What happens when your AI develops a sense of self-preservation?"

Brandon frowned. "I'll cross that bridge if we come to it. We're a long way from developing artificially based sentience, Ms. Moon."

"I hope you're right." Alisha turned her attention back to the drone, which had ignored a frightened family of refugees and incapacitated another threatening figure as it reached its northern-most goal, a white flag. *Incapacitated.* Alisha gave an almost silent snort. *More like obliterated.* "Can its program be changed so it just returns by the most expedient route?"

"In a real-life situation it would always do that," Brandon said with a nod. "It's a matter of turning it over to the AI. Here." He brushed his finger over the tablet, indicating the sequence Alisha should put in. She echoed the actions, then sent the command, watching the drone break off from its original eastern path and simply flow back toward the platform in an almost straight line. Its only deviations were to avoid the landmines that cropped up on its sensors, which Alisha watched on the screen she held. When it encountered a half-circle of mines directly in front of it, it paused, scooping up stones to throw, and moments later swarmed through the smoke and rubble unharmed.

"Have you tested it against living targets yet?"

"Only in extremely controlled situations." Discomfort still strained Rafe's voice, as if he hadn't gotten over the drone's malfunction earlier. And he shouldn't have, as far as Alisha was concerned. "We've arranged for a demonstration in the morning. Will that suit?"

"That'll be fine. I'll have time to make a written assessment of the drone's capabilities as I've seen them so far for my employers." The clinical answer covered the truth: a morning demonstration would give her all night to snoop around the base and search its computers.

The drone glided up, dropping the white flag onto the platform before hunching back down to its hobbit-height to await further orders. Alisha crouched to pick the flag up, smiling over her shoulder at the two scientists. "A truce," she said lightly. "In the name of scientific exploration."

"Why, Ms. Moon." Brandon offered his hand. "We're not on opposite sides."

"Of course not." She took his hand, letting him help her to her feet. *Of course not.*

Six

Brandon escorted her to a small, spartan dorm room in the main building's second level, and offered her a door key that Alisha bet almost everyone had a copy of. "All yours for the duration, Ms. Moon."

"Thank you, Dr. Parker. Is dinner a communal affair?"

"Much to General Hashikov's dismay. The officers' mess is downstairs to the left. I'll come by around six to escort you, if you like."

"That would be lovely." Alisha closed the door on him, locked it, and leaned against to observe the room. Someone had already brought the carry-on suitcase she'd traveled with to the room and placed it on the most utilitarian luggage rack she'd ever seen, which was saying something, since luggage racks weren't usually built to be visually pleasing in the first place. A security camera lodged above the bed swept the room at an angle that left the bed itself mostly unobserved, but the only real privacy in the gray-walled room was the bathroom. She crossed the room to use it. A frosted window in there had a glow of artificial light behind it and a shower, toilet, and sink so close to one another Alisha could reach everything in the room while sitting on the toilet.

At least the main room was a little better than that, a plain black desk and a plastic chair beside the luggage rack, with a large, dusty vent cover above the desk. A narrow window set close to the room side of the base's deep concrete walls. An industrial-grade olive green carpet emerged from under the bed and stretched toward the desk without quite reaching the far wall. The whole thing felt exactly like what it was: a Cold-War-era bunker, built to—hopefully—withstand a nuclear strike.

Aloud, but under her breath, Alisha murmured, "I've stayed in worse," and sat on the chair to kick her shoes off and massage her ankle. The swelling had gone down, but walking across the drone's demonstration grounds in low heels hadn't done it any particular favors. With a sigh, Alisha unzipped her carry-on and took out a sheaf of paperwork, literally handwriting the report for her erstwhile employers. Nothing—*nothing*—sent online could be absolutely confident of remaining secure, and the sort of people she supposedly worked for liked absolute confidentiality.

Around six, as promised, a knock sounded on the door and Brandon Parker escorted her down to dinner, past a host of young military men whose allegiance lay, she knew, with the highest bidder, rather than any country or creed.

General Oleksiy Hashikov had once followed the Soviet, and then the Russian, flag, but in his later years the appellation *General* was honorary, referring to his previous service rather than his current status. He'd been a freelancer for close to a decade now, and the Kazakhstani mountains offered him a place to be king of his own command. Those mountains offered a lot of people a great deal of freedom, so long as they paid bribes in the right places, and didn't bring obvious international trouble to its long-serving president's door. That, above everything else, was most likely why Brandon and his research team were holed up here, although the almost total inaccessibility couldn't hurt.

She rather liked Hashikov at first blush. From the tone of his voice he clearly hated the idea of the drone, and thought war was best left to men. *Men*, specifically, of course, but humans, at the very least. He obviously felt there was no honor in sending a robot out to fight man's battles, but as dinner wore on, he grudgingly admitted that the prototype might have its uses as a front-line combatant and scout.

Alisha saw more potential for the drones than the general did, and enjoyed arguing in their favor while Brandon, Rafe, and the rest of the all-male research team struggled to keep their opinions out of it. A couple of times Alisha caught Brandon taking notes, as if making sure he'd remember the thrust of her arguments later. The Alpha-10-Gamma's movement capability was considerably superior to the current robot warriors in use, Alisha said; those functioned on track treads, like a tank, but without the weight that allowed tanks to inexorably crush almost anything in their path. Besides that, the prototype could actually scale walls without reducing them to rubble first, making it dangerous not just on a ground level, but even up into buildings. Individuals could be sought out and destroyed by the artificially intelligent drone in a way that current robotic soldiers couldn't match. Alisha could see the resentment in Hashikov's acknowledgments of her points, and steered the conversation to less incendiary topics, like the Ural mountains weather, rather than rile the General up any more.

Besides, although she knew all her arguments were good ones, she also knew there were far too many places in the world that A-10-G tech could be put to use immediately. The Crimea, the Middle East; between India and Pakistan. Even Northern Ireland, where the fragile peace process had been badly shaken by Brexit. Elisa Moon might be enthusiastic about the drones' potential, but Alisha Mac-Aleer was shaken by it.

Hashikov thawed as she kept away from political and military discussions, and by the time dinner ended she'd been treated to photographs of his grandchildren and, to her delight, his Corgis, a breed he'd become enamored with after learning Elizabeth II of England bred them. Brandon, walking her back to her room after dinner, murmured, "I didn't even know he'd been married, much less bred dogs."

"And here I thought you were supposed to be a people person. I'm looking forward to the demo tomorrow, Dr. Parker. I'll see you in the morning." Alisha closed herself into her room, and, with a sigh, began preparations for her night's work.

The first part was dull, scene-setting work. She finished her preliminary report, went over it, did some stretching—her ankle still twinged —and finally crawled into bed beneath the camera's watchful eye. After a few minutes of settling in and pushing pillows around, she'd stuffed enough of them under the covers to create a crude facsimile of her sleeping body. As soon as the camera's sweep was at its furthest point from her corner, she rolled under the bed, waited, then slipped into the bathroom. A vent above its door was easier to access than the one in her bedroom, and she swiftly worked the screws out and lowered the vent cover to the toilet seat.

The downward trill of the *Mission: Impossible* theme song played in the back of her mind as she lifted herself into the vent. Not every job gave a girl the chance to play along to that music and actually have good reason to. She'd trained herself out of mouthing the sounds as she edged along; it'd taken longer to break the habit of shifting her shoulders in isolations, like a dancer, at the sharp beats in the music. But both those practices had been abandoned a long time ago now, even if the thoughts that provoked them were ingrained, part and parcel.

The ventilation shafts in the building had been built to cut off any outside circulation in the event of nuclear war. Generators beneath the building, according to fifty-year-old blueprints, would keep the bunker's air fresh and provide heat to anyone lucky enough to survive the anticipated war.

The ducts' narrowness was handy in a second way, too, although probably not one that had been considered in the architecture of the building: generally speaking, they prevented someone from doing exactly what Alisha was doing now. Few men—at least few men in a military organization that had height and weight requirements—would have fit through the cool narrow tunnels. There were places where Alisha regretted eating dinner.

There had been a few moments toward the end of that dinner where she'd considered whether General Hashikov might have been seduced—in mind, through open adoration, if not physically—by a fragile-seeming female. But she'd concluded he was too dedicated to his job—or at least being king of his own domain—to fall for that, and pushing it too far would have instigated outrage at a woman trying to invade his domain.

So she simply had to invade it the old-fashioned way. Alisha rolled onto her back as she reached a ninety-degree upright connection in the ventilation tunnels. There was no room to stand, but thin grooves in the shaft walls—grooves that would rotate and fold closed in case of nuclear war—gave her enough purchase to slowly pull herself up through the walls. Her fingers trembled and ached with the effort, shivers of stress working down through her arms and into her shoulders. She took deep, deliberate breaths, making certain to get enough oxygen to the overworked muscles. The air tasted faintly of metal and dust, as if it had been tainted by long years of lingering in the ventilation shafts. It lay in the back of her throat, a sweet tangy taste like blood. There was barely enough room to pull in those cloying breaths, and each expansion of her ribs made her feel as if she would crush herself against the close-set walls. Her toes—clad in rip-stop nylon with tiny rubber pebbles on the soles, as were her palms—dug into the grooves, barely earning her any more purchase, and her ankle muttered irritation as she strained it. There wasn't nearly enough room to draw her legs up so she could wedge herself in the ventilation ducts.

Brandon's lab had to be in the bunkers beneath the old base. Not that it was impossible for it to be elsewhere, but the bunkers were by far the safest location in the base. Whoever funded his research would want to be certain their investment was well protected.

The *who* was a question worth pursuing. She would have to ask Greg if he knew who was funding the presumably considerable cost of Brandon's work. Anyone with that kind of money and the taste for building mechanical warriors was an inherent danger to the security of the United States and the world at large.

The vents went a long way toward making certain whoever had put his money up wasn't in danger of losing the research he paid for. It was all but impossible for anyone to slip in that way. Twenty feet of upright metal to climb through before another right angle and finally a third would lead her straight down, as dangerous in its way as the upward climb. One slip and she would fall four stories. A broken bone in the shafts would finish her.

Alisha pushed the thought away. There was never time for that sort of what-if-ing. At best it was frivolous and at worst it would get her killed. Besides, she had the backup she needed for the descent. Filament line trailed behind her, anchored just inside her bathroom's ventilation grate. Chances were that no one would physically check up on her during the night.

She hoped.

Concentrate. Alisha mouthed the word, inching higher. If she'd been discovered, she'd deal with it later.

She inhaled sharply as open space gave behind her head. A glance upward ascertained the shaft ended above her. Alisha let go the breath again, squirming backward into the new shaft. For a moment the metal just above her face seemed to press down on her, squeezing the air from her lungs. Alisha closed her eyes, envisioning the space around her as larger, then squirmed backward into the claustrophobic tunnel. From there on out, it was a cake-walk.

Even as she thought it, Alisha shook her head in a scold. Over-confidence led to mistakes. Still, it was a matter of minutes to drop the filament line, clip a pulley ratchet to it, and slide headfirst into the ventilation ducts leading down to the base's underground laboratories. She landed fingertips first, edging her way forward into the boxy shafts toward dim emergency lights that glowed in the room beyond.

The tiny *tink*s as the screws from the grate hit the floor sounded to her ears like a doomsday bell tolling, blaring an announcement of her presence to anyone with a care to hear. Alisha slid down the wall, still headfirst, then reversed herself, landing on the balls of her feet. The rubber nodes on her soles felt odd, wriggling slightly with the pressure of her weight against them. She collected the screws, fixing the grate closed so that it would pass a perfunctory inspection. The filament line remained coiled behind it, the lifeline she would need to return to her room. She closed her eyes briefly, pulling up the blueprints in her mind's eye, graying lines against grayer paper.

There was a central control room overlooking a cavernous hub room, what would have been the eye of activity if nuclear war had broken out and the base evacuated to the below-ground bunkers. It should be two corridors to her right, on the same level. Alisha nodded, tight motion to herself, and ran silently on her toes through the bunkers, her ankle whinging at the speed.

The walls were unadorned concrete, floors unmarred by the passage of feet, but also well cared for: there was no dust to betray her trail, nor, for several doors, any locks to inhibit her. Ancient surveillance cameras creaked in the corners, their sweep of the hallways so slow that she counted out the long seconds before darting to the next camera's blind spot.

The last door was locked, a modern keypad set into the wall beside it. Alisha curled her lip, mouthing a curse rather than risking it aloud. At least it wasn't biometric. She shot a glance at the lugubrious camera at the end of the hall. Nine seconds. She slid a penlight out of the belt at her waistband, flicking it on. Ultraviolet brightened the keypad, illuminating fingerprints left on the keys. Seven seconds. Five keys were smudged: 1 2 8 9 0. Cold lifted the hairs on Alisha's arms as she stared at the numbers, grasping for a meaningful sequence. Three seconds.

My life, she thought, *is an endless countdown of numbers.* The sequence popped into her mind and she punched it in without hesitating, 2101890. The door slid open and she stepped through, taking in the layout of the control room with a single glance. A surveillance camera clicked and began its rotation back toward her. She darted forward, folding herself into the space beneath a desk, making sure the chair obscured her. Only then did she exhale through pursed lips, as near a whistle as she dared make, and drop her head against her forearms for a moment.

Two ten eighteen ninety. Groucho Marx's birthday, written European style: 2 October, 1890. Thank God for the shared humor between father and son. Alisha's heart slammed against her ribs, excited relief threatening to bubble into laughter. She allowed herself a fierce grin against her arms, then nudged the chair a few inches, studying the room more closely from her hiding spot.

There was only the one visible camera from where she sat, but a second had been in the opposite corner. There was something wrong with their angles. Alisha closed her eyes, this time visualizing the sweep of the cameras. A few seconds passed before she tightened a fist in triumph and lifted her eyes to study the nearest computers.

The cameras couldn't see their screens. There were distinct blind spots in the room; it was merely a question of navigating to them. Alisha offered thanks to whatever saint ensured the paranoia of great programmers, and skittered from one blind spot to another until she sat crouched behind one of the terminals, hidden entirely from the security cameras.

Objective one: get the schematics. White letters on a black command screen blinked at her as she punched out commands, listing the files and directories on the mainframe. It was too much, far too much, to download it all. That was okay. The integral pieces were all she needed, enough to reverse engineer the prototype. The screens to her left and right hummed on, various stages of the prototype's development flashing by as she scanned through the files. There were half a dozen that seemed promising before stalling out. Alisha gnawed her lower lip, resisting the urge to bounce with impatience. Too much movement would put her in the cameras' line of sight despite the dimness of the room. She couldn't risk being seen.

There. A schematic flashed up and held, blue-white lines against the screen catching her attention. The drone she'd seen in action that afternoon, Prototype Alpha-10-Gamma. Alisha clenched her fists in triumph and fished a USB stick out of her belt. A *truly* paranoid programmer would have computers without USB ports at all, and passwords to keep people out of files that weren't their own. Brandon's programming team were clearly trusted: she found a port and got the stick into it on only the second try. A handful of quick commands started the download, though Alisha noticed herself baring her teeth as she typed, as if threatening the computer itself into behaving.

Or proving to the computer that she was brave enough to face it. Accessing the mainframe was dangerous, too easily trackable. If anyone was watching, they'd see the spike that indicated her subterfuge.

Second objective: destroy the schematics. Alisha took one rough breath to steady herself and turned to another computer. A second USB went into its port, and she reversed the transfer protocol, now uploading a new file to the servers. A seventy-two hour Trojan; once set, it would lurk in the mainframe, silent for three days before a simple command—accessing one of the text editors on the mainframe—would set it loose. All data on the servers would be destroyed before anyone had a chance to react. And it would happen days after she was gone, more than enough time for her to disappear completely. Brandon might be forced to suspect her, as one of the few outsiders the base ever saw, but the development servers were strictly off-limits: no one except authorized personnel should have access. Alisha flashed a tight grin at the screens, watching percentages of uploads and downloads scroll by. It was a tidy job, and she was already proud of it.

File transfer complete. Alisha tightened her

fingers in triumph again and reached for the first USB, the one with the newly downloaded schematics. Excitement shivered over her, an almost sexual pleasure of another move in the spy game well played.

"I don't like making contact when there are strangers in the base." Brandon's voice came through the door, muffled.

Alisha had time to think, *oh, fuck*, before the door slid open.

Seven

Nowhere in her job description was it written that when in trouble, a refrain of, "Fuckity fuck fuck," more or less to the tune of "Here Comes Santa Claus" should play in her head. Alisha doubted anyone else had ever come near that particular idiosyncrasy, and it wasn't the sort of query she'd ever wanted to put to anyone. She made herself a solemn promise that she would at least *ask* Greg if he'd ever done such a thing, if she got out of the base unscathed.

She slid under the desk, stomach muscles bunched with contained nausea and excitement. The lights were still off, and her black suit would help hide her, but there was no way out without betraying herself. A shadow passed beside her hand, Brandon's footsteps sounding flat against the concrete floor as he walked between the desks.

"I'm losing you. I'll put the internet phone through in a second." He sat down, a chair creaking. Alisha closed her eyes, a hot shudder of relief making her shoulders sag momentarily. She snaked her fingertips out, reaching for the nearest USB stick, then hesitated. If the virus hadn't finished uploading yet—Alisha bit her lower lip, withdrawing her hand. The second stick was too far away to be reached from beneath the desk. The computer beeped, making her flinch, and she snaked her hand out again, trusting the sound had been the file finishing its transfer. USB sticks made almost no noise going in and out of their slots, but the tiny pop of release sounded like a thunderstorm in Alisha's straining ears. Brandon's chair creaked as he turned, but he didn't move.

"Security system's on a loop," he said a moment later. Alisha almost laughed despite the danger. The scientist had spoken to his contact, whomever it was, even out in the hall. The security system had to have been looped for at least a few minutes. Her dramatic sneak across the computer lab had been for her own benefit. Ah well, she thought: there was no way she could have known.

"We're clear," Brandon added. Alisha squirmed beneath the desk, searching for a crack that might allow her to see him as he spoke.

"How did the demonstration go?" The new voice came through the computer's speakers, mechanically distorted so Alisha couldn't tell if it was male or female. A thin break in the soldering on the desk's corner allowed her to watch the conversation, Brandon's shoulder turned toward her. He lifted it slightly, a shrug that betrayed faint tension.

"A hitch or two. The protocols were still set to live targets. Rafe covered it. Otherwise, not bad. Tomorrow we've got another demo, this time with appropriately live targets."

Alisha turned her palm up, staring at the black stick in her hand. The faintest bit of light reflected off it: she would have to carry matte-covered data sticks from now on. Its dim reflection of light danced swam in her gaze as she assimilated Brandon's words: *still* set to live targets. Who had the targets been? Alisha set her teeth together, racing through possibilities in her mind. The words implied either tests run with live targets—the more innocuous choice— or that the drone had actually been used already in real-world scenarios. If the latter was true, there was more urgency to her mission than she'd known. Maybe even more urgency than Greg or Director Boyer had known. Alisha mouthed a curse and turned away from the crack, eyeing the second computer.

"As opposed to inappropriately live ones." Despite the alteration, the dryness of the speaker's tone came through clearly. Hair stood up on the back of Alisha's neck, a warning of familiarity that she couldn't place. She twisted back to frown through the slit, Brandon's shoulder no more revealing than it had been. The screen beyond him had a graphical interface, but no image to go along with the video chat. Alisha set her teeth together in soundless frustration.

"The Russians are sending a man in," the mechanized voice said. "He'll be there in the morning."

"Dammit!" Brandon's hand came down with a sharp crack. Alisha flashed her hand out, moving beyond the dark safety of the desk to snatch the second USB under the sound of Brandon's anger. "I don't like having even one agent here at a time! Two's a disaster!"

Ice formed deep in Alisha's belly, spreading through her in such clear increments she felt as if she was watching frost grow on a window. It froze her motion, fingers stretched toward the USB stick. A knot of cold lay in her throat, catching her repetition of the word *agent* there before it could be uttered aloud.

"You couldn't expect the Russians to hold off when a Middle Eastern conglomerate has moved in. They send in an agent, the Russians send in an agent."

"And what about the Americans?" Brandon demanded. Alisha relaxed, the chill draining away from her bones. *Agent* didn't necessarily mean CIA. *But just because you're paranoid*, she thought, *doesn't mean they're not out to get you.*

"You are the Americans." The distorted voice sounded chiding. Alisha's shoulders went back, her head turning toward the source of the conversation again. Brandon's response was abruptly weary.

"Yeah. Some days it's hard to remember."

"Others it's hard to forget." Chiding faded from the computerized speaker, as if the speaker felt sympathy, or even empathy. Alisha had a brief, unsubstantiated conviction that the speaker was a woman, and rejected it: she couldn't know that with the weird, flat edge to the voice, and women weren't the only people who could feel sympathy. Whomever they were, they'd say *you* are *the Americans*. Not according to Greg or Brandon's CIA files, he wasn't, and the idea that there was more going on than she knew set Alisha's teeth on edge. She had far too many questions and absolutely no answers. Nor could she contact Greg to find out what the hell was going on. Until her scheduled departure, she was on her own.

On her own and possessed of two very dangerous pieces of material. Still listening to Brandon and his contact—they were discussing when the Russian agent would arrive—she turned her gaze upward, studying the room for exit points. Knowing the security cameras were temporarily disabled left her considerably more freedom, though she didn't want to make her move until Brandon was gone.

"The live demo's at ten. If he's not here by then—"

"Then you'll do it again when he arrives. This isn't just about the Russians, Parker. It's about the Sicarii."

"Son of a bitch," Brandon said so mildly Alisha checked the impulse to peek over the edge of the desk to see his expression. The very low-keyness of his delivery made her feel it hid much deeper emotion. "All right."

Curiosity itched at the back of Alisha's mind, her palms tingling with adrenaline. *Sicarii*. It meant nothing to her, though she thought it sounded Italian. The need to escape the computer lab began to pound at the base of Alisha's skull, a throb that said her body felt as if it had been put into a danger zone well beyond what she'd prepared for.

She crept forward, trusting the conversation to be her cover. A staircase spiraled up into what the blueprints indicated was a ready room of some sort, above the computer lab and overlooking the enormous hub room. Brandon continued talking, more deferential than he'd been before. Alisha hesitated at the end of the row of desks and computers, frowning at the windows that made up the larger part of the room's front wall. Lights were on in the hub room beyond it; her reflection would go unseen if she risked the stairs. But it would put her on a new level, one she might not be able to access her escape route from so easily. She closed her eyes, building the blueprints in her mind again, tracing the route in the air with a fingertip.

"I heard something." Wheels squeaked as Brandon stood, pushing his chair back. Alisha winced, casting a sharp look over her shoulder. She caught a glimpse of the blond man striding down the rows of desks toward the door, the opposite direction she faced. She took one quick breath and sprang forward as noiselessly as she could, landing on the steel stairs with a soft thump that fell in time with Brandon's footsteps. She scampered upward, casting one more glance over her shoulder.

The screen on the second computer, where she'd uploaded the virus, was still awake, leaving her activities visible for anyone to see.

Right down Santa Claus Lane, Alisha sang to herself, and ran up the stairs in silence.

She could hear with astounding precision. It always happened when things went badly. Her own heartbeat was too loud, but somehow only served as a backdrop for every other minute sound in the bunker. Pipes behind concrete walls creaked, air circulation thrummed with a deep, bone-shaking rattle normally reserved for film scenes set in deep space, and above all of that, Brandon's voice cut through: "I don't know. This isn't exactly the easiest place in the world to compromise."

The room she'd come into was dominated by an oval table and windows overlooking the hub. One of the windows was open; Alisha darted through it without taking time to think, vivid image from the blueprint giving her faith. Faith well rewarded: immediately to the window's left were fire rungs, grooves cut into the wall. She scrambled up, rubber pads on fingers and toes giving her extra security, and within seconds was among the open pipes and florescent lights of the hub room's ceiling. Preternaturally aware hearing picked out Brandon's footsteps on the steel stairs below the lights' hum, and a few seconds later he looked out the open window, frowning.

Looked out, but not up. Alisha stopped breathing, making herself a shadow behind the lights. A prey species' flight instinct: run for the higher ground. That was still hard-wired into humanity, even though they'd become a predatory species themselves. The funny thing was that as predators, human apes didn't tend to look up. Except Brandon did, chin tilted up and eyebrows drawn down into a deeper scowl as he squinted against the brightness of the lights. Alisha felt a flash of exasperated humor. Greg Parker's son hadn't forgotten his CIA training—always look to the high ground —which would be excellent hunter behavior if it wasn't Alisha he was looking for. She would have much preferred he looked for things like most people did: at eye level or lower.

But he turned his gaze away from the shadowy ceiling after only a cursory glance. Alisha pressed her eyes shut briefly in relief so faint she could barely feel it. The window whooshed shut with a quiet puff of air, Brandon's departing footsteps muffled by the seal. Alisha let go of the breath she'd been holding and opened her eyes again, looking down twenty feet to the hub room's floor.

Domes and spheres bounced silver light back at her from a dozen different areas, scattered across the floor. Corners of matte black swallowed light in the peculiarly distinct way that deadly weapons often did, barrels and ratcheting legs making a tangled mess. Alisha stared at the machines littering the floor for what felt like a very long time, not breathing, not blinking. She knew, on one level, what she was looking at; on another she waited, breath held, to accept what she saw and make sense of it. Then all at once, with painful clarity, it all came together so she could understand.

Her third objective, obtaining the prototype drone, had always been going to be the hardest of the tasks to perform. Physically, at least; the emotional difficulty of her potential fourth task, terminating Brandon Parker, was far worse than the logistical difficulty of stealing a hobbit-sized drone programmed to protect itself at almost all costs. But that aside, the stealing the drone was always going to be risky, something she would have to do in the very last minutes before leaving the base, and even then, managing it without getting caught would be chancy. Out of the objectives, it was the one most likely to go unfinished, although as a matter of pride Alisha had always intended to come out with the drone.

A growing discomfort in her chest turned to

a burn and she inhaled sharply, not knowing when she'd last taken a breath. Her eyes were hot from not blinking. She did so, hard, then forced them open, as if she might somehow change what she'd seen below with the fierceness of the blink.

It didn't work. The drone she'd watched that afternoon—the Prototype Alpha-10-Gamma—sat in a corner, scuffs from use very slightly marring its gleaming surface.

Opposite it, cargo crates with their tops ripped off revealed five more drones hunkered down like silver-headed dwarves. They were identical to the A-10-G, the same size and shape, and even half-wrapped in packing hay and foam, they seemed to give off a sense of malevolence. Goose bumps crawled over Alisha's skin, leaving her shivering against the pipes.

She was looking at the beginnings of an army.

And there was no way she could steal it all.

Eight

The return to her quarters was a blur. She could pick the details out if she focused, but it wasn't the trip back that had kept her awake all night. Alisha lay on her back, eyes closed, racing fruitlessly through the same thoughts that had haunted her for the past several hours.

Brandon had created an *army* of prototypes. His work was much further along than the CIA's intelligence had suggested. He had an outside contact, but not his employers, or he wouldn't be making clandestine midnight calls. Someone else, then. Someone who considered him one of the Americans.

Alisha clenched her jaw, trying to keep a curse locked behind her teeth. If Brandon Parker was working for the Americans—for the CIA—then his cover was so deep that Greg didn't know about it. Which meant a hundred different things. It meant Alisha's presence at the base was potentially dangerous to Brandon, an inexcusable chance that his cover might be blown. It could mean Brandon Parker was not at all the threat that his work presented him as.

And if that was the case, someone so high up in government had placed him that not even Director Boyer had known that sending Alisha in might expose an operative. It meant, as too often happened, the left hand didn't know what the right was doing. Secrets upon secrets: they were the lifeblood of the CIA, but functioning without full disclosure in a situation like this was disastrous.

There were too many unknown variables, questions that couldn't be answered until she'd left the security of the Kazakhstani base. Impatient nerves made Alisha's stomach ache, not from fear, but from anger and distress at her path being unclear. She'd lain in bed, sleepless, for nearly five hours. It was enough. More than enough.

She shoved the covers off and reached for her bag as she sat up. The red glow of a digital clock told her it was minutes before 6:00 a.m., a veritable lie-in for someone on a military base. Brandon had pointed out a utilitarian gym as he'd shown her to her room the night before, and it was late enough to go make use of it. It had to be: her body was trembling with the need to move. She pulled on a sports bra and running tights, put bare feet into tennies, slid her earphones into her ears. Her phone—obviously not *her* phone, but an Agency-provided phone belonging to Elisa Moon, and filled with all the apps and calendars Elisa used—went into a bulky casing that she could strap to her arm with soft-sided Velcro. The big ugly case helped disguise the fact that it hid thin USB sticks: one with the virus she'd brought in, and one now laden with the Alpha-10-Gamma's specs. Those specs had been prizes only a few hours earlier. Now they seemed to taunt her, like the visible ten percent of an iceberg.

Alisha curled her lip in frustration as she jogged through the base to the exercise room. There was nothing she could do at the moment. Yoga, at least, would help her think more clearly.

"Ms. Moon." Brandon's voice cut through the music, a greeting that interrupted Alisha's *bakasana*, the crane pose that put her weight on her hands, body curled in a ball and supported by the strength of her arms. She lifted a fingertip, uncertain if he'd see it, but it was the only action she could take without disrupting her pose. A moment later she heard the grate of weights being moved as she brought her knees out of their tuck and placed them even with her feet, remaining doubled for the space of a long exhalation. Then she reversed herself into a slow standing pose, opening her eyes to study Brandon as he loaded weights onto a chest press. He wore sweats and a T-shirt and looked like he'd had enough sleep, though she knew perfectly well that he hadn't retired any earlier than she had.

So, she asked silently, *who's Sicarii? Are you really still working for the CIA? Who's your contact outside of this base?* She at least got a moment's satisfaction out of imagining his expression if she asked the questions, but aloud, she said, "Good morning. I wasn't ignoring you."

"Yeah, I saw." Brandon waggled a finger, repeating her gesture of a moment earlier as he slid the last weight on the bar. "Glad the weight room's useful to you."

Alisha nodded, lifting a shoulder. "Need a spotter?"

She could see him about to refuse and then reconsidering the offer. "Sure, thanks. If I've got a spotter..." He pulled another set of twenty pound weights off the rack and slid them onto the bar. "You always so helpful in the morning?"

Alisha pursed her lips, considering, and came down on the side of *what the hell.* She dropped her voice into a purr, her smile growing into a wholehearted, flirtatious grin. At the worst he wouldn't respond. At the best, he might open up, maybe let something slip. "Sometimes I'm much more helpful. On your back, Jack." She pointed at the bench, smiling playfully. Brandon lifted his hands in acquiescence and laughed, rolling onto the bench as Alisha came over to stand behind the bar. "How many?"

"Three sets of fifteen."

"So're you, if you can catch this thing." He began his reps, gaze focused hard on the ceiling.

"I can't," Alisha said with perfect honesty. "Three hundred's too much for me. But I can keep it from crushing you."

"Two-eighty," he said through his teeth.

Alisha's eyebrows rose. "How pedantic."

Brandon's gaze flickered from the ceiling to her. He split a tiny grin, almost a grimace as he concentrated on the press, and finished his set before speaking again. "I'd rather be admired for what I can actually do."

Alisha squinted. "Are you sure you're a guy?"

He barked laughter, half crunching up toward her. "Pretty sure."

"Lie down," she said, mock-severely. "Fortunately for you, you've got some pretty impressive..." Her gaze trailed over his chest before she brought it back to his face and grinned again. "Accomplishments."

Brandon laughed out loud. "Are you supposed to flirt with your business associates, Ms. Moon?"

"Of course not." But then, her business associates weren't usually young blonds with broad shoulders and teen-idol smiles. "Do you always do what you're told?"

Darkness glittered in Brandon's eyes. "Not always."

Alisha cocked an eyebrow, a jolt of interest making her stomach jump. "Fill me in." *For example, tell me about the army of prototypes you've got downstairs, when my intelligence suggested a single drone.*

"Ms. Moon—"

"Elisa," she reminded him. "I told you that yesterday."

"And then you started calling me Dr. Parker again," he pointed out. "You weren't exactly happy when the prototype was misprogrammed. I couldn't tell if you'd thawed out over dinner."

Alisha spread her hands in a touché motion. "I thawed. I think being pissed off about being the prototype's target was reasonable." She tapped the bar again. "Back to work."

Brandon settled back down and curled his hands around the bar. "It was. So anyway, Elisa," he said with faint strain on her name, "I doubt my history is a secret to a woman like you."

"Intelligent, attractive and highly paid for illicit work, you mean?"

Brandon grunted an acknowledgment, making Alisha grin again. "Not much of it," she agreed. "So why'd you do it?" She left the question deliberately vague, curious to see what he'd choose to answer.

Nothing, for the space of his sets, and then he let his arms fall to either side of the bench and sighed tremendously. "Oversight committees."

Alisha's eyebrows shot up. "Excuse me?"

Brandon chuckled. "Government organizations have accountability for everything. It takes forever to get anything done." He shook his arms, then folded his fingers together, cracking his knuckles. "My prototypes would have gotten caught up in committee and debated for years. I didn't want to wait."

"Come on." Alisha infused her voice with disbelief. "With the Attengee's military potential? I thought enormous amounts of money were funneled into research and development."

"Attengee." Brandon breathed laughter. "That's got kind of a ring to it. Easier than A-10-G." He shrugged. "Sure, and with it you get almost no autonomy. This project has been my life. I wanted to do it my way."

"Last set. You and Frankie, huh? So you opted for the highest bidder?"

Brandon flashed her a glance beyond the weight bar. "The most idealistic bidder."

"Idealistic. You're telling me that whoever is paying for this research site really believes your drones will be used for nothing more aggressive than peacekeeping?" Alisha's brows rose in genuine curiosity. "Who is this fount of decency?" *Your Sicarii?* she wondered, without voicing the question aloud.

Brandon stretched his forearms, then reached for the bar again. "I'm hardly at liberty to tell you that."

"Eh, it was worth a shot."

Brandon chuckled, quick sound beneath his labored breathing as he began his set. "I guess.

Anyway, even if he's naive, I don't have a lot of illusions about how my work will be used."

"Then why do it at all?"

"Because someone would." Brandon spoke through his teeth again, huffing out the count for his repetitions at the end of the comment.

"And it might as well be you?"

He shot her another look. "Why do you do it?"

"Money." It was Elisa Moon's motivation, at least. Moon had grown up poor, her only commodity her pretty face. It hadn't been enough to get her through college, but drug couriering had. Elisa's allegiance was to whomever could pay her, plain and simple.

Just like Reichart.

"Someday," Brandon grunted, "I'm going to ask you that question again."

Alisha's forehead wrinkled as she looked down at him. He gave her a thin smile, then turned all his concentration to the weight bar. "Eleven," Alisha murmured, picking up the count for him. "Why? Twelve. Three more." She curled her fingers around the bar more solidly, watching his biceps tremble with strain.

"Because." Cords stood out in his neck as he spoke through his teeth, focusing on lifting the weights. "I don't—" he thrust the bar up, Alisha's hands clenching around it, then relaxing "—believe money. Is a legitimate answer. There's always—" He broke off again with another grunt.

"Fourteen. One more. C'mon, Parker."

"—another—*reason!*" He shoved the weight bar up with one last burst of energy. Alisha caught it, guiding it back to the braces, and stepped back from the bench.

"Nice job," she said quietly. "I'm going to grab a shower. I'll see you in the mess hall." She took another step backward, then turned away, keeping the length of her strides steady as she headed for the door. It felt too much like a retreat, as if Brandon had gained an upper hand she hadn't known they'd been playing for. She paused at the door, looking back. "Maybe if you ask another time I'll have another answer."

But not until she knew more about Brandon Parker and his associates.

Unfortunately, with no way to contact Greg or anyone outside the base until she'd left Kazakhstan, finding out more would have to wait. Alisha showered, grabbed a bowl of slightly stale cereal in the mess hall, and approached the demonstration location a few minutes early. Rafe Denison paced the hall nervously, but pulled himself together to give her a tense smile. "Good morning. Ms. Moon. Dr. Parker will be with us in a few minutes. There'll be another potential buyer joining us for the live demonstration. Please, come this way."

Alisha arched an eyebrow, giving the lab assistant a sideways look as he guided her down a concrete hall. His nostrils were pinched with consternation, though he gave her another brief smile in an obvious attempt to belie the distress his body language admitted to. "An unexpected addition," he said apologetically. "Brandon insisted."

"Really." Alisha kept her voice neutral, just a hint of curiosity in it. "Who's he representing?"

Rafe gave her another pained smile. "I'm sure you understand I can't answer that, any more than I'd discuss whom you're affiliated with."

"Of course not." Alisha gave the fidgeting Englishman a quick smile. "But it was worth trying."

"It must be exhausting, living a life where you're always wondering which side everyone's on. How do you do it?"

By scribbling down all the things that drive me crazy about it. By keeping a record purely for myself, that allows me to be as honest as I can be before facing the blacks and whites of my reality. Answers she couldn't really—*wouldn't* really—give. Aloud, easily, she replied, "Practice. "I imagine it can't be so different for you, Dr. Denison. Rafe," she corrected herself, before he had a chance. "You probably don't tell much of your family that you're working on secret weapons research, after all, do you?"

"No," Rafe said. Alisha could all but hear him adding, *but I don't buy and sell weapons on a black market, either.* He opened a door for her and she stepped past him into a control room very like the one she'd infiltrated the night before: enormous windows overlooked an open hub area, thick concrete walls rising up into a tangle of pipes and lights at the ceiling. Alisha glanced up, studying it briefly, before looking down into the belly of the room.

The Attengee drone squatted there, half-hidden amongst a maze of wood and concrete walls. Four men in stiff-looking fatigues stood together, another three scattered in the maze. "Those aren't standard issue," Alisha said, nodding at the closest group of men. Rafe shook his head, expression approving.

"We had to develop an armor that could stand up to the lasers if we wanted to be able to test the drone against live targets. It absorbs and dissipates most of the energy, although the knock-back is still a problem."

"But better than a burning hole through your stomach," Alisha said. "Now all you need to do is find a way to convert the absorbed energy into a battery pack for charging soldier-carried laser weapons."

Rafe shot her a startled look that turned to furrows of interest. Alisha's shoulders rounded in dismay as he paused to take a few quick notes on a phone he produced from inside his hip pocket. *Good going, Leesh. Suggest a way to vastly improve the bad guys' system.* But if they could do it—which they couldn't, once she'd delivered the schematics to the CIA and the virus she'd set had destroyed the rest—but if they could, it really would be a tremendously efficient war system.

Once she'd delivered the schematics. Alisha nodded like she was approving of Rafe's notes, but really she realized a plan had crystallized in the back of her mind. Brandon's project was just too big for an individual to take it out, at least without sufficient preparation. Extraction would require a team, and she could put that together once on the outside and back in contact with Greg. It would have to be swift and efficient, and they would have very little time to prepare. Even the slightest delay could compromise the materials inside the base, and with a second buyer coming in, Alisha couldn't risk it.

The door behind them swung open, ushering Brandon's words: "—will take place here. This is my assistant, Rafe Denison, and Elisa Moon."

"Another assistant?" The deep voice made a jolt of physical pain lance through Alisha's chest, just above her heart. She opened her fingers wide to prevent herself from rubbing it and swallowed against a thrill of sick panic as she turned.

"An interested party," she corrected, giving the dark-eyed man with Brandon a tight smile. His hair was even longer than it had looked when she'd caught sight of him at the Scottish observatory, tending toward a little curl. It suited him, giving him just a touch of impishness to temper the thin smirk he so often wore, like a promise that the bad boy could be tamed. Alisha's hands were cold as she offered one to him, an infuriating tell that he couldn't fail to notice.

Frank Reichart clicked his heels together and performed a short, sarcastic bow over her hand. "My apologies, Ms. Moon. It's a pleasure. Michael Clarke, at your service."

"Mr. Clarke," Alisha said neutrally, and turned away again, forcing her breathing to remain steady so that the hammering of her heart wouldn't be betrayed by the rapid-fire pulse in her throat. Brandon launched into a lecture, apparently oblivious to Alisha's discomfort, as he should be. It was the only thing in the mission that was going right. She listened and watched the room below as the demonstration began, recording detail without yet absorbing it.

Reichart was working for the Russians. Parker might be working for the Americans. The former, at least, could blow her cover with a single word, as easily as she could break his. The situation bordered on out of control.

No battle plan, Alisha thought wryly, *survives the first encounter with the enemy.*

Nine

"Elisa—" Minutes later, Reichart hissed her alias down the hall at her, full of quiet urgency. She turned to face him, her jaw set as if the physical gesture would deny him anything he asked.

"Don't tell me you didn't know I was here," she said in as low a voice as he'd used. "What the hell are you doing here? The *Russians,* Frank?" She used his real name deliberately, taking out frustration and anger in the only way she could. "Did you follow me?"

"Off that cliff? Are you nuts? Elisa—"

Alisha rolled her eyes, an expression so violent she turned her whole head with it, cutting off the name with a jerk of her hand. Reichart bared his teeth, then set them and said, even more quietly, *"Alisha."* She could all but hear his unspoken, *Are you happy now?* in the pause before he continued. "I'm not here because of you—"

"Of course not," she snapped. "You're here for the money."

Reichart's nostrils flared, a sign that he'd nearly taken the bait. "You're in over your head."

"I wasn't until you showed up and screwed the whole equation." It was a blatant lie, and worse, Reichart's expression gentled slightly, suggesting he knew it. "Who's Sicarii?" Alisha demanded, grateful for the confused surprise that wiped sympathy from his eyes.

"Alisha, this isn't the place—"

"No shit." Alisha flexed her fingers, trying to pull her emotions back under control. Reichart brought out the worst in her in the best of circumstances—and, she admitted sullenly, the best in the worst—but in the midst of a mission was not the place to let old anger get the best of her. She dropped her chin to her chest, lifting a hand, palm forward, to stop anything Reichart had to say. When she raised her eyes again, her breathing was steady, heartbeat calm. "Step back," she murmured. "You're in my personal space. Nobody who comes around a corner is going to think this is a casual conversation."

Reichart did as she asked, to her surprise and his credit. His shoulders straightened as he uncurled from the intense, hovering posture he'd held, though his frown stayed in place. Almost, Alisha thought, as if he was genuinely concerned. "How'd you know it was the Russians?"

"It doesn't matter."

"Meet me in Paris on Friday." Reichart's voice was low, deep enough to be hardly more than a rumble. "There's a lot to talk about, Alisha." He turned his head a fraction of an inch, hearing footsteps falling in the hall behind them. "Adequate?" he asked, amusement suddenly tracing his tone. "You're a hard woman to please, Ms. Moon. I thought the demonstration was more than adequate."

"You weren't here yesterday," Alisha replied coolly. "A malfunction in the programming decided I was the target. It was corrected, but I'm sure my employers are going to be cautious about artificially intelligent drones that make that kind of mistake. Don't forget that in the report to your own."

"Conspiring?" Brandon asked pleasantly as he came up to them. Alisha turned a brief, meaningless smile on him. Out of the corner of her eye, she saw Reichart stiffen, and her smile deepened. The man couldn't possibly be jealous. No: he couldn't *reasonably* be jealous. But reason had little to do with jealousy.

"Comparing notes," she said. "Mr. Clarke thinks highly of your prototypes."

"Thus damning me with faint praise."

"Not at all," Alisha said. Never mind that she'd done just that a few moments earlier, and never mind the amused look Reichart gave her for the lie. "Despite yesterday's hitch, you know perfectly well it's an amazing machine."

"I hope you'll be telling your employers as much."

Alisha's gaze slid to Reichart. "You can count on it. For now, though..." She turned her wrist up, making a show of looking at her watch. "I should get my things. The plane is at two." And with the plane went her chances to find a way to steal the half a dozen drones that were hidden beneath the base. Frustration surged through her, hot enough to make her feel as though she blushed.

"There's time for you to stay for the second demo, if you like. I have something of a surprise planned."

Alisha exchanged a look with Reichart, whose dark eyebrows rose as he turned the look onto Brandon. "I assume it's not one involving me being shot at?"

"Scout's honor," Brandon said. "Elisa?"

Reichart's eyes darkened at Parker's informality. Alisha, catching the faint change of expression, smiled. "How could I resist?"

"You couldn't. I'm irresistible. This way, please." Brandon offered Alisha his arm and she took it with a laugh.

"So noted."

It was petty, but she couldn't help enjoying the sensation of Reichart's gaze boring between her shoulder blades as Brandon escorted her down the hall.

The Attengee drones swarmed the broken wall, ratcheting legs and trifold feet locking together to pull each other up. Two, perched atop the wall, lay down fire, covering the others as they crossed into the battlefield. Alisha watched, lips parted with astonishment, and turned to Brandon.

"They arrived last night," he said, the note of pride in his voice so smothered it was all the more obvious.

"You have a production facility?" Alisha asked, strain audible to her own ears. Brandon all but bounced on his toes as he nodded. "That's considerably more development than we'd been led to believe." Alisha struggled to keep the distress out of her voice, though Reichart's sideways glance told her she didn't entirely succeed. At least sounding shaken helped keep her cover. Brandon should have no hint that she'd been in the bunkers the night before and had already seen his new stash of drones.

"I didn't want to show our hand until I was sure the first-run drones would work well." Brandon nodded again, pointing toward the squad of machines as they laced their way across the field and began scaling the mountainside. "You asked about their handling of rough terrain. I think this demonstrates their capabilities nicely."

"Extremely." Alisha dared a glance toward Reichart, whose expression was carefully schooled. Well enough that she thought he, too, was hiding surprise. Good. It was the least he deserved for showing up in the middle of her missions. His surprise helped level the playing field after her own shock at his arrival.

"Your patrons have put a great deal of money into this, Brandon. I'm impressed. They must be very sure of turning an eventual profit."

"I think so." He flashed her a smile. "Not that I expect the CIA will be providing it."

Sound thunderclapped around Alisha's ears, a deep boom that made her feel as if she'd been hollowed out. She crinkled her forehead, privately astonished that her heart rate wasn't soaring, for all that every bit of her training taught her to stay cool in just such a situation. "The CIA?"

"Central Intelligence Agency," Brandon said, voice light and mocking. "I think you're familiar with it."

Alisha's eyebrows crinkled further, a deliberate expression of confusion that she hoped masked the impulse to reach out and throttle Frank Reichart. "Who isn't?"

"Don't embarrass us both, Alisha," Brandon murmured. Cold plunged through Alisha's hands, her feet itching with the need to move. "Did you really think I wouldn't know my father's protégé? I'm not that out of touch."

"Your father?" Alisha turned the adrenaline churning in her belly into bewilderment, filling her voice with it. "I know your father's CIA, Brandon. You used to be yourself. What does that have to do with me?" She could see Reichart taking a slow step backward, his hands partially lifted, as if to say he was not involved in the situation. It was possible, barely possible,

Alisha acknowledged deep inside herself, that Brandon was telling the truth, and that Reichart hadn't betrayed her.

It was barely possible that pigs with wings might be pigeons, too.

It could wait. Who'd set her up was irrelevant, right now. Getting out was all that mattered, and there *was* no good way out: she didn't have to look around to verify that. The best chance might be across the minefield, up the mountains with the drones—and then there'd be the drones themselves to deal with. "Brandon—"

"Rafe." Brandon turned his head a fraction of an inch as he issued the one-word order that brought the Englishman forward.

"Ms. Moon," Rafe said apologetically. "If you'll come with me."

"Are you out of your mind?" Alisha turned toward Rafe, rocking her weight back, hands spread compliantly as she saw that he held a gun with easy competence. "You checked my credentials yourself."

"Brandon had some compelling evi—"

Alisha lashed out with a kick, smashing her toe into the joint nerve in Rafe's wrist. Her twisted ankle, shocked at the sudden impact, flared with pain as Rafe's fingers spasmed open. Alisha ducked forward, wrapping her hand around the barrel of the gun as it fell. She reversed it, sliding her hand over the grip and checking the safety—it had been on; it wasn't as she curved her arm around Rafe's neck and held the gun to his temple. "I have no idea what you're talking about," she said through clenched teeth. "Are we at an impasse?"

Brandon had taken one step forward in the time it took her to take Rafe hostage. Reichart stayed back, hands still held wide, though he watched her as intently as Parker did. Alisha wanted to shout *He's FSB!* Alisha wanted to shout, but knew it was useless. Brandon's mysterious contact had warned him that a Russian agent was on the way. He knew what Reichart was. And there was the very slightest chance Reichart would opt to help her, if she didn't out him.

She was better off counting on flying pigs.

"Alisha, you can't get out of this alive unless we agree to help one another," Brandon said.

"Elisa," Alisha said. Beyond Brandon, Reichart cast a faint smile at the platform floor. She saw his mouth move, and for all that she didn't hear anything, she knew what he said: *Leesh.* Rafe's fingers were curled against her arm, digging in. She could see his eyes were crushed shut, and felt his breath came short and quick over her arm. He didn't have the combat training that she —that any of the others—did, or he'd have thrown her already. "Drawing a gun on me is not a good way to earn my cooperation, Dr. Parker. How exactly do you think we can help each other?"

Brandon's voice was gentle, like he spoke to

a frightened animal. "Well, right now you've got Rafe, and I've got your only way out of here. I think that might be one way to help one another."

Alisha barked laughter, not caring that Rafe flinched at the sharp sound in his ear. "I didn't think you were a hostage negotiator for the Agency, Parker."

"I wasn't," Brandon said in the same calming tone, "but we're all trained in it. You know that."

Alisha curled her lip into a snarl. "All I want is out of here." Fourth objective, part of her mind whispered. Determine if Brandon Parker is a clear and present danger and be prepared to terminate. She could certainly fulfill that part of her mission right now.

But it wouldn't get her out of there alive. "I'm listening."

"We'll take a Jeep. All three of us." Brandon's voice remained soothing. "Rafe will board the plane with you."

Rafe's eyes flew open, shock making his body go rigid in Alisha's grip. "It's all right," Brandon said to him. "She won't hurt you unless she's forced to. Unnecessary casualties don't look good on CIA records."

"Then what makes you think she'll shoot him now?" Reichart asked, faint amusement in his deep voice.

It didn't matter if he'd been the one to betray her to Brandon or not, Alisha decided. She was going to shoot him on general principle.

"I don't," Brandon said softly. "But she's in a corner, and I'd rather not have Rafe's brains splattered over the field if I'm wrong."

"You have a deal," Alisha interrupted. "But one thing." She nodded over Rafe's shoulder, toward the distant drones. "Shut them all down and give me the remote."

Annoyed admiration flashed through Brandon's eyes. "I hoped you wouldn't remember them."

Alisha smirked. "Not likely." She waggled the gun a centimeter or two, still keeping it against Rafe's temple. "Turn them off. Give me the remote. And tie him up." She nodded toward Reichart. "Then we go."

"Me?" Reichart's voice rose. "What'd I do?"

"As if you have to ask," Alisha muttered. "For caution's sake," she said aloud. "I don't know whose side you're on, and I'd rather not have a squadron of soldiers waiting for me down at the airport."

Resigned exasperation crossed Reichart's face, as clear as words saying *you're enjoying this, aren't you?* Brandon curled a lip in irritation, then followed Alisha's orders. Rafe sagged against her, relief obvious in the lines of his body. He hadn't been sure—*Alisha* hadn't been sure—that Brandon would negotiate with what amounted to a terrorist.

He started it, Alisha thought childishly. She heard him mutter, "Sorry," to Reichart, who shrugged acceptance and sat down against a platform post so Brandon could lash him in place. He cut Alisha one sharp glance through dark eyelashes, and she twitched an eyebrow back, acknowledging that he hadn't caused the kind of trouble he was more than capable of. He lifted his shoulders in a minute shrug and thumped his head back against the post as Brandon turned away. Alisha almost wished she could be there when Brandon returned, as she was certain Reichart would be gone, and she wanted to see Brandon's face

Brandon offered her the remote, but she nudged Rafe to take it. "You two first." Her voice was rough, nerves stressing it. They filed down the ladder and she jumped down after them, absorbing the impact with her knees and grimacing as her ankle objected. Brandon tensed, precursor to action, and Alisha straightened, gun held low but threatening. "Don't," she said. "Just don't."

He managed a brief smile. "Can't blame me for trying."

"Yes." The word came out flat. "I can." Her stomach twisted in a sour knot. Too much had gone wrong, with too many ramifications to consider, at least until she no longer had a Damocles sword hanging over her. Alisha jerked the gun toward the distant Jeep.

"Let's go."

Ten

The plane taking Alisha out of Kazakhstan theoretically belonged to her employer, and as such, was theoretically sacrosanct. With her cover blown, though, there was little, save the hostage she'd taken, to make them allow her to even board the plane, much less take off or fly out of the base's airspace. The fact that she escaped at all, while much appreciated, sent warning notes down her spine. *You* are *the Americans,* Brandon's contact had said. Alisha's survival suggested maybe the unknown handler was right. She *knew* there had been half a dozen opportunities to take her out as she fled to the plane with Rafe, opportunities she would have taken if one of her own people had been seized as a hostage and dragged unwillingly out of territory she controlled. Granted, no one who wanted Rafe to survive would have risked a head shot while she was driving on the treacherously narrow mountain road, but there had been moments of exposure while they'd gotten in the Jeep, and others while they boarded the plane.

Someone apparently didn't want to kill her.

That brought up even more questions than she'd started with.

She sent the pilot south through Azerbaijan, landing at a private airport on the Caspian Sea to drop Rafe off without a mobile phone or money. It wouldn't take him long to get back in contact with Brandon, but every delay helped Alisha a little. She had the pilot take her farther south, into Iran, abandoned the private plane then for a commercial flight out of Tehran, and changed flights and passports twice more before reaching Istanbul a full eighteen hours after she'd been scheduled to meet Greg Parker there. Leaving the air-conditioned airport for the humid heat of a Turkish summer hadn't improved her temper any, and by the time she got to the hotel safe room, she was ready to flay herself and anyone who got in her way for her own sheer stupidity.

Greg Parker waited for her in the little room, sitting on one side of a two-person table in front of windows open to let in heat and flies and the rising scent of street food. Aside from a minimum of electric wiring and a wire-framed bed, the room looked, to Alisha's eyes, the same way it probably had two, three, or even five hundred years earlier. There were days when she would take not just comfort, but delight, from that: things endured, despite humanity's best efforts. Today, though, all she knew was that she was sweaty, smelly, and professionally compromised. She flung her phone across the table and threw herself into a chair with equal violence before the phone had finished spinning and clattering its way to Greg. "It was a complete disaster, Greg. A total mess."

"Is anyone dead?"

"No."

"Then it wasn't a *complete* disaster."

"My cover got blown. Brandon knew who I was." Alisha pulled her lips back from her teeth, as if baring them would frighten the next thing she had to say into submission. "Reichart was there."

Greg's mouth pinched, weary resignation in his eyes. "I'll take you off the assignment."

"What?" Alisha jolted upright and brought her palm down on the table with a crack. "Like hell you will!"

"Alisha, it was a mistake to send you in the first place. You're too close, by dint of being close to me. And if Frank Reichart's involved, it's—"

"Not," Alisha growled. "It's not an emotional complication, Greg. Dammit, I've got too many questions. You can't take me off this. *You* should have questions." She straightened up, shoving a finger at the papers beneath Greg's hand. "Have you read my preliminary report?" A wave of guilt stabbed through her. The report was barely more than one of her illegal journal entries, filled with unanswered questions and exclamation marks.

"I've glanced at the first page or two." Greg

pursed his lips, tapping a finger on the papers before looking up at her. "It's..."

"Sketchy." She doubted that was the word Greg had been going for. Emotional, more likely, or compromised. On an intellectual level, she knew he was right: she didn't belong on this mission. But on a deeper level—an emotional one—sticking with it felt important. "I don't like turning in preliminary reports, Greg, you know that. I like presenting the whole picture. But this time I feel like I'm missing too much already. Like, who the hell is Sicarii?"

The shadow of a frown passed over Greg's face and he tapped the papers again, circling his fingertip against them. "The name doesn't mean anything to me. Are you certain about this information, about Brandon working for the CIA?"

Alisha sighed explosively, sinking down in her chair. "I'm not certain of anything right now. It's what I overheard. I'm going to follow his old trail here and see if I can get as far as a dead end." It was frequently what she couldn't find that told her the most. An agent who'd genuinely gone rogue would have a current operation file as long as her arm. One who'd been buried in secret operations was far more likely to come up as a red flag and a warning not to pursue him any further.

She wanted very much to find a dead end. For Greg, she told herself, and that was true. A son buried so deep in an undercover mission that even the father didn't know about it was a better ending to their story than resentment between the two having driven Brandon away.

But her own pride was tied up in it as well. She'd been compromised, whether by Reichart or by Brandon himself, and it had left with more questions than she'd begun with. Being unable to see the whole picture was often the price of being a player in the spy game, and usually she could accept that. But Brandon's possible continuing involvement with the CIA, his contact, and the name Sicarii that had so quickly silenced his objections, all piqued her interest beyond the norm. There was a trail to be followed there, a significance that itched to be discovered, but Alisha pushed that away for the moment, focusing on the concrete. "He's got a prototype army of his AIs in that base, Greg. Half a dozen of the Attengee drones, way too many for me to take out. I didn't know until it was too late that I should be looking for more. With any sort of luck—" she cast her gaze upward, supplication to the sky "—the virus will be uploaded to their main servers by now, as part of the daily backup, and all the schematics will be destroyed when the virus is triggered. But we need those prototypes. They could be reverse engineered. I've been in there. No one else has."

"How much of this is loyalty to king and country, and how much is revenge for being discovered, Alisha?"

That was the second time Greg had used her full name, just in case Alisha hadn't already realized how serious he was. She straightened in her seat, leaning across the table with her hands spread in a gesture of earnestness. "Some of it's revenge. I'm—" She jerked her shoulders in a tight shrug. "Embarrassed. Angry. To have been betrayed." Later she might examine her own choice of words there, but for now she went on with a quick shake of her head.

"But I genuinely believe returning to the base is vital, sir. The Attengee drones are highly effective combat machines. It's of paramount importance that a trustworthy organization hold all copies of that design—" Alisha broke off at the glitter of amusement in Greg's eyes, giving him a tight, rueful smile. "Let's at least pretend to believe the U.S. government is a trustworthy organization," she said, teasing as much as she dared.

Greg brushed it away with a brief smile of his own. "Yes, let's. Go on."

Alisha stood, crossing to the room's balcony so she could scowl out at the ancient city. Their safe room hotel had been part of a smaller village engulfed by Istanbul's 20th century growth, and hints of the village remained in the shop fronts and street widths. The distance was littered with factories in various states of repair rather than any of Istanbul's historic beauty, but voices chattered up from below, the musical Turkish language rising in an indistinguishable cacophony. The relentless humanity of it, the steady wash of people involved with their own lives, washed away some of Alisha's anger, and she sighed. If she had time, she'd go out and lose herself in the press of bodies and the noise of the marketplace, singing scraps of Western songs to herself.

"I don't doubt for an instant that Reichart will be reporting back to the FSB and they'll try something similar. We need to not waste time." It was too precious a commodity to be spent forgotten in the narrow streets among the vendors. Alisha touched the flaking paint of the window frame with a modicum of regret.

"And what about Reichart himself?"

"Permission to kick his ass requested, sir."

Greg laughed aloud, an unexpected sound of genuine delight. Alisha turned from the window, modestly pleased with herself. "Permission granted," Greg said, "if you can find him. All right, Alisha. You've got a go on this thing. Good luck."

"Thank you, sir."

The Kazakhstani base was deserted.

Alisha hadn't been the only one to sense the wrongness as they'd approached, military helicopters dropping them just on the other side of the valley's mountaintops. She'd seen the exchanged glances, the wordless warnings, as they'd come down the mountainside into the silent, dark valley. No one liked it: it had the feel of a place rigged to blow, a recognizable quality to those with combat experience. The walls held their breath, listening for the countdown that would rupture them and blow the world asunder. The silence had purpose, and in the heart of enemy territory, purpose could be deadly.

She found the first bomb herself, a block of C4 as big as her two fists. She lifted a black-covered hand, shrilling a soft whistle to gain the attention of the rest of her team as the numbers worked their way backward toward zero. Thirty-nine minutes until detonation. She uncovered her watch—no longer the delicate fashion piece she so often wore, but instead a heavy black-banded thing with dim numbers —and synchronized its alarm with the countdown as she spoke. "The prototypes aren't going to be here."

"You want us to check anyway?" The squadron leader eyed the timer before turning his attention to Alisha. She pressed her lips together, then nodded once.

"I'll bring two men down. The rest of you see if there are any surface-to-air-defenses. If not we can just call the choppers in and get out of here before the whole place blows to kingdom come."

"Yes, ma'am." The sergeant flicked a salute and motioned to his men, splitting two of the eight off to join Alisha. Overriding the elevator protocols took seconds, and despite the bombs counting down overhead, Alisha smiled as they took the shaft down. Much easier than sneaking through air ducts.

Black acrid smoke rolled over them as the elevator doors swept open. Lights dimmed and brightened, sparking out with hisses and splatters. Alisha muffled a cough in the back of her hand, then pulled her turtleneck up over her nose and mouth, eyes watering. Her two guards stepped forward, one dragging infrared glasses over his eyes. They checked the hall, then Infrared nodded. Alisha pointed to her eyes, then down the hall; Infrared nodded again and she darted through the wispy fumes.

Brandon could not have conceivably de-stroyed the prototypes, and yet Alisha was relieved to punch the pass code—unbeliev-ably, it still worked—into the computer lab's lock pad and find that it was only the comput-ers that had been destroyed. "We're clear," she said into her radio a moment later, voice hoarse. "They let out the magic black smoke."

A chuckle answered her as she hurried through the sizzling computer remains, search-ing for any hard drives that might have gone unscathed. There were none. Brandon, or Hashikov and his men, had been thorough. Al-isha muttered, "Shit," philosophically. It would have surprised her more to find something sal-vageable.

"Ma'am?"

"Nothing," she said. "Two minutes and we're out of here."

"Yes, ma'am," the soldier said, sounding considerably more cheerful. Alisha crawled over the row of desks against the viewing windows, peering down into the hub room. It was clear of the smoke that roiled through the other levels, its ventilation system cut off from the rest of the bunker. Alisha coughed again, wiping the back of her hand across her eyes. There was a single piece of paper in the middle of the hub room floor.

"Conspiracy, or coincidence?" She tested the windows, finding them sealed, and crawled off the desks to run for the steel stairway. Bits of debris and wiring littered the floor, a few hot spots glowing as if determined to hang on just a little longer.

The control room above was as hazy, but less damaged, than the computer lab. Alisha gulped air and yanked the window open, taking the wall-cut rungs down with abandon, which made her realize, gratefully, that her ankle had finally healed up. She jumped the last few feet, landing in a roll that brought her to the sheet of paper.

A cardinal on an ornate dome, drawn in black ink on heavy parchment paper, dominated the page. Written in small block letters at the bottom of the page was a Latin phrase: *cave retro*. Alisha stared at the dome, something itching at the back of her mind. It was familiar, the ink lines edging a memory into place before fading into blackness. She shook her head, unable to grasp it, then frowned at the letters, searching for what little Latin she knew. The phrase was neither *carpe diem* nor *illigitemi non corundum,* but it took several seconds to get those translations, especially the second, *don't let the bastards grind you down,* out of her head. Alisha shook herself, wiping the phrases from her mind, and studied the paper again. *Retro* was behind. *Cave* meant beware. In modern English—

Look behind you.

Alisha's shoulders went rigid as a tendril of cold slithered around her spine, stiffening her posture, while simultaneously, heat filled her belly, blood rushing from her core to her limbs, making her hands and feet itch and burn. Every impulse told her to run, even without knowing what she was running from. Alisha clamped down on the urge, swallowing thickly.

Don't run. The order, spoken silently, felt slow and stupid, words a barrier against a million years of instinct. *Don't run. Look first, Leesh. Don't run.*

The tiny muscles in her neck bunched, vertebrae creaking as she turned her head so carefully she couldn't tell at first that she was moving. The steadying breath she took felt cold against the heat of adrenaline spilling through her body in preparation for action.

An Attengee drone crouched in the shadow

of the back wall, its blaster compartments already open. She could see the shimmer of guidance dots against her shoulder, red on black. The soft whir of the weapons training on her told her the initial assessment—threat or not—had already been performed, and she had been found wanting.

"Son of a *bitch*."

Eleven

"Ma'am?" The polite question on the radio was so incongruous with the lasers aimed at her that Alisha nearly laughed. She quelled the impulse, clutched the cardinal drawing in her fist, and flung herself into a roll, seeking cover.

Laser fire smashed after her, bursts of heat that sent the concrete floor into smoking striations. Alisha jolted back, twisting her hip so hard it popped. Heat seared the air above her head as the drone overshot. *Evasive action maneuvers.* She heard the words spoken in Jean-Luc Picard's voice inside her mind as she hit the floor on her back, rolling again. It was almost impossible for a human to make truly random choices, and the drone's AI would likely recognize the pattern in random choices before she herself would.

The alternative, then, was to out-think the machine. Make deliberate and irrational choices. Alisha snatched the gun off her hip, taking two purposefully wild shots in hopes of distracting the drone's AI for a few seconds. She heard the crackle of the radio as her guards recognized weapons fire and came running, but she didn't have time to wait on them. Rolling onto her belly and scrambling to her feet gave her the momentum to dive for one of the drone's three legs. The trifold foot snaked out of her reach, clanking down against the concrete floor hard enough to mar its surface. Alisha took another two shots, the first ricocheting off the drone's metallic ankle. The second hit, not shattering the bolt as she'd hoped, but at least wedging it in place and reducing the mechanism's ability to rotate. Combat-trained preternatural hearing kicked in despite the ringing in her ears from the gunshots, and a low buzz warning her the Attengee's blasters were focused on her again.

She flung herself forward again, rolling beneath the drone and coming up flat against the wall. The silver dome whipped around, weapons firing and turning the wall behind her to slag.

Alisha was no longer there, already flinging herself at another leg. They *had* to be the weak points. She wrapped both hands around one, just above the ankle, and scrambled backward, ducking laser fire to haul the drone off balance with all her strength.

It toppled with an ear-shattering clang against the concrete, legs flailing like an over-turned spider, and for one blessed moment, lay still.

Alisha scrambled out of reach, fumbling with the utility belt at the small of her back. Her hands shook, endorphins pumping through her system so powerfully she could hardly control her own movements. The buttons popped open and she slid the Attengee's remote—the one advantage she'd thought she might have, in trying to bring the prototype army out of the base—free of its pocket.

A ratcheting leg slammed into her diaphragm, throwing her backward across the room. Tears leaked down her cheeks, blocking her vision of the commands on the remote pad as she struggled for air. The drone swayed to its feet and lurched forward, reacquiring her as a target with another low whir. Alisha choked against the knot of breathlessness in her stomach and only succeeded in exhaling more of what little air she had left.

Don't look up, Leesh. Just do it. Just find the right key combination. Her hearing wouldn't let her ignore the whine of the lasers preparing to fire. She'd forgotten to ask Greg about the Santa Claus song.

Gunfire splattered the room, as precious as the sound of a knight in white armor riding down the evil king. The drone whipped around, spattering the concrete walls with bursts of laser fire. One of the soldiers bellowed, "Hit the deck!" and Alisha wheezed a little laugh, a tiny gasp of air that felt like the first promise she might someday breathe normally again. She wiped her arm across her eyes, coughing another insignificant breath out, and finally, weakly, punched the disabling code into the remote.

The drone folded down into its resting state,

lasers settling back into place and leaving the AI's silver dome unmarred once more. Alisha rolled onto her back, arms flung wide, and dragged in a painful breath around the baseball-sized knot beneath her sternum. Another fit of coughing brought tears to her eyes, but she lifted a hand in triumph, ignoring the cardinal drawing still crumpled there. "Drone acquired. Third objective accomplished, sir."

"Ma'am?" The infrared-goggles-wearing soldier appeared in Alisha's line of vision and offered her a hand up. She took it, wheezing, and jerked a thumb at the drone.

"My boss needs to see this. Can we pack it up and fly it out of here in the next ten minutes?"

The soldier made a brief show of looking at his watch. "We can do it in seven, ma'am."

"Seven. Seven is good." Alisha got the hell out of there with a squadron—this one friendly—on her tail. Minutes later, the reverberating explosions that confirmed the base's destruction were a deep echo of the helicopter blades, and Alisha, relieved, fell asleep to the sounds of destruction.

Returning to base with a successful mission under her belt lightened Alisha's step considerably as she helped Infrared—his name was Harrison, yes, like that one, he said—offload the drone in England after an all-night flight paused only for refueling. He'd insisted his men would do the heavy lifting, but having blown one mission, physically helping to deliver the drone into Greg's waiting hands felt important to Alisha. Satisfaction lit her handler's eyes as she and Harrison walked the drone off the chopper, and she watched with a pleasure close to glee as military nerds swept down on it like a holiday gift.

"You did well, Ali."

"I made up for a colossal error," she conceded, but Greg shook his head.

"Sending you in to Kazakhstan after my own son was my mistake, not yours. None of us knew Reichart would be there, and despite his presence you got out of that base with no casualties and the information we needed, and went back for the hardware. Don't belittle that."

"Yes, sir. What's next?"

Greg pressed his lips together as they watched the tech team bundle the Attengee drone off to their lab. "I need you to find Brandon."

"*You* need me to, or the Company needs me to?"

He gave her a sideways look. "I'm surprised you're splitting that hair."

Alisha's eyebrows rose. "Are you really."

A breath of laughter escaped him. "Maybe not. In either case, the answer is both. I've spoken with the director, who claims no knowledge of Brandon having deep cover status, so the Company wants answers as much as I do on a personal level. I already tried to take you off this once and that didn't take, so I'm going to use the assets I've got. Find Brandon, whatever it takes, and find out what the hell is going on."

"It'll be my pleasure, sir." Alisha strode away, leaving the techs to do their job, then stopped suddenly, turning back to catch Greg's attention. "Do you ever sing 'fuckity fuck fuck' to the tune of 'Here Comes Santa Claus' when things have gone wrong?"

Gregory Parker's eyes widened as an incredulous smile spread across his face. "Do I *what*?"

"Yeah, okay. I didn't think so." Alisha waved and left him behind, laughter and hope blooming in her chest. She had a task and no specific orders as to how to accomplish it, which meant she could take as direct or as circuitous a route to finding Brandon Parker as she needed to.

And she had a date waiting for her in Paris. One she didn't want her handler, or anybody else, to know about.

Meet me in Paris. Four words, spoken with intimacy, urgency, and a certain degree of confidence. Paris was a big city, and a man expecting a woman to meet him there might well have been wise to be a little more specific.

Not Frank Reichart, though. Not when he was talking to Alisha MacAleer, anyway. The flight from England lasted just over an hour, not even enough time to get uncomfortable in the cheap, last-minute-airline seats. Alisha entertained the little kid beside her with shadow puppets cast with her phone's flashlight, smiled at the grateful mother as they disembarked, and took the Metro from the airport in to city center to find a once-familiar café that had changed just enough, over the years, to be slightly jarring. It spilled out its own doors and over to the riverbank as it always had, though, burbling with cheerful noise, umbrellas catching voices and echoing them down again. Students forgot their haute couture cool in favor of too much rich French coffee and passionate political arguments. A word or two spoken in English caught Alisha's attention now and again, but largely the free flow of French spun by her as a comforting babble she could choose not to understand.

Reichart wasn't there. Hadn't been, any of the dozens of times she'd glanced up, searching for him. Wouldn't be the next time, either. Alisha smoothed the wrinkles out of the cardinal drawing for the hundredth time, staring not at it, but through it. The heavy lines of the dome it perched on swam through her line of vision, bringing with them a sense of nagging familiarity, but she pushed it away. She probably shouldn't have come to Paris. Reichart wasn't the most reliable man she'd ever met, and the reality was he'd probably set her up just to see if she'd jump. She smoothed the drawing again, gaze unfocused. She knew better, dammit. She knew he wouldn't be here. That disappointment was inevitable.

Although that was bullshit, really. Alisha pushed the drawing aside, picking up her coffee cup in both hands to blow on the hot liquid. Reichart never disappointed. He betrayed, he lied and he endangered, but mere disappointment was too blasé for him. Alisha huffed a breath into the coffee and sipped before putting the cup down again, her eyes closed. All that, and she'd still be disappointed if he didn't show up. She muttered, "Bastard," and Frank Reichart—blasély—shifted the table as he sat down, saying, "I think that's my cue."

Alisha shook her head minutely, eyes still closed, mouth twisted with amused irritation.. After five years, his nonchalant arrival, always with the perfect line, could still make her heart jump. In spite of everything. *Bastard.* She opened her eyes to find him sprawled in the chair across from her, long denim-clad legs crossed at the ankle and hands folded behind his head. "It's good to see you, Alisha."

"You've seen a lot of me lately."

"Glimpses stolen in the midst of flight don't count." Reichart leaned forward, snaking a hand toward Alisha's coffee as familiarly as if they were still engaged. She smacked his knuckles, and he withdrew, looking injured. "It's been a long time."

"The Russians, Frank?" God, she fell right into the old patterns. Trying to understand the motivations of a man whose base desires were diametrically different from her own. Asking questions she already knew the answers to, in hopes of hearing something other than the answers she knew were coming. Asking questions she knew the answers to, because he wouldn't answer the other ones anyway.

Reichart shrugged, a lazy action that shifted his whole torso. He wore a white T-shirt under a thigh-length soft leather jacket, more fashion model than Fonzie. "They pay in euros."

Alisha let go a breath of humorless laughter and looked up at the café umbrella that blocked the gray Parisian sky. She'd warned herself, more than once. He never disappointed, and he never changed. "You're a greedy son of a bitch."

"Some things don't change."

"Too much." Once upon a time the fact that his thoughts paralleled hers so closely would have pleased her. Now it annoyed her, in an old, worn-out way. "You said we had a lot to talk about."

"We do." Reichart's voice dropped. "We never talked about it, Leesh."

Ice formed in Alisha's lungs, chilling her voice. "There was nothing to talk about." Hairs lifted on her arms, and she fought back a shiver, her expression cool as she met Reichart's eyes.

"Did it ever occur to you that it might've been Cristina?"

Rage spilled down Alisha's spine, wiping out the cold. Just like always, she thought. If there'd been any room left in her for laughter, she might have let it come, but there was only the shadow of past mistakes. "Yes. Obviously. Years later. Was it?"

Something dark flickered in Reichart's eyes before he deliberately looked away. Alisha tightened her hands around her coffee cup, wishing the mug was smaller, less sturdy, so she might shatter it with her hands. So that hot coffee might spill over her, shards embedded in her hands: any excuse to walk away from the man sitting across from her. She shouldn't have come. Five years wasn't enough to wipe out old emotion. Maybe a lifetime wouldn't be enough. And Reichart's failure to answer—well, she'd known better than to ask.

"That's what I thought," she said, working to keep her voice steady. "This is how talking goes with you, Frank. This is why there was nothing to say." Once upon a time his reticence had been enticing. Once upon a time it had been mysterious, exciting, a challenge.

Once upon a time.

"Then why did you come?"

Pain jolted through Alisha's heart, like a contraction around a knife. It zinged upward, lingering just below her collarbone before it faded again. She pressed her eyelids closed, clutching the mug hard enough to turn her knuckles white. "Because you asked me to."

"Is that all it ever would have taken?"

Cords stood out in Alisha's neck as she lifted her gaze to him. "Don't. Don't do this, all right, Reichart? It's over." She could hear tension making her voice tremble, the frustrated amusement of his arrival dissipated. "You've played your get out of jail free card. This isn't a date or a reconciliation. I'm here because you said we needed to talk and I thought you might have something to say that I needed to hear."

Reichart's expression, never easily read, shuttered further. "Fine. Where'd you hear about the Sicarii?"

"Oh, for God's sake, Frank." Alisha put her cup down again. "Interrogating me isn't talking, either. We can go on like this for hours. Flat statements and answering questions with questions. I don't have time for it, and if that's what you're going to play, this conversation is over. I don't want to see you again." She shoved her chair back from the café table. His hand flashed out and caught her wrist, then let go so quickly it barely left the impression of warmth against her skin.

"Ever?" The question came and went as rapidly as his grasp. "I'm not playing a game, Alisha. The Sicarii's outside your realm of expertise. You're too straight."

"Straight." Alisha snorted. "Nobody with my

day job is straight, Frank."

A smile flickered through Reichart's dark eyes, warming them. "Some are straighter than others." Alisha spread her fingers, granting him the point, and he glanced around. "This isn't the best place to talk."

"You said Paris. Where else but here?" Alisha shrugged at the café in general, carefully not looking toward the riverbank tables. Reichart did look, and for a moment Alisha could see memory play across his features. Memory of the man getting down on one knee at the end of a muggy Parisian evening, fog starting to roll in off the river and giving the light the misty blueness that seemed to haunt old paintings and romantic movies. Reichart, always so circumspect, deliberately raising his voice and speaking fluid French, the better to gain attention from the lingering crowd at the café. Alisha, laughing, her hands cupped over her mouth, knowing what was going on but not quite able to believe it.

The ring was a round-cut diamond set directly into gold, so that there was nothing to snag or catch on. Yellow topaz, Alisha's favorite stone, hugged the clear center jewel. Subtle, discreet, beautiful: the perfect engagement ring for a spy. Alisha hadn't needed to ask to know Reichart had designed it just for her.

The café patrons had erupted into applause and cheers when Alisha, embarrassingly tearful, had flung herself into his arms, whispering,

"Yes, of course. Of course!" Someone bought them a bottle of wine older than the two of them put together, and everyone had a splash, just enough to taste the rich old flavor in celebration.

Reichart pulled his gaze back to Alisha, looking almost guilty. "Yeah, where else. Look, Leesh..." He reached for her hand again, more cautiously. Alisha curled her fingers around her coffee cup, holding it tightly enough to turn her knuckles white. Reichart pressed his lips together and pulled his hand back, drumming his fingers against the table. "Yeah," he said again. "I don't think I ever told you I'm sorry."

Old anger burst inside her chest, becoming weariness. Alisha slumped back in her chair, shaking her head. "For which part, Frank? For choosing cash over country? For selling me out? For shooting me?" She stilled her hand, refusing to rub the scar between her collarbone and her heart. It was faded now, careful surgery blurring the edges away, but she could still feel it. Especially now, another sharp pang that felt like it cut through her heart. "There are a million things to be sorry for. It doesn't matter anymore."

"It does."

"No." Alisha straightened, shaking her head. "No, Frank, it doesn't. I don't understand you, I don't like you and I don't trust you."

"I didn't sell you out."

"Which time?"

"This time."

Alisha's cheeks burned hot, anger flooding

through her. "I don't believe you. The timing's too pat." There was no doubt in her tone, though a modicum remained in her mind: Brandon *might* have known all along. But why bother with the charade, then? Unless he *was* working for the Americans and Reichart's presence had forced his hand, somehow. Alisha curled a lip, pulling her thoughts back into order. "Do you have anything useful to say, or am I wasting my time here?"

Reichart raked a hand through his hair, disheveling it into slicked-back curls. "Sicarii's a conspiracy theory, Leesh, that's all. Secret organizations, trying to take over the world. I didn't think you were into that kind of thing."

An exasperated smile broke through Alisha's rancor. "I thought that was the Illuminati. Come on, Reichart. Conspiracy theories?"

"I've just heard the word bandied around, Leesh. It's crap."

"And I haven't heard it because...?"

Reichart performed another loose shrug. "Because people on the legitimate side of this business don't waste their time with conspiracy theories. There's enough scary shit to follow up on in the real world without adding layers of monsters in the dark to it all."

"Do you ever miss it?" Alisha regretted the question as soon as it was asked. Reichart's gaze came up, meeting hers, then flickered away again. Back to the table at the riverside.

"Not it," he said. Alisha folded her thumb

across her left palm, rubbing it against her ring finger, then closed her hand into a fist, all as betraying as Reichart's glance. He saw it, and offered a faint smile.

"It wasn't all bad, was it?"

"Not at all." Alisha looked down at her hand, feeling the missing shape of an engagement ring she hadn't worn for years. She would never admit to Reichart—or anyone else —that the ring lay in a strongbox in a Parisian bank, along with a journal so full of pain the scrawled words were almost illegible. The ring was gone, but not irretrievable.

Like, apparently, the feelings she had for Frank Reichart. "I've got to go." She stood, digging in her pocket for a coin or two to throw down on the table as she scooped up the wrinkled drawing.

"Is that Rome?"

"What?" Alisha looked down, catching Reichart's nod at the piece of paper.

"The dome. It's the Basilica dome, isn't it? St. Peter's Basilica's dome on the Vatican. It would've been the last thing you saw after—"

Alisha pressed her eyes shut, the black lines on the parchment finally leaping into sunset-stained color in her mind's eye. The memory of astonishing pain exploding in her left shoulder hit her, crushing the breath out of her. Body memory, physical memory: her right hand, working of its own will, touching the spot of agony and lifting into her line of vision. Hot blood trickling down her fingers. Her hand falling away, leaving her gaping in disbelief at the Vatican's dome, blazing golden and red in the sunset, like God's own holy light.

Then blackness, fading in around the crowning globe atop the dome, and nothing at all until the bright white light of a hospital room.

"After you shot me." Not the words Reichart would have chosen, Alisha was sure. "Yeah." She crumpled the drawing again, pressing the rumpled paper against her shoulder as if it would stop the wound from five years earlier. *Look behind you.* The Latin phrase and the drawing itself suddenly seemed layered, filled with far more portent than the simple warning she'd taken it for in the bunker. It was that, certainly, but a sense of confidence settled into Alisha's bones. It was a warning, but it was also an invitation. Sent, she was sure, by Brandon.

Reichart's low voice drew her back to the moment: "I have nightmares about it."

Alisha studied him briefly, then folded the cardinal into her pocket and walked away. "I don't."

Twelve

A few hours later, Alisha stood in the midst of Roman foot traffic, shifting her shoulders enough to allow passersby to sweep past without jostling her from her place. There was no bloodstain on the stones, no dark spot to say she'd fallen there, almost dead, five years earlier.

Five years, and she'd never come back to this place. To Rome, yes: it was like getting back on the horse, and she knew it. But she'd avoided the Piazza San Pietro without consciously realizing it.

Now sunset flared around the Vatican's dome, the long shadow of its crown bending and stretching down toward the plaza, just as it had then. Shadows that matched the cardinal sketch Alisha held tightly in her hand. *Look behind you.* She fought the impulse for another moment or two, still watching the colors gleam and fade off the dome.

The scar under her collarbone throbbed, insistent bump of discomfort. Reminding her that she was still alive. Reminding her how close she'd come to death.

It was easy to replay, standing there under

the same light. Like a dream unwinding in her waking vision, the faces around her changed, becoming the ghosts of other strangers burned into her memory. An older woman with the enviable Mediterranean graying at the temples, chin held high and regal. A handsome man twenty years the woman's junior, turning to watch her with admiration. A bevy of nuns, flocked together like black-headed birds, at odds with breathless teens wearing jeans cut low and shirts cut high. Five years after the fact, if any of them walked by Alisha on a city street, she would know them all with a pang of recognition that cut just above her heart.

There had been a disturbance in the crowd: a thin man in the red robes of a cardinal, making his way against the flow of traffic. Ripples spread out, an opening and closing of the waters as people created space for the holy man, adjusting to his presence, then resuming their normal course as if nothing had bothered them. In moments he was at Alisha's side, brushing against her: papers neatly folded into his palm slipped into hers instead, and then he was past. One step. Two steps.

Gunfire. One violent shot from above. The cardinal fell, the crimson of his life's blood hidden by the crimson of his robes. All of it stained gold by the setting sun.

Made! The word screamed inside Alisha's mind as she shrieked with the passersby, falling back a step against every impulse to run forward, to see if the cardinal had somehow survived. She had been his contact for four years, almost her whole CIA career. They'd exchanged no words in that time, nothing more than the brief touch of hands at sunset. There was almost a romance to it, illicit, secret, stimulating: but then, that was part of the fun. The sensuality of clandestine work was one thing that kept her coming back for more.

Three people. Three people had known where she'd be at sunset. Greg, who'd set up the meeting. Impossible for him to have betrayed her; Alisha rejected the thought out of hand.

Cristina. Her partner for more than three years. Alisha's cover, in the plaza, watching, keeping her safe. Even as she scanned the rooftops for the shooter, Alisha sought Cristina's bright blond hair in the plaza itself, unable to believe that three years of trust could be destroyed with a single bullet.

No: there was Cristina, her own weapon pulled—an action Alisha didn't dare take herself, for fear that if she was unknown to the shooter, she'd betray herself to him by being armed in a city where civilians didn't carry guns—as she searched the roofs herself.

Relief and horror cascaded together, making sick chills in Alisha's stomach, forcing tears to her eyes. A casual statement, an invitation to dinner: "I'll be at the Vatican plaza at sunset." Spoken to her fiancé, who'd waved a hand agreeably and gone back to sleep.

No one else. No one else knew. Reichart was the third.

Another desperate scan of the skyline, sunlight shafts piercing around the buildings. Highlighting a man with a gun and no expression on his face.

"Frank," Alisha whispered.

She was never certain if she heard the shot or merely felt it, explosive pain beneath her collarbone. It shocked her breath away, her very heart seeming to shatter, and knocked her around a few inches, bringing the sunlit cross atop the basilica into view. Numb fingers touched the hurting place, then lifted, blocking her view of the dome. Blood crept into the thin lifeline in her palm, trickling down, filling it. When it was full, Alisha wondered, would she be dead? But she couldn't see it anymore, the strength to hold her hand up lost. There was only the Vatican's dome, glowing with the beauty of sunset, and then encroaching darkness that dimmed all further thought.

Sunset faded from behind the Vatican, leaving twilight less potent than the blackness of memory. Alisha took one careful step back from the place she'd fallen—funny that she remembered it so clearly, one square foot among thousands—and slowly turned to look across the square.

Look behind you.

Brandon Parker leaned in a doorway hundreds of feet away, an arm above his head and his weight cocked on one hip. A mocking smile, just visible in the blue light of early evening, flickered across his face. He inclined his head, then he turned and walked inside, leaving the empty doorway a dark rectangle of challenge infused in the pale stone walls.

"Son of a bitch." Alisha heard herself infuse the words with the same mildness Brandon had used a few nights earlier. Too many thoughts crowded against each other: how had he known, why was he doing this, what was he doing? One thing was certain, at least: there was no longer any point in protesting her own innocence. Elisa Moon had run her gamut of usefulness. Alisha would face Brandon as herself. She swore again, softly, and pushed against traffic, ducking through the throngs of people.

The doorway was empty, no wires or notes or traps hidden within the darkness, only a narrow stairway leading up to a second door. Alisha tattooed a beat against the downstairs door frame, waiting for a sense of danger to forbid her to go. Instead, the scent of baking bread wafted down, more startling than a trap. She clicked her tongue, muttered an oath and took the steps two at a time. Curiosity had killed the cat. Evidently fresh bread would be her undoing. She put a hand on the second door, leaning in to listen warily.

"It's open. I don't suppose you brought wine."

Alisha nudged the door open, still wary. "I didn't know I was meeting a date."

Brandon stood in a room filled with candle-light, the wooden table beside him bearing a broken loaf of bread that steamed in the air despite the evening's heat. A small kitchen with a pot bubbling on its stove lay at the back of the room beside a door that led into darkness. Directly above the table, a skylight was propped open with a stick. Alisha took it all in with a glance, her fingers curled against the door frame.

"Didn't you?" Brandon looked skeptical. "It's all right. I have some. I just thought you might bring something better." He stepped around the table to take a bottle and two glasses from the kitchen counter, making a musical clink as they knocked together.

Alisha looked back over her shoulder, down the staircase she'd taken, as if the answer was there. *Look behind you.* Had she expected him?

Yes. From the moment Reichart had recognized the cardinal on the cross, Alisha had known. She had expected Parker to be here in Rome more than she'd trusted that Reichart would show up in Paris. Alisha twisted her mouth and repeated, "Son of a bitch," still mildly. "How did you know about the cardinal?" Her code name for years now, an homage to the man who had died to pass information along to the right people. She would have to talk to Greg about changing it.

"I told you. I pay attention to my father's protégé. Come in, eat." Brandon gestured her in, waving at the bread with the wine bottle. A bottle of olive oil and a tin of butter sat on the table beside it. "We can talk here," he added. "The room has been swept for bugs. Come on in. I'll put the pasta on."

Alisha closed the door behind her, amusement warring with irritation. "Is this your usual method of seduction? Leave a cryptic note, blow a girl up, and if she survives prepare an Italian dinner? How's that working for you?"

"I'll let you know." Brandon shot her a smile. "I wasn't sure you'd come."

"You look confident." She gestured at the bread and cooking pasta. "How did you even know I'd find the drawing?"

"I didn't. I took a chance. What happened to the drone? Rafe," he added, "may have post-traumatic stress syndrome. I don't think grad school prepared him for being a hostage."

Alisha said, "I'm sorry about Rafe," without meaning a word of it. "Why'd you let me go?"

"Because whether the rock strikes the pitcher or the pitcher strikes the rock, it's going to be bad for the pitcher. I genuinely didn't want anyone to get shot, and letting you go was the only way to make sure that didn't happen. Besides, they had me over a barrel."

"Thank you," Alisha said dryly. "Who are they? Who are you working for?"

"I spend two days waiting in a dramatically lit doorway and cooking extravagant meals, and you want to cut to the chase just like that?"

"Well..." Alisha put as much thoughtful consideration into the single word as she could. "...yes." Then, after a moment of actual thoughtful consideration, she admitted, "It *was* very dramatic." *Watch it, Leesh.* She didn't need to play up to him to get what she wanted.

No, but it was a lot more fun that way. Brandon Parker was charming in a boy-next-door way, much safer than the dangerous edge that had drawn her to Frank Reichart. She'd known going in that dating Reichart was playing with fire. Brandon had none of that threat to him, and letting herself relax and banter was incredibly appealing.

And comparing one agent's charms to another's would inevitably end in tears. She had a job to do, and Parker might have the answers she was looking for.

Brandon laughed aloud and sketched an elaborate bow, complete with hand flourishes. "Thank you. I'm glad you came. I couldn't have waited more than one more day."

"I almost didn't come." She wouldn't have, if Reichart hadn't recognized the dome. A detail Brandon certainly didn't need to know. "All things considered, I'd say my timing is excellent. Why the deadline?"

"Because I'm in the midst of a complex mess, and my loyalties are being tested. Which is why your ex-fiancé was present at Project ACUTE three days ago. I'm sorry, Alisha, but Reichart is working for the Sicarii, and has for years."

Cold formed at the back of Alisha's throat, spilling down to spread through her stomach. The chill extended itself to her expression: she felt her cheeks pale and her eyes widen in confusion.

Someone was lying. If the Sicarii was real, if Reichart was working for it—them?—he had every reason to debunk it. And the very word had been enough to make Brandon kowtow to his handler. Anger replaced confusion, heat filling the cold spaces inside her. For now, it didn't matter who was lying. For now, any information she could get was priceless, and for information, Alisha would play Parker's game. All the impulse to flirt drained away, leaving her tight-jawed and staring at Brandon.

His eyes crinkled with apology and sympathy. He crooked his fingers, beckoning. "Come on, sit down. There's a lot to tell you. Things you can't tell my father, Alisha. This goes beyond him."

"Then why include me?" Alisha swallowed against sudden roughness in her voice.

"Because you're extraordinarily loyal, Alisha." Brandon poured her a glass of wine, elevated his eyebrows and offered the glass as an invitation.

"Loyalty. An admiral quality in dogs," Alisha took the glass without sipping. Brandon noticed and laughed, pouring himself a splash.

"*Salute.*" He lifted the glass and drank, then arched his eyebrows again, challenging. Alisha nodded and took a small sip, satisfied the wine wasn't drugged, or at least that Brandon had spent years building up an immunity to iocane powder. "Loyalty is as valuable in spies," he said. "Everybody's got a price, but no one seems to have found yours yet."

"Are you looking for it?" Alisha kept her gaze steady on Brandon's, feeling that even one small hesitation, the slightest faltering, and she might reveal what her price was. Not that even *she* was sure. Her sister's family, certainly; she would do anything to protect them. But so long as she remained good at her job, there should be no connection to them. If she had a price, it was something else.

Frank Reichart, the back of her mind whispered. Alisha took another sip of wine, watching Brandon and hoping her gaze was shuttered.

Brandon shrugged. "Only clinically. In the way that anybody in espionage is interested in someone's price. It's information, and that's power, but I'm not trying to buy you, Alisha. I know you've got a personal stake in this mission. You've worked with Dad too long to be neutral, no matter what you might tell him. You're tenacious when it's personal, and I'd rather have that tenacity working for me."

"I already have a job," Alisha said icily.

Brandon winced. "That wasn't what I meant. Look, I'm making a mess of this. Could we start again, please?"

Alisha sang, "I think you've made your point now," in a clear soprano, startling Brandon, whose eyebrows rose once more, questioning. "Nothing. Never mind. Confident, aren't you? What if I don't give a damn whether you're Greg's son or not?"

Brandon pulled a faint grin. "You'd have arrested me already if that was true."

Alisha pursed her lips, examining the man across from her. "All right. You have the space of a meal to convince me, Parker. If I'm not dead certain you're one of the good guys at the end of it, I'm going to clobber you over the head with that wine bottle and drag you back to Langley in cuffs."

Brandon cast her an uncertain glance, the beginnings of a smile fading as he determined she wasn't making a joke. "Fair enough. Where do I start?"

Alisha pulled a wooden chair out from the table and sat down, arms folded across her chest. "With the Sicarii."

Thirteen

Brandon turned back to the stove with a heavy exhalation. "How much do you know?"

"Assume that I'm a novice."

He startled, then chuckled. "Was that deliberate? No, I can see it wasn't. The Sicarii call their initiates novices. A coincidence."

"Initiates. They're a cult?" Alisha shook her head. "I thought I was aware of most of the major religious cults with any sort of decent intelligence network."

"Not religious. Not exactly, anyway." Brandon focused on whisking together a white sauce, cream and butter and flour, as he spoke. "More along the lines of the Masons. The Illuminati. Domination based on divine right rather than wealth or world order."

"Divine right?" Alisha snorted dismissively. "Didn't that go out with the Magna Carta?"

Brandon gave her a half smile over his shoulder. "And so you see the problem. Deposed and displaced royalty have always sought a way back into power, but in general they've been sufficiently isolated from others of their ilk as to be ineffective on a large scale."

"You're lecturing," Alisha said. "Nobody says 'ilk' in real life."

"You wanted the history," Brandon said, offended. Alisha lifted her hands in semi-serious apology and he continued. "The Sicarii were born of an attempt to unite those deposed leaders. The literal translation is *dagger people*. I personally think the word was chosen for a bit of the 'Et tu, Brute?' implication, although I can't find any proof of that. At any rate, they've had their periodic successes—James of Scotland inherited the English throne from Elizabeth despite it all, for example."

"That was four hundred years ago, Parker." Alisha picked up her wineglass, swirling the dark liquid without tasting it again. "Any recent history, or are you going to tell me they all disappeared mysteriously after that?"

"On the contrary. They began coming into their own with the Bolshevik revolution."

"I didn't think any royalty survived that."

"Except Anastasia."

"Right, exc—oh, you've got to be kidding."

Brandon shook his head, turning back to the roux. "No. Her descendants are part of the Sicarii now, maybe even ruling it. She was one of the purer recent royal bloodlines, after all. Maybe the purest, given the questions about the Hanover family in the Victorian age."

"You lost me." Alisha frowned, watching him stir the sauce. "But that's starting to smell good."

"Thanks. You know they say the best way to a woman's heart is through her stomach."

"Rib cage," Alisha corrected absently. Brandon gave her a look that she shrugged off. "Hanovers?"

"Victoria carried hemophilia and passed it on to several of her children. There's some question as to how she ended up a carrier. There's a theory that she was a bastard child. Anyway, I digress. The point is, with communication becoming easier and easier, with DNA testing, with genealogy sites, all of it, the Sicarii have gathered more and more of themselves together. Tracing bloodlines and histories back centuries, building a base of supporters and candidates who believe God actually intended for them to rule the world."

"And this has what to do with Reichart?"

"He's a Tudor."

Alisha dropped her forehead to the table in exasperation. "You know," she said to the table, "I agreed to listen because I thought there might actually be a possibility that you weren't chock full of shit." She set her wineglass aside and stood, picking up the bottle to examine the label. "I should have known better. Who're you waiting for, Parker? Somebody to come pick me up while you distract me with tall tales?" Her heartbeat was steady, breathing deep and even: this was how combat should be entered. The powerful rush of endorphins and adrenaline were useful for battle itself, but it was far better to begin without fear or panic clouding the mind. Alisha flipped the wine bottle into the air, catching the neck. "Because I can see the holes in this story right now. For one thing, there weren't any more Tudors, that's why the Stuarts got the throne. For another, *Frank?* It was a nice try. How about you don't make me hit you with this?"

"Whoa! Whoa, whoa whoa! Wait! Hang on here!" Brandon backed up, away from the stove, hands held high. "Alisha, listen to me. I knew you wouldn't believe me."

"Well, at least you got that right." She shoved the table aside, making a show of strength that was meant less to impress than to distract. Olive oil and candles tumbled over, the oil's glass bottle top bouncing loose. Pale greenish liquid spilled across the tabletop with a faintly flat, metallic scent, gleaming as it rolled near a guttering candle.

"Listen! Listen!" Brandon backed up against the wall, hands still lifted as she advanced on him, bottle raised. Alisha had almost no intention of using it as a weapon, but like the table, it was an excellent tool for distraction.

"There aren't any legitimate Tudors, you're right, the family name died out, but Henry the Eighth wasn't known for keeping it in his pants," Brandon blurted. "More than one country girl had his bastard, long before he got syphilis and —" The last words were delivered as he abruptly reversed himself, ducking forward to launch himself at Alisha's midriff. "—poisoned the royal seed!"

Alisha sidestepped, clobbering Brandon's outstretched arm with the wine bottle. A satisfying, bone-deep *thunk* sounded, knocking him off balance. Alisha planted her hand on his shoulder, shoving him farther off center and sending him into a roll that ended beneath the table. For one instant he looked genuinely startled, blue eyes wide with boyish surprise, before scrambling backward and scooting out from under the table.

"Henry the Eighth married anything that moved, Parker. Why would he let a pregnant country girl go, even if she wasn't royalty herself?" Calmness was settled in her bones, a deep-set sense of inevitability that guided her actions without the fog of emotion. It was better to be remote; she knew that. It made it easier to accept the fact that she had to arrest Greg Parker's son.

It wasn't enough. Alisha wanted it to hurt.

"He didn't know how badly he'd need one of them." Brandon watched her more warily, hands spread out to his sides as they both circled the table. Oil crept up to a still-burning candle wick, a sudden tiny burst of flame flaring between them. "If you'd stop trying to beat me up—"

Alisha, almost solemnly, said, "*Apprehend* you," and felt a smile break through the chill that had risen in her.

"Whatever. Stop it and I'll prove it."

Alisha lowered the wine bottle a few inches, curiosity piqued, another break in her repose, though she knew she needed the distance. She asked anyway. "You can prove that Frank Reichart is Henry the Eighth's bastard great-to-the-somethingth-grandson?"

"Why do you think I wanted you to come to the Vatican?"

"For dinner and drinks?" Alisha shifted the bottle in her hand again, testing its weight as a weapon. "You have ninety seconds. I'm listening."

"Will you put the wine bottle down?"

"No."

Mild dismay, but no surprise, passed over Brandon's face and darkened his eyes. "Spare royalty, the second and third sons given over to the church, have kept meticulous records of royal lineages for centuries, Alisha. It's part of what they do. Parish reports going back a thousand years are in there, records of dates visited and children born. There is an unbroken line of descent from an English king to your former fiancé, and I will bring you to the records to read it yourself." Brandon straightened cautiously, keeping his hands spread wide. "After dinner."

"After dinner," Alisha repeated. Brandon nodded. Alisha sighed, lowering the wine bottle further, knowing she was looking for excuses not to arrest—*apprehend*—Greg Parker's son. "You're really determined to make this a date, aren't you?"

Brandon finally brought his hands back together to rub at the reddened spot on his arm where the bottle had bruised him. "Yeah."

"Why?"

"Because it'd be nice to bring a girl I already know he'd approve of home to Dad?"

"You're not using me to smooth the waters with your father, Parker." She was already going too far down that road herself, hesitating when she should act, in hopes of finding a reason to clear the man.

It wasn't just that. Largely, perhaps, but not entirely. There was the question of the Sicarii, as well. If Brandon was right, if Frank worked for such an organization—it didn't excuse, Alisha thought, but it might explain.

Brandon's smile fell away. "I liked it better when you called me Brandon."

"I liked it better when you hadn't blown my cover in the middle of an op. All right, fine. Dinner, the Vatican, and you can tell me who the hell you're working for, in the meantime."

Brandon's shoulders dropped and he turned back to the stove, his good humor gone. "Fix the table, would you? Somebody set it on fire."

"Sorry," Alisha said without a hint of genuine contriteness. "Talk."

"I had to blow your cover. Anything else would have blown mine, and I've been on this case a long time. The roux's burned."

"You shouldn't have tried fighting me. How long?"

Brandon frowned over his shoulder, scraping the bottom of the saucepan with the whisk. "I was approached three years ago by a covert agent, deep undercover. I'd been gone from the Agency for years at that point, no contact at all. With my programming background I was a good candidate for insinuation into the Sicarii as a double agent. I'd just finished the work on the quantum chip and wanted to move into developing my drones, and they were looking for a technological advantage in a war they had no other chance of winning. The situation was ideal for everyone."

"And the cover?"

"My CIA contact warned me a Sicarii representative was coming in. When it turned out to be Reichart, I knew I was being tested. They had to know it was you there for the CIA. If I hadn't made you, they'd have believed I was covering for you."

"That's a lot of supposition, Parker."

"Yeah," he agreed, "but you were expendable."

A knot tied and loosened in Alisha's stomach. "Honesty. How refreshing. You know I'm going to check you on all of this."

"That's why I'm telling the truth." Brandon put the saucepan on a back burner, checking a second pot to see if it was boiling before pouring fettuccine in. "You'll run into red tape. I doubt you've got the clearance to get the details."

"Then I'll find someone who does." Alisha pushed the table back into place, mopping up some of the spilled oil with a piece of bread. "Do you have a lighter?"

Brandon frowned over his shoulder. "For the candles," Alisha said patiently.

"Oh." He dug into his pocket. "I didn't think you smoked."

"Only after sex," Alisha muttered.

"Then you're doing something terribly wrong." Brandon handed her the lighter, smiling hopefully. Alisha curved a reluctant smile in return as she bumped the flame into life and lit the candles.

"That's a high school joke, Parker." She ran her thumb over a raised emblem in the lighter's smooth silver casing, turning it toward the candles to investigate the shape—a crown—before handing it back. "I didn't think you smoked either."

"But you smiled. I'll take it. And I don't. Dad gave me this when he quit and I've kept it." Brandon pocketed the lighter again. "I'll even stay here through tomorrow evening if you want to check up on me. This is for real, Alisha. It's been my life for the past three years. It would be nice to have someone I could actually talk to about it once in a while."

"We'll see," Alisha said, pushing sympathy aside. It was one of the prices paid for the life she'd chosen: intimacy, real intimacy, was a rare thing, to be treasured when it could be shared. "Dinner first. The Vatican, research and possible handcuffs come later."

Brandon's grin turned into a slow leer. "I've never had a better offer."

"You'll never get one, either. Dinner first," Alisha repeated.

Dinner hadn't led to handcuffs, and the Vatican wasn't looking promising, either. Alisha cracked her neck, pushing a tome half the size of her torso a few inches away. It slid across the mahogany desk with a whisper, musty scent receding, and Alisha put a fingertip between the pages she'd been reading, marking her place as she closed the cover to stare at the embossing. It was a veritable work of art:, circles of swords with blades nearly as long as her hand, pointed inward, worked into the heavy leather.

Maybe not swords, Alisha thought. Maybe daggers. Her eyes stung from reading black ink, faded with the years to brown, on page after yellowed page of cramped writing. The image of the daggers swam, her tired eyes looking for depth perception where it didn't exist. A pattern formed at the center of the daggers, where their points came together, then blurred away again before she could resolve it into any kind of imagery. Alisha sat back, raising a shoulder so she could wipe her eyes without dampening her hands and risking damage to the ancient parchment.

The antiquity of the Vatican records was convincing, at least. Written painstakingly in Latin, they recorded centuries' worth of what Alisha presumed were legitimate, minute details of royal lives, from birth on. The records were the stuff of legend: Alisha wasn't sure how Brandon had gotten them into the nearly mythical Vatican archives, reputedly the heir to the lost Library at Alexandria, and it killed something inside of her to know these records existed but weren't public. But victors wrote the histories, and the Church had enough invested in the world's history being written as it was to make no mention of their own extensive and possibly contradictory records.

Or maybe there was more truth to the Sicarii story than she wanted to believe. The Sicarii were never mentioned in the archives, unless she was to take the passing reference of "we" as the—Alisha's impulse was to call it the Brotherhood, which sounded so affected the whole concept was clearly getting to her. But if a secret organization devoted to the divine right of rulers existed, the Church quietly supporting it made a certain amount of sense. If the Sicarii were ever to regain the power they felt they'd once had, the Church itself might end up with secular power unlike anything it had had for centuries.

"God." Alisha flopped the book open again, wincing as the heavy cover smacked against the desk and reverberated through the archival halls. Brandon, drowsing in a tall-backed chair a few tables away, flinched awake, looking guilty.

"Find what you were looking for?" he asked.

"I don't know." She was finding enough to at least entertain the possibility that this could be real. And the pages in front of her detailed a line of descent that, against all probability, began with Henry Tudor and ended with Frank Reichart.

Reichart was hardly the only bastard descendant of royalty; his ancestor alone had spawned literally hundreds of descendants in the centuries since his death. Genghis Khan, Alisha remembered reading somewhere, was a direct ancestor of something like sixteen million present-day males: Henry the Eighth of England had been conservative, by those standards. The only real hitch in the line was the very first one: there was no way to be absolutely certain the barmaid's child was fathered by the young Prince Henry.

But there were other places where the chroniclers had found conclusive enough evidence to strike through the names of children they'd once believed to be bastard sons and daughters. Reichart's line had no such mark-through. Alisha, staring at the pages, wondered if there was any Tudor DNA that could be used to determine the absolute truth of the matter, now, five centuries after the fact. A lock of hair tangled in a comb or kept safe in a locket. Exhuming royal bones was probably not an option.

Brandon appeared at her shoulder, looking down at the page with her. "Well?"

"I don't see how you could've faked any of this," Alisha said grudgingly. "How'd you get us in here?"

"I called in a favor." Brandon took a deep breath. "A favor that will probably come back to haunt me, since this is a lot bigger than what I was owed. Getting permission to come down here usually comes from the Pope."

"Gosh," Alisha muttered. "I hope they didn't bother him on my behalf." She brushed her fingers over the page again, tracing names down through the centuries until she reached Reichart's, then sighed, closing the book. "All right. I'm done."

"You believe me?"

"No," Alisha said, "but you've earned some reasonable doubt." She stood, standing close enough to Brandon that it gave her an excuse to slide her fingers through his belt loops for balance. Pindrop pressure, nothing more. "I need to verify everything you've told me through the Agency."

Brandon tilted his head down to meet her eyes. "Maybe you could get started in the morning," he suggested in a low voice.

Alisha couldn't tell if the sound she made was a laugh or a groan. Whatever she thought she was doing, it was clearly a bad idea. She didn't know what was going on here.

No. She didn't know which side Brandon was on. She knew very well what was going on there, and wanted to revel in the quickness of her heartbeat and the awareness of Brandon's warmth so close to her. He smelled good, the lingering scent of pasta in white sauce mixed up with simple masculinity. She sighed. "I'd love to," and took half a step back.

Brandon's body heat dissipated as she moved away. "Can't blame a guy for trying."

"Try," Alisha said, with a little emphasis on the word, "not to get in trouble while I cross-check your story. You come up straight and maybe we can pick up this conversation later." She gave him a brief smile, then brushed past him, leaving the archives.

Fourteen

"Come on." Alisha paced her hotel room, tugging a curl out of her ponytail, then fixing it again. The phone rang a fourth time and Alisha snapped at the air with her teeth, hanging up and dialing again. "Come on, Q, pick up the phone, I know you're there." She bent double, hair brushing the floor as she stretched into downward, then three-legged, dog. Her muscles loosened and a vertebrae popped, making her grunt with contentment. "Eeeerika."

"Ali?" Surprise but no weariness filled the warm alto voice that answered the phone. "Thought you were on no contact. Oh, you are, aren't you, which is why you're calling my personal phone and not leaving messages when the voice mail picks up." Erika became cheerier with each passing word, until she sounded as exuberant as a kid at a circus. "Which means you want me to do something I'll get in trouble for. What's up?"

"I thought *you* were supposed to be on vacation," Alisha said with a grin. She heard an exasperated snort and the rush of wheels across a plastic mat.

"This *is* vacation. You should see what I came up with last ni—"

"It's eleven at night, Erika."

A pause. "So?"

"So people on vacation aren't usually at work at eleven at night."

"Oh." Another pause; Erika's speech was littered with them, as if much of what she heard was being assimilated and examined for veracity before she responded. "Are you sure? Everybody I know is."

"How many people are in the office, Erika?"

"Well, just me, but—oh, I see what you mean. But this one's really cool, Ali. With enough of a sample it'll do real-time voice distortion. Want to sound like Princess Di?"

"Erika!"

"No, no, you're right, she's dead, no one would believe it. Okay, choose your favorite smoking hot bisexual leading lady. You could nail anybody you wanted."

"Erika!" Alisha laughed. "I need your help."

"Oh! Right. The thing I could get in trouble for."

"Only if you get caught."

Offended pride filled Erika's voice. "I never get caught."

"Then I'd say you won't get in trouble for it. Did you know Brandon Parker?"

"Oh jeez," Erika said, a Yooper Michigan accent suddenly coming through strong. "I don't do recon on exes, Ali."

Alisha stopped mid-stretch, pulling the phone away from her ear to gaze at it in astonishment. "You dated him?"

"Oh yah." The accent stayed in place: Alisha had startled the hell out of the CIA tech geek. Erika had worked hard to eradicate the telltale long vowels, and was always sensitive about teasing for a few days after she came home from visiting family. "In college, you know?" That time she heard her own idiomatic slip. Alisha could all but see her stiffening her spine and watching her enunciation. "We broke up after I beat him in a collegiate math competition."

Alisha rolled out of her pose onto her back, laughing. "So he's a little competitive?"

"No," Erika said, surprised again. "I figured, who wants to make babies with somebody you can trounce that easily?"

Alisha blinked at the dark ceiling. "If all the guys you know take that attitude, you might never get a chance."

Erika made a dismissive sound. "You sound like my mother. I keep telling her, that's what the Stanford artificial insemination program is for."

"You haven't got a romantic bone in your body, Erika."

"No, but I've got one of the world's greatest brains. So what's the deal? You sleeping with him?"

Alisha laughed out loud a second time. She'd meant to call her technical consultant for help, not an unexpected dose of good cheer. She'd needed it, though. She was still mentally struggling with the records Brandon had shown her, trying to arrange their meaning in the greater scheme. A simple girl-gossip phone call was going a long way toward helping her stop worrying so much. "No, I'm not sleeping with him!"

"Why not?"

Alisha found herself blinking at the ceiling again, then grinning. "I dunno. It gets complicated. Is he worth it?"

"I think I gave him a seven point eight. But he was only nineteen," Erika added generously.

"You actually scored him?"

Considering pause. Alisha wondered how she could tell the difference between a regular hesitation and one that seemed more thoughtful than usual. "Isn't that why it's called scoring?" Erika asked eventually.

Alisha laughed again. "Sometimes I'm not sure you're for real, E. Anyway, look, no, I'm not sleeping with him, although I could've been if I hadn't wanted to come call you and get you to do recon on him. So how solid is that rule?"

"Ooh," Erika said, Yooper coming through again, "not so solid. More a matter of principle. To be discarded as soon as someone asks me to. Alisha, honey, if you passed up a pretty face like that for talking to me, I mean, I'm flattered and all, but you need to straighten out your priorities. You don't get out enough."

"This from the woman whose idea of a romantic evening is looking over a file folder of sperm-bank donors?"

"We're talking about you, not me," Erika pointed out. "Brandon'd be good for you. He's blond."

Alisha's eyebrows went up. "So?"

"Nothing!" Erika protested. "I'm just saying. A change of pace'd be good for you."

"And a blond is a change of pace?" Alisha squinted one eye, making a face at the ceiling. She didn't like to admit it, but—

"Yup," Erika said, finishing Alisha's own thought. "The whole tall, dark and dangerous thing leaves you moody."

"I am not," Alisha said, "hung up on Frank Reichart."

"Did I say that? I didn't say that."

Alisha groaned and rolled over onto her stomach, burying her face in the hotel pillow for a moment. Then she lifted her head enough to be able to speak. "So are you going to discard your principles and follow Brandon's files until you hit red tape or a wall or whatever?"

"You're changing the subject," Erika accused. Alisha wobbled her head at the pillow in silent agreement. "Arright," Erika said. "How soon you want it?"

"As soon as you can get it, and call me back at this number."

"This isn't your official phone, is it?"

"It's a throwaway. I bought it with cash."

Erika sounded intrigued. "You're gonna have to give me the dirt someday, Ali."

"Someday," Alisha promised. "Call as soon as you can?"

"Yup," Erika agreed. "Bye."

Alisha folded her phone closed, dropping her face into the pillow again. The temptation to call Erika back and argue over Reichart was embarrassing in its strength, and telling. Alisha made a face into the pillow, then sat up, smearing her fingers across her eyes before wincing and studying them. Mascara and eyeliner, what little she usually wore, now colored her fingertips. She blew out an exasperated breath and stood, going into the bathroom without turning on the light.

Her reflection looked bruised, dark brown smudges across her eyelid an ill-made black eye. It stirred memory and a quiet laugh as she dropped her gaze, turning the water on to splash it over her face.

"Lovely shiner." The first thing Reichart'd ever said to her, a droll opening salvo. She was only twenty-one, an agent for just two years, and the bar fight that had destroyed her outfit had been a distraction. *Start a fight,* she'd been ordered. *Your contact will know the one who starts the fight is his cargo.*

His cargo. Alisha had been prepped for a

mission deep inside Afghanistan, and a mercenary agent had been hired to bring her into the dangerous territory. He'd followed her into the unisex European bathroom like he'd been supposed to, but he wasn't what she'd expected. His voice was deep enough to rumble, and carried an American accent. Alisha remembered the word very specifically: *lovely*. One of the first times she'd heard an American man use it seriously, back when she still found it startling, even effeminate, coming from a man.

There had been nothing effeminate about the man leaning in the door behind her though. Black hair buzzed a quarter inch from bald, eyes dark enough to be as black as his hair, in some light. Not then: they were dark brown then, clear and depthless as water. He was tanned, not from a booth, but a genuine tan that left faint white smile wrinkles around his eyes and mouth, his hands stained dark from the sun, enough that he might have been a wood-worker too familiar with his own varnishes.

His hands were too refined for that, though. Thumbs hooked in his jeans pockets, his fingernails were clean and pale, neatly trimmed. Alisha remembered looking through her fingers at his reflection, then at her own bruised knuckles and broken nails. At the damp spikes of black hair—not her own, but a punk-cut wig she was particularly fond of—trailing over her swollen eye. At the cut lip and the ankh earring and the plastic choker around her throat, and then back at Reichart's reflection.

He ought, she remembered thinking, to have been wearing a fedora. It didn't fit the biker jacket or the white T-shirt—some combination of leather and denim was always Reichart's uniform du jour, when he had a choice—but it fit the noir smirk and the easy confidence. He made her own beaten-up self look that much more bedraggled. Her black bodice, deliberately ripped at the ribcage to show off a slender midriff, barely stayed on now, since the straps that had held it in place had snapped in the fight that had blackened her eye. And the wig she liked so much now looked like a sad mop dog-flopped on her head.

Then Reichart's reflection grinned, and Alisha knew she was in the best kind of trouble possible.

She remembered writing the chronicle for the Afghanistan mission, so full of fresh new love and enthusiasm that it made her blush even now. Everything had gone right with that mission, from spiriting out the defecting FSB agent that was her primary objective to the intense blossoming relationship with Reichart. It had started so well, she thought wryly, and lifted her head, pushing away memory as surely as she blinked away water, the remains of her makeup cleaned from her face.

The woman looking back at her was almost eight years older than the girl who'd recognized trouble when she saw it in Frank Reichart's leggy reflection. Her own hair, colored dark by the night and highlighted with paleness from streetlights, fell in loose curls and braids around a face that was exactly what she needed it to be: unremarkably pretty, with the ability to be transformed into beauty or plainness with the right makeup and attitude. Any natural color was leeched from her skin by the light coming in the hotel window from the street, but most of a decade hadn't yet added fine wrinkles around almond-shaped eyes.

She could see a greater ability to judge and calculate in those eyes now, and a certain cynicism around the corners of her mouth, but not enough to jade her. Not yet, at least. Not as long as she had it in her to let Frank Reichart walk free. Not as long as she could still extend the benefit of the doubt to Brandon Parker.

"Older," Alisha said to her reflection. "Not that much wiser."

The woman in the mirror gave her a one-sided smile and shrugged, as if to say *we can live with that*.

"You and I can," Alisha said wryly. "Let's not tell Greg, though, okay?" Then she laughed and pushed away from the counter, wandering back into the main room. Talking to herself in the mirror had to be a bad sign. Better to drop onto the couch and study her own memories and desires behind closed eyelids, without making it a conversation.

It'd begun as almost a dare. No, not a dare: a challenge. Taming the bad boy, of all the impossible tasks, for her; corrupting the good girl, for Reichart. He'd asked, early on, why she'd become a spy. The answer had been easy then. It'd been about idealism and apple pie, a response that, in retrospect, must have made him laugh at her. He'd answered, "Adventure," when she'd put the question back to him.

And it was only in retrospect that she understood how shallow the answer had been. Nothing opened him up: not alcohol, not sex—though both brought out a possessive streak that had been, like so much else, charming at first and increasingly irritating as Alisha outgrew girlishness and progressed into womanhood.

She supposed it was only a matter of course that CIA agents looked up their lovers in the records, official and unofficial alike. The wiser among them probably didn't then confront said lover with the scraps of detail, trying to wring more out of him, but hints hadn't been enough. Alisha wanted to know.

She half opened her eyes, looking at the gold light from the street bouncing against the ceiling. She wanted to know.

Which was the crux of the matter, every time. It was what made her let Brandon walk away when policy said otherwise. His Sicarii story might answer questions about him, but even more, it might answer questions about Frank Reichart.

Answers she might have forced, if she hadn't blown it.

Except she hadn't blown it. She'd opened her fingers and let it go, and Reichart had never known the difference.

It had been London, three years ago now. A blustery afternoon; they usually were, when she was there. Alisha was almost certain it wasn't personal. Besides, the weather suited her mood as she tromped through Trafalgar Square, a rare space in London, in that it was a square that was actually square. Small thoughts, was how she thought of things like that. Small thoughts, filling up her mind so she didn't have to think about the larger things. A gray wool cap pulled down to her eyebrows, shoulders coated in a well-lined trench hunched up to her ears. Boots with tall square heels and blocky toes. Alisha felt like a Londoner in that outfit, one of a million costume changes that redefined her very self. Small thoughts.

A bus roared to a stop in front of her and she walked up to it without looking for its destination. Anywhere was warmer than the square with its host of pigeons and bird ladies. She dug into a pocket for change as she stepped up. Looked past the coin box, past the driver, through the fountain spray that added unnecessary water to the damp London afternoon.

Looked at Frank Reichart swinging a little girl up onto his hip, putting his hand into a pretty woman's, and lifting the conjoined fingers to hail a popcorn seller, to the child's delight.

A heartbeat of pain stabbed through her, just below the collarbone. Alisha stepped backward again, so gracefully it was the man behind her who apologized, as if he'd been in the wrong. The bus rumbled away, leaving Alisha with her hands in her pockets, staring across a hundred feet at the man who'd betrayed her.

She followed him. It was what spies did, and she was a spy whether she was on duty or not. *Snooping*, memory supplied. As a little girl she'd snuck around, hiding behind corners and under tables, *snooping*, as her mother called it. It had come naturally to her. She'd called it *an active interest in the community around her*, as a teen. *Nosy*, her mother had said. Alisha'd laughed and hugged her.

He had a life, her former fiancé. The man she hadn't talked to in two years, not since the bullet had knocked her to the ground after she'd seen him with a gun in his hands. The little girl was called Mazie, and her mother was Emma. Mazie wasn't Frank's, which made Alisha's heart contract with relief close to tears. They'd been dating eight months. Frank had a straight job as an accountant. An accountant, Alisha kept thinking. Of all things. An accountant.

It had to be a cover.

She stood at his elbow once in the three days she followed him, a step behind him in a tea shop she'd chosen as her place to approach because it had no mirrors. She could change her mind and disappear without much chance of being noticed.

His mobile rang and he dug it out of an oversized pocket, thumbing it on while Alisha studied her feet and thought of the questions she'd like to ask. *Hello, Frank, how've you been? Hello, Frank. What were you doing at the Vatican with a gun? Hello, Frank, did you think I'd survive? Did you ever love me? Was it a game I didn't understand?*

"Emma," he said into the phone. A low softness that Alisha knew was audible in his voice. Softness that had once been reserved for her, a familiar purr of sensuality and love and desire, all wrapped up in a single word.

It had to be a cover.

By the time Frank Reichart turned to see who'd rung the bells on the tea shop door, there was nothing more to glimpse than a bit of scarf blown back by the London wind.

Fifteen

Sleep had claimed her somewhere in the midst of memory, and morning came too early. Strains of Beethoven's Fifth startled Alisha awake, and she answered the phone without opening her eyes.

"God himself couldn't have made a thicker wall of red tape," Erika said.

For all that she was flat on her back in bed, Alisha sagged, feeling as if she'd dropped another few inches through the mattress. She lifted her hand to press fingertips against her still-closed eyes and let out a long sigh. Legitimacy. A dead end of red tape was a kind of legitimacy for Brandon's story, and far beyond anything Alisha had thought she might fine. "Tell me more."

"Well, you know, the file follows him all over the place, meandering, after he left the Agency. Then a little more than three years ago—"

Energy surged through Alisha, propelling her out of bed and into motion. The Roman sunlight poured in as she yanked her hotel room curtains open, and she squinted into a view that caught a distant corner of the Colosseum. She pulled a camisole out of her suitcase, sliding it on as she held the phone to her ear with two fingers, listening avidly. "—it all turns red," Erika went on. "Everything on top of it says they lost him, that he went totally underground."

"Which is in keeping with what I know," Alisha said. The satin was cool against her skin, soft brush of fabric making her breathe deeply to feel its caress. She dragged a pair of jeans out of the suitcase and went into the bathroom alcove to brush her teeth, phone pressed awkwardly between shoulder and ear.

"So you sent me looking for stuff you already knew?" Erika let out a "hnf" of air, and Alisha all but heard her follow-up shrug. "Anyway, scratch a lawyer, get a liar. There was a phrase in his paperwork that struck me as funny, I don't remember what it was—"

"Baloney," Alisha said around her toothbrush. "Maybe you can't tell me what it was, but I don't believe you don't remember it."

Erika laughed. "Whatever, Ali." It was as good as a confession: Erika's security clearance was different from Alisha's, and Alisha had no doubt Erika was aware of key phrases and sentence structures that would tell her worlds of information that Alisha herself would never recognize. "The point is, beneath the dead end I found red tape."

"And beneath the red tape?"

"I would never break into secure CIA files to find something called 'prodfac one' located in backwater Beijing," Erika said, sounding hurt, innocent, and totally culpable all at once.

"Made in China." Alisha leaned on the counter, head dropped. "Go figure. Who's handling him?"

"There are only a handful of reports buried under this tape, Alisha. Assuming your boy—"

"*My* boy," Alisha protested. "You're the ex."

"I'm not the one digging up files on him." Erika fell silent. "I mean, I am, but you know what I mean."

Alisha grinned at the sink and pulled her jeans on as she put her toothbrush away. "Yeah. Anyway, my boy what?"

"Assuming he's undercover, he's so far undercover that he can't even make reports regularly. I don't even know who's handling him. Couldn't find it behind the dead ends. So watch yourself, okay? You don't want to blow an op like that."

"No kidding. Okay. You rock my world, Q. Thanks for the help."

"I still think you oughta pounce him," Erika said. "See if he's improved that seven point eight I gave him."

Brandon's warmth and easy smile flashed through Alisha's mind and she smiled. "Sure, maybe. If I get the chance."

"There's a girl." Erika hung up without further ado. Alisha put the phone against her mouth, studying her bare toes, then wiggled them and went to pack for a trip to China.

✝

Backwater Beijing covered a lot of territory; that was the downside. The upside was that a few euros went a long way toward answers, and a few more bought discretion.

As much discretion as a tallish American woman traveling alone could buy, at least. She wore a short black wig, since any hair color besides black stood out in a major Asian city, and her own rough tawny curls would draw attention. She didn't want that today, as she searched for 'prodfac one', Production Facility One. The abbreviation might have meant something else, but Alisha knew in her bones that she was right.

And when she found the place, she was gonna compromise the shit out of it. If Parker's operation was legitimate, she'd have hell to pay, but she was still following orders. Second objective: destroy the drone schematics. If Greg —and consequently Alisha—hadn't been let in on a secret op, they could hardly be blamed for disrupting it. And no matter how pure his intentions, the combat drones Brandon had developed were only going to press war on to a new, nastier level. She didn't believe for a minute that they'd reduce the human casualties. At best they'd make them more one-sided.

Your job is not to die for your country, but if necessary, to make the other son of a bitch die for his. That was the real strength of the robotic army: making the other guy die for *his* country.

Alisha had enough idealism left to think it a bitter dreg, if not enough naiveté to believe it could all be avoided.

It was possible she was carrying Greg's orders a little too far, by searching for and— face it, intending to destroy—the production facility that she suspected was building an army of Brandon's drones. The CIA—the U.S.A.—didn't really want them destroyed. They wanted to control them. She was going to get her ass busted so far down the ranks she'd be lucky to break the chains locking her to a desk for the rest of her career.

And if that happened, so be it. Even in the most perfect of worlds—which this most as- suredly was not—she knew it would be a setback in the drone development, not a mora- torium. The CIA had the drone she'd disabled in Kazakhstan, and if Brandon was working undercover—

You do your part, Leesh. Stop worrying about the rest.

The thoughts, the consideration of her path —metaphorically, if not physically—had taken her through half a dozen contacts and the streets of Beijing, into a warehouse district that looked bad and smelled worse. Alisha bowed low to a bored young woman popping bubble gum, showed the girl a well-faked company ID, and passed through the factory doors. Euros bought more than information.

There were no underground structures to

these warehouses, all of them built without basements or sub-flooring. Alisha went up instead, brazen strides taking her through areas that menial workers weren't allowed to go. But confidence gave her the aura of belonging, and within minutes she was beyond the warehouse gates, through the building, and on its rooftop.

Her contacts had suggested easily a dozen different addresses to investigate as the possible production facility. Factories where wealthy-looking Americans oversaw the work; places that the men and women she'd spoken to were quietly certain were not clothing manufacturers, or toymakers.

Sun glared off corrugated roofs, ribbons of heat waving upward to blur Alisha's vision. She boxed her hands around her eyes, cutting off brightness from both above and below. Within the shadows of her hands, the world leaped into focus.

One factory stood out in the afternoon glare. There was an inexplicable *something* to it, although not in its fading paint or sun-cracked windows. Instead the ineffable something was in the shoulders of the men she saw entering the building, and in the sharpness of the guards at the front gates, whose uniforms were pressed and crisp despite the midday heat. There were no white men immediately visible, no one to make an obvious and easy tie back to Brandon and his work, but there was new heavy machinery toward the enormous building's back end. It had been scoured and chipped at, yellow paint deliberately dimmed, but no rust graced the unwieldy silver buckets and prongs.

Alisha sat down, hands still cupped around her eyes, to watch the distant factory and its people until the sun sank behind her, setting the district alight with gold and red fire.

There were half a dozen ways in, starting with the most obvious: the front gate, which was so obvious as to be unexpected, and therefore tempting. But the open windows just beneath the roofline were more likely. They hadn't been closed at sunset, probably to relieve some of the heat that built up inside the building. If there was air conditioning in there, it was for the benefit of overheating machines, not the people who ran them. The tractor bays toward the back offered another entrance, but Alisha's gaze returned to the windows. They were gaping black holes in the fading twilight, maws that she could slip into with a filament line and grapple. There were at least two buildings nearby, on different campuses and almost certainly less secure than the one she felt housed the Attengee production facility. She could come in from either of them; scale the exterior and shoot a grapple gun the hundred feet or so to her target. It would take a few hours in the morning to acquire the equipment she needed, and she could go in when sunset came again.

Alisha cracked her knuckles and stood up for the first time in hours, stretching muscles that protested moving from the position they'd settled into. Tree pose, very simple, grounding herself and straightening to her fullest height. The muscles in the small of her back groaned as they tightened, then relaxed suddenly, the warmth of fresh blood flowing through them. Alisha twisted around, eliciting pops all the way up her spine, and repeated the motion to the other side, earning another satisfying series of crackles.

Motion caught her eye as she came back to tree pose, her shoulders back and chin held high. No sound: it was too far for it to carry, especially over the noise of the city factories. Just a flash at the corner of her eye, a wrongness that made a thread of caution tighten in her belly. Looking directly didn't work: darkness swallowed detail. Alisha curled a lip and looked away, finding a point on the skyline to study.

Again: motion. The faint wavering of a line stretching from one building to another, black against black. Alisha held her breath, pulse bumping high in her throat. She knew, with terrible certainty, what would come into her line of vision, and just as fundamentally didn't believe it.

There. A bulk too large to be hidden by the night or the eye's blind spot, if she knew where to look. A man sliding hand over hand along a filament line, from a nearby building to the factory she'd scouted.

Outrage flooded her, so sharp and hot she nearly laughed with it. That was *her* factory! That was *her* plan! How dare someone else sneak into it before she did? Alisha darted to the edge of her rooftop, lifting her hands again, as if she might somehow make binoculars out of her cupped fingers.

But she couldn't see clearly, not at that distance, not at night. He moved elegantly, despite dangling upside down on a handful of wiring. Despite the sixty-foot drop beneath him; despite the black, close-fitting clothing that must have been too warm in the night's heat. He moved with strength and grace, approaching the factory quickly. He curled his hands around one of the window frames and folded himself inside, disappearing from sight. He could have been anyone.

Could have.

Alisha's outrage faded into a new certainty, then flared up again. She'd been followed, spied on, *used!* And she'd known better. She should have known better. Should have looked for a tail, for the man who wouldn't have let her simply walk away.

She should have known that Frank Reichart would find a way to betray her again.

Sixteen

The thing that separated humanity from the beasts was the ability to apply intellect over instinct.

Alisha had reminded herself of that more times than she cared to think about in the last twenty-four hours. Her every impulse had been to dash in, helter-skelter, after Reichart, and to hell with good sense or preparation. He'd followed her, and worse, he'd *beaten* her, entering the production factory the way she'd intended to, but earlier.

She wanted to kick his ass.

But following him in unprepared would have been the moral equivalent of signing her own death warrant. Worse, if he'd been compromised while inside, the entrance he'd used would have been discovered and she'd be walking into a trap.

And Alisha had yet to see him come out.

True, she hadn't watched the place for the whole twenty-four hours. Despite her anger, she'd had preparations to make. Things to buy, and a difficult phone call to put through to Langley.

She could still hear Greg's voice, the strain in it echoing louder in her memory than it had when they'd actually spoken. "Carry on," he'd said. "I'll contact you if I can find any verification on him being deep undercover. Otherwise, complete your mission objectives." That was when his voice had almost broken, that sign of weakness sending a chill through Alisha that she felt again now, even in the close heat of the Beijing night.

Brandon had asked her not to involve his father, and she was sure he would have liked that very much. It had never been likely, though. First off, Greg deserved to know the truth. Brandon's departure from the CIA had cut his father deeply, and Alisha thought the truth—if it was the truth—would help Greg rest better. But more, she wasn't quite reckless enough to charge into what Brandon claimed was a deep undercover op without some kind of backup from home base.

An almost silent hiss of fire sprang from the tip of the soldering iron she held. Chain link glowed and melted, an arch cut into the bottom of the fence just large enough for Alisha to wriggle through. The sky route was too dangerous now: Reichart had already used it, and if he hadn't made it out—

—then she would get a chance to kick his ass after all. Alisha thrust the idea away, even as it brought the ghost of a smile to her lips. She tugged her backpack—so compact she probably could have fit through the arch wearing it—through after her.

Evidence was stacking up against her ex-fiancé. Not that she'd been inclined to trust him anyway, but his sunset entrance into the factory only seemed to prove Brandon's story had merit. She would still talk first and hit later, assuming she even saw him again. It was hard, remembering that stories usually had two sides. Her job was to see one side as the important one. The CIA's side. *Her* side.

It raised the question of why she'd let Brandon go.

She pushed the thought away. The answers were there, clear enough, but it wasn't the time to go into them. One of the roughed-up bulldozers loomed in front of her and she sidled along it, watching the darkness for signs of motion. The tractor bays were the best option for entering the factory, since Reichart had already used the windows. She could have tried buying an ID off a factory worker, or having a false one made up, but if she was right and the Attengee facility lay inside, she doubted security would be lax enough to let her get away with either of those attempts.

Alisha pressed into a shadow beside the tractor bay doors, searching for locks or key-pads. The latter sat in a recess that she could only barely fit glove-clad fingers into. With effort, she popped the pad forward and pulled its base off so she could clip rerouting wiring into place. Dim numbers appeared on the code breaker display, changing faster than she could read. They slowly settled, and she slashed a blank key card through the narrow gap. There was a hesitation in which she held her breath, and then the door rolled up, surprisingly quietly, given its size. She rolled through as soon as there was room, pausing only long enough to pull a block of C4 from her backpack and press it into the darkness next to the door.

It was already late, nearing midnight. The factory was almost empty. A fire alarm should empty it of the remaining workers before she detonated the bombs. She knew it was only a temporary solution to the drone army question, but for the moment, it would do. It would provide time to regroup and consider, before Brandon's life's work rolled out onto the market.

Greg's voice filtered through her memory again, stressed and tight. "I don't know what this Sicarii thing is, Alisha. I've never heard of it, or them. I can follow Brandon's trail beyond what you can, but for now the mission is a go. Obtain what information you can. Destroy what you can't. I'll be in contact as soon as I learn anything."

She touched a fingertip to her ear, checking to be certain the bud was still there. It was set to receive so Greg could make that contact if necessary, but she had no intention of broadcasting on it. It still lay snug against her skin, almost invisible, barely there even to the touch.

She'd studied the plant's layout through the walls in the small hours of the morning with illegally-obtained infrared goggles. *Legano, illegano,* she thought. *Is gray area.* The contact she'd used had been a legitimate CIA asset, which didn't make it any less illegal, just sanctioned. Only a few bodies had moved through the factory at that hour, while warm water pipes blazed the walls and providing her with the mental map she required. There was no sign of Reichart.

He had gotten out, she told herself. Maybe. *Maybe* he'd left while she hadn't been watching, but there were underground structures to this factory. Unlike its neighbors, it had a foundation, possibly more, beneath it. The earth had blocked her ability to see those foundations with the goggles from outside, but now, as she pulled them over her eyes, the building lit up, heat spots blossoming below her. An itch between her shoulder blades told her she would find her quarry under the factory.

Her quarry, whether it was the drone production facility, or Frank Reichart.

She placed another block of C4 by the front entrance, obscuring to some degree the way she'd come in, then made a rapid exploration of the main floor with no narrow escapes. The guards were timely in their rounds, and Alisha slipped behind them without fuss. She saved the bulk of the explosives she'd brought in her backpack for the lower levels of the factory.

Which, on the surface—literally—produced stuffed toys with soft glossy looped fur: red bears and blue rabbits, the kind she'd seen in vending machines with claws too weak to lift and hold the weight of the toys they were meant to fetch. Alisha felt a stab of dismay for the honest workers whose livelihoods would be lost when the factory went up in flames. At least, with a late-night explosion, their lives would be spared.

And besides, she might be lucky. Greg might get back to her, in which case, the electric current that would set off the C4 would never be discharged. Alisha cast a brief glance upward, as if to say *Are you listening, God?* and went on.

There. A private door in the midst of the factory, marked **Keep Out**, with a lock and keypad. Alisha shot a look over her shoulder, searching for guards, then retrieved the descrambler from her backpack and put it to work. The blur of flashing numbers on the screen seemed interminable, though both her watch and her mental countdown said only fourteen seconds passed before the lock opened. Alisha disengaged the scrambler and slipped through the door to the head of a well-lit stairway. It was only partially finished, the ceiling open, pipes exposed and so close to the top of her head Alisha felt the impulse to duck. A camera above her whirred and she took in its angle with one glance, then flexed her fingers and leaped.

As she did, the humor of potential catastrophe

hit her. If the pipes wouldn't bear her weight, or if they proved too hot for the rubber-pebbled gloves she wore to handle, she would tumble, pipes breaking and hissing all around her, to the bottom of the stairs. Steam billowed in this scenario, the clang and tear of metal loud enough to wake the dead. It would be a hell of an entrance, but in the worst possible way.

Fortunately, the pipe she grabbed held. Alisha crunched upward, folding herself into the black and silver metal above the lights. She spread her weight across them, spider-like, angled precariously down.

And none too soon. Voices—neither speaking English—preceded two men, their footsteps clacking rapidly down a hall Alisha couldn't yet see. She froze, heartbeat accelerated for the first time, preferring to maintain silence and stealth than to see who might be coming. At the best, they'd continue on; at the worst they'd pass directly below her, and look up.

A curl of hair escaped the hood she wore, tickling the corner of her eye. Exasperation and amusement flooded Alisha as she winked against it, the only move she dared make to alleviate the itch. Then the tickle was swept away into a coldness that seemed to come from her bones as the men came jogging up the stairs, one after the other.

The younger man, in the lead, was almost no surprise. Sandy blond hair and good shoulders, even viewed from above. Brandon Parker took the steps up two at a time, a jaunt in his step that suggested pure confidence.

Behind him, following his son's long-legged steps but using the stair railing to help make the stairs in equally good time, came Greg Parker.

This is your local spy network radio station, said a sonorous voice inside Alisha's head. *Welcome to today's broadcast on KFQD, where you are FQD day in and day out.*

The door at the head of the stairs banged shut, leaving Alisha numb and alone, tangled in the open pipes. It was not possible. She'd spoken to Greg only a few hours earlier, nowhere near enough time to get from D.C. to China.

Although it was now obvious he hadn't *been* in D.C. Phones could be forwarded, and it certainly explained the stress in her handler's voice. Alisha moved again, self-preservation overtaking the white shock that hissed through her like static. That was the combat pilot, moving her along regardless of the situation. It left her mind free to run in circles as she edged forward.

Compromised. Somehow, she'd been compromised. Whether Greg had known about Brandon's assignment and hadn't told her, or whether she'd been entirely sold out. Whether there was something so real to the Sicarii Brotherhood that Greg couldn't allow her to know about it. Whether—

She stopped again, this time on purpose, spidered over the pipes. One deep breath, then two, cleansing, sending strength into muscles that felt watery. Sending the clarity of breath through her mind. That was the center of yoga: breathing. Giving herself the ability to shake off the cares and worries of the world, and to focus on one singular thing. It could help her feel more deeply, or it could remove her entirely, taking her a step away from any situation so she might see it more clearly and make her choices more wisely.

It was the ability that had let her assess and determine that Brandon Parker needed arresting, in Rome. It was the ability she'd deliberately shaken off then, needing to be reminded of her own humanity by accepting her own strong emotions. But now she embraced it, desperate for the clarity that removal brought. Ironic to spend so much time trying to *feel*, only to willingly banish feelings now.

She had an assignment. Until her orders were contradicted by the man she'd just watched leave, she would continue. That was her job. But by God, this time she would find a way to see the bigger picture and understand what, exactly, she was in the middle of. Promise made, she crept forward, sliding over pipes to take in the factory layout, and to be vindicated in an unsettling way.

The underground floors of the factory contained exactly what she'd feared they would: assembly lines that gleamed a purposeful silver in the scattered overhead lighting, diagrams and schematics littering the walls. The stairwell was the best-lit part of the floor. Everywhere else the lighting was periodic, turned down for the evening. Even in the dim lighting, the breadth of the hall was enormous, stretching well beyond the confines of the building above.

Alisha scampered across the pipes, moving with surprising ease, until she could drop into one of the darker spaces on the assembly-line floor. Cameras were visible here and there, but between her black clothing and the lighting, she thought she could go undetected.

Not that it mattered tremendously, if Greg had any intention of turning her in. He had to know she was in the building by now. The question was whether he'd encouraged Brandon to leave in order to give Alisha the time she needed to set the explosives, or whether he was acting out of forewarning and self-preservation.

Alisha sighed out a breath that verged on laughter, more frustrated than humorous. She'd know soon enough if she'd been betrayed.

Voices cut through the air again, sending her diving beneath one of the burnished metal machines. She held herself still beneath it through force of will, suddenly more afraid of assembly line being turned on than of being caught. She'd obviously watched too many movies that involved the heroine being nearly crushed in huge metallic teeth, and for a moment her mood lightened at her own silliness.

The voices were closer now, though still far enough away that she only knew they were speaking Mandarin, rather than understanding what they said. She lay on her belly, trying to catch a glimpse of the speakers, who came into sight, and into her range of understanding, as they spoke. Two men, this time—thankfully—strangers to her. Discussing saboteurs under-ground, a comment that made Alisha's belly cramp with panic. She drew in a slow breath through flared nostrils, forcing herself to listen instead of run.

The *laowai*—Alisha felt a trickle of humor warm some of the nervousness in her belly; the word meant foreigner, with less than flattering connotations—wanted the saboteur kept alive. The speaker was not inclined to oblige: one of his men had already suffered a broken kneecap at the devil's hands.

The second man shrugged. "We do as *laowai* Parker says."

Alisha made a slow fist and, even more slowly, punched the metal rack she hid beneath. It made no sound as her knuckles contacted the heavy steel, and didn't do her any injury, but the touch seemed to rebound inside her, lending her the strength that the gleaming material had.

Frank Reichart was alive somewhere inside the factory. Personal feelings aside, the CIA wanted him alive, and he was certainly going to be last on the list of people the workers would save if the building went up in flames.

Alisha rolled out from beneath the assembly line treads and went to rescue her ex.

Seventeen

Frank Reichart did not deserve her.

Alisha hung upside down from the pipes again, a full level deeper into the earth than she'd been. The vents in the factory were much wider and easier to traverse than the bunker's had been, for which Alisha was both grateful and mildly annoyed. The irritation came largely from the vague idea that rescuing ex-fiancés ought somehow to be more difficult than stealing top-secret plans. The plans, after all, couldn't possibly appreciate the trouble she'd gone to.

Not that Reichart was likely to either.

The second underground level of the factory was much smaller than the first. The vents she'd followed angled in so sharply that it'd been a near thing keeping herself from just sliding down and bursting out through a grate. Alisha was almost certain the guards would shoot first and ask questions later. She would have.

There were secure offices beneath the factory, their small windows casting ghostly light on computer labs as extensive as the ones at the Kazakhstani bunker. Some had drafting tables littered with papers, and a couple were small, individual spaces with one desk and land-line telephones beside surprisingly old, clunky-looking computers. One room had neither ventilation nor any other sort of access besides a lone door.

Odds were good that Reichart was behind that door.

He didn't deserve her, Alisha thought again as she studied both ends of the hall she dangled over. Then again, he didn't have her, either, so maybe it all worked out. She allowed herself a breath of amusement at that, then let it go.

She'd finished her rounds on the first level, planting C4 in enough spots to bring the military production facility to its knees. As she'd worked, she'd realized that the plant wasn't functional yet. Not for mass production, at least, although she suspected the drones she'd seen in Kazakhstan had been largely constructed here. Still, there was no oil, no last vestiges of heat, no dings or scratches in any of the equipment to suggest it had been heavily used. She wasn't stopping an already-producing system, but rather destroying it before it began.

It lit a flicker of hope inside her, offered the slightest kernel of chance that a setback this severe, this early in the drone army's developmental stage, might bankrupt the whole process. It was a slender thread to hang idealism on, but it was more than she'd had.

Alisha unwound from the pipes with slow, deliberate actions, as graceful as a gymnast as she dropped to the concrete floor. The faint thunk of her weight hitting the ground, knees bent to absorb the impact, was swallowed by the hallway, though she held herself still an extra instant or two, listening hard. Then she darted forward, tempted to take one of the last C4 charges and simply blow the door apart.

Now that would be an entrance. A disaster for anyone on the other side, but an entrance to remember. She tested the knob, unsurprised to find it locked. There was no keypad, just an old-fashioned lock. Presumably whomever had commissioned the underground facilities assumed it was safe enough that extra electronic security measures were unnecessary. Fine by Alisha: she delved into her backpack again and came out with solid steel lock picks.

There was a certain earthy joy to picking locks. Alisha had never broken herself of the habit of closing her eyes, head tilted to the side as she listened and felt through the cool steel. She rarely remembered to breathe until the tumblers gave their satisfying rattle of clicks. A smile of delight split her face as she tested the door a second time and the knob turned easily.

She opened the door a fraction of an inch, listening. There were no voices within. Satisfied, she pushed it open farther.

White light flooded her eyes. Reichart bellowed, "Look out!" as a shadow flickered in the light. Alisha flung her arms up, crossed at the forearm, and caught the broken leg of a chair in the X. Another flash in the brightness: the shadowed expression of surprise on a man's face as she grabbed the end of the leg and pulled it straight between her hands, turning it into a blockade against the next hit. She stepped forward, bringing her knee up sharply into his groin, and caught the man by the hair as he doubled. One step to the side, and she used her own momentum to crash him into the door she'd just come through. He slithered to the floor and Alisha turned back, the chair leg held as a weapon.

There was no one else in the white-lit room. No hostiles, at least: Reichart, shirtless, was clamped to a chair, a smile of appreciation crooked across his bruised face. "Guard has the keys," he said, which struck Alisha as both ungrateful and entirely appropriate. She turned back to the man she'd disabled, tugging keys off his belt and pushing him into the corner. The overhead light—a bare incandescent bulb, burning with heat—glared hard enough to make her squint as she hurried to unshackle Reichart's wrists, then handed him the keys so he could free his own ankles. Alisha ducked beneath the light to crack the door open a few centimeters, checking the hall.

"Really went all out, didn't they? Did they say, 'Ve hoff vays of making you tok?'" She heard Reichart's chuckle as he stood, and barely cast him a glance as he grabbed the guard's ankle and dragged him into the chair he'd just vacated. Within seconds the guard was sagging in the chair, locked in place. "I took the vents in. You up to climbing out that way?"

"Do we have another choice?"

"Sure. It just might get us killed."

Reichart chuckled again, the sound more like a groan this time. Alisha cast a more careful look over her shoulder at him, taking in his injuries. His face was swollen, bruised, the sharp angle of his cheekbone more than blurred with mottled purple flesh. There was water in his hair, curls half dry and for once completely untamed, making him look younger. His torso was bruised and burned in places, telltale marks that made Alisha glance around for the electric nodes that had left the burns. Nothing looked broken, not even the delicate bones in his fingers, though the back of his left hand had a deep red burn on it. "You okay?" she asked, more gently than she'd intended to.

She could see pride coming down over him like a cloak, straightening him out of a weary slouch. "I'll make it."

"That's not what I asked." Alisha bent to pull the tacky rubber-soled shoes off her feet, tossing them to Reichart. "It's all I've got that'll provide you with any kind of grip for climbing the vents."

Reichart slid one over his right hand, flexing his fingers inside it. "Not much to it."

"That's the idea. Come on." Alisha slipped out

the door, stopping across the hall to make a stirrup of her hands. "Vent's above the pipes."

"You sure they're going to hold me?"

"No," Alisha said, "but this is my rescue. Come on, go."

"You should go first."

"Frank." Alisha set her jaw. "I can't lift you from up there, but you can lift me if need be. Just shut up and go."

He hesitated one moment longer, looking down at her with an inscrutable expression. Then his lip curled and he stepped into the stirrup she'd made. Alisha grunted, pushing through her thighs to give him a boost of several inches. He grabbed the pipes and swung up with an alarming creak that reverberated down the hall. Distant footsteps sounded immediately. "The vent's to your left," Alisha hissed. "Go!"

"Alisha—"

"Go!"

The echoes of his quick scramble and the soft clang of the vent cover closing sounded like the walls of Jericho falling, to Alisha's ears. She crouched, ready to make her own leap for the pipes, even as she listened with all her being for the booted feet, running on concrete. Raised voices called out warnings in Chinese. At least two, possibly more. Alisha's face crumpled in concentration as she tried to count individual footfalls and pick out voices. Three. She swore voicelessly and bolted down the hall.

Toward the guards.

She met them at the nearest corner, her body coiled in preparation. The first of them skidded around the corner and she lashed out, a closed fist smashing into his larynx. He dropped with the horrifying silence of someone whose breath has been taken, clutching at his throat.

His compatriots nearly trampled him. Alisha dove between their feet, snatching for the downed guard's club, his gun—anything that might be a weapon, all the while cursing herself for leaving the broken chair leg behind in the interrogation room.

The awful clarity of combat training fell over her, slowing down everyone's actions until each play of muscle became visible. Her hearing ratcheted up, until the swiff of a gun leaving its holster sounded as loud as a freight train barreling down on her. There was no time to disarm: she was too low, too off balance, facing the wrong direction.

Alisha planted her hands on either side of the downed guard's head, stopping her own forward motion, and lashed back with a powerful donkey kick, aiming low. She could feel the floor's solidity adding to her own strength, as if the building's weight passed through her and into the kick, pure kinetic energy flowing as easily as a stream. She felt cartilage give as the kick connected with his knee, heard his scream as if it came through water: audible but distant. A gunshot fired, bullet going wild. Alisha thought if she turned her head she might see the bullet's flight. Instead she heard it, a slow whine that ripped the air apart without its path being visible before it clanged noisily against a wall, the pang of metal against metal.

A boot connected with her ribs, lifting her into the air and slamming her back against the wall. The final guard's hands crashed into the wall above her head: she hadn't been lifted as high as he'd expected. There was no breath left in her body, the boot having claimed it all, but she pulled strength from somewhere and thrust her arm out, heel of her hand leading. It connected solidly, just above the man's solar plexus. She felt bone snap, even thought she heard it, and looked up to see an expression of breathless horror bloom over the guard's face.

She had two guns in her waistband and the third in her left hand before he hit the floor. She crouched beside him, yanking his radio from his belt, and stopped long enough to knock the other two radios away from the others before she was running again, every motion so fueled by adrenaline and awareness she felt like a machine, honed to combat perfection.

Dry amusement rasped through her at the idea, too distant from her immediate needs to break through into laughter. The drones she was trying so hard to destroy were only a literal mechanization of what she felt now. God forbid the artificial intelligences that supported the drones' abilities should be able to learn to feel emotion. Humans who enjoyed destruction were dangerous enough. A drone that could take pleasure in a job well done would destroy the world.

Not a thought for here and now. She had almost no idea where she was, trusting instinct to guide her through the unknown halls beneath the production facility. Her feet burned with the cold roughness of concrete beneath them, dull warnings of pain warming her heels: she would pay for the shoeless run later.

Later. That was all that mattered. She spun around another corner, startling a young man with such sleepy eyes that Alisha felt a spark of guilt as she clobbered him with the butt of the gun she carried. He dropped without a sound or change of expression, and Alisha yanked open the door he'd guarded.

Stairs led up. Alisha shuddered with relief that her internal guidance system had brought her there, and bounded up the stairs, three at a time. These steps were metal grate, cutting into her feet with the weight and pressure of her run. She'd have hell to pay later, but for now she breathed through it, absorbing the pain, as if welcoming it would spread it through her whole body and make it bearable.

She banged the door at the top open, whipping her pistol out to the right and smashing another startled guard in the nose. He howled, doubling over, and she brought her elbow down on the soft spot at the base of the skull. He went down, a surge of remorseless relief firing fresh adrenaline through Alisha's system.

There was no time for subtlety or staying to the shadows. Alisha sprinted across the factory floor, not daring to look back at her own bloody footprints following her. Voices lifted, a security alarm finally going off. Time had shifted until it was meaningless. It felt like hours since she'd begun her escape, and the jangling alarm seemed to be terribly slow on the uptake. She vaulted an assembly line tread, then threw herself toward the floor. Bullets spattered over her head and as she rolled she fired, bright sparks smashing off the new equipment as none of the volleys, neither hers nor theirs, hit.

She couldn't allow them to encircle her. Alisha popped to her feet, firing again, but this time taking the necessary instant to aim. Curses filled the air along with the sound of bullets, and for a moment everything was clear. She put on a burst of speed, launching herself over another piece of equipment. She could see the stairs and the door she'd entered through now, the ones that led back to the teddy bear factory. A matter of yards, her life as a series of countdowns again.

Heat blazed against her arm, making her fingers spasm so she lost the gun she held. Not a deadly hit, just a shockingly painful sting. Alisha drew a second pistol, right-handed, and shot wildly over her shoulder, providing herself with what cover she could as she lengthened her stride and ran. No one was dead yet. One minute more and it would be over.

She hit the metal grate stairs running so fast she missed a step and stumbled, clawing her way back to upright. She could feel the sharp points of the metal grating puncturing through the calluses on her feet and muscle cramping around the injuries. Genuine horrors might await her at the head of those steps, but she kept returning to the image of Greg Parker's face as the worst of them. Alisha set her teeth together and surged forward, bursting into a dark silence so complete that for a moment she was bewildered at the calm that surrounded her. A brittle laugh of confusion escaped her, pain suddenly bright and hot in her feet. She broke into a hobbling run again, trying to breathe away the stabbing agony as her own weight bore down on fresh wounds. She would need medical care soon. Running through city streets would certainly infect the punctures in her soles.

Alisha limped to a fire alarm, weariness sweeping over her, and yanked it with everything she had left. Shrieking bells rang so loudly it jolted her into wakefulness again, making her aware that she'd better escape while she still could. She breathed deeply again, digging deep for her last vestiges of strength, and lurched through the tractor bay doors into a staggering run. She made it several blocks before she paused, exhaustion wracking her as she fumbled in her backpack for the C4 detonator.

The bud in her ear chirruped, melodic and at odds with her harsh breathing. "Cardinal," Greg's voice said, "do not proceed. Repeat, do not proceed. Return home. The mission is aborted."

Alisha swayed, slinging her backpack on again. "Roger that," she said, voice torn with tiredness. "Mission aborted. Cardinal returning to the nest." She no longer had any idea what was going on above her security clearance, and just then, didn't care. She would figure it out later. For the moment, not having to blow up a building was enough.

An eruption loud as Judgment Day exploded behind her, knocking her off her feet and into the dirty street. Alisha rolled on her back, staring in shock as plumes of fire leaped into the air, smoke billowing in thick stinking waves from the remains of the building she'd just been ordered not to destroy.

Eighteen

There was beauty in destruction. The warehouse district lit to golden tones that spoke of sunset, not death; fire cast sparks into the sky, dancing like stars. Heat rolled through the streets, breaking comfortably around her, wrapping her in warmth and safety. It made her feel as if she were floating, disassociated from gravity's call. Perfect solidarity with the universe, nothing wanting, nothing given. There seemed to be no sound associated with the booms she could feel in her breastbone, so deep that the beat of her heart was altered, and unconsciousness claimed her so peacefully she didn't know it until she woke on the ground, acrid smoke burning her lungs.

Its bitter taste made her cough a word. A name. *Reichart*. There was almost nothing to her own voice, little more than the shape of the word and a hard click. Reichart couldn't have gotten out. She'd only taken moments to escape herself, and *she* hadn't been forced to climb up awkward ventilation shafts to get away.

The heat and the sting of smoke made her

vision blur with tears. That was all: the heat and the smoke, nothing more. There was nothing inside her, just a cool empty place waiting to be filled.

Brandon. *Greg.*

That empty place twisted and filled with bile, horror cramping her belly as she rolled, barely able to hold her head up as she heaved a few bitter mouthfuls. Her forearms lay against the ground, stomach stretched long on the littered streets. She couldn't remember falling, nor could she bear to hold the weight of her head up. New tears gritted through her eyelashes, catching on her cheeks with an infuriating tickle. Alisha slapped her hand against them, sagging with her own weight. More than her own weight: it felt as if the fire pressed down on her shoulders, trying to pin her to the earth.

She didn't need to look to know the fire had faces. Brandon's face, Greg's face. Reichart's, and even Cristina's. All the dead, weighing her down. Joining them might be a blessing. It had to hurt less than the pain in her lungs that wouldn't let her draw breath. That kept thick tears etching their way down her cheeks. It would be so much easier to lie down and die, instead of losing anyone else.

Alisha shoved to her hands and knees, swaying in the fire-lit darkness. Easier. Not acceptable. Just easier. Her head dangled between her arms, gaze unfocused on the ground beneath her as she worked her toes under her feet. Curled her lip and pushed into downward dog, struggling to stabilize herself.

There. She could breathe now, a long shuddering breath that loosened, but didn't unbind, the knots caught in her lungs. Pain, purely physical and therefore welcome, shot up through her toes, the cuts on her feet shrieking as she put weight on them. Alisha gritted her teeth and walked her hands in, bent double. It took her breath again, but gave her the ability to bend her knees, to push herself upright through the thighs. Agony lanced through the soles of her feet all the way to her stomach, threatening to force another coughing mouthful of bile from her.

She had a detonator. She was dressed for infiltration. She could *not* afford to be found in the warehouse district, a thing growing more likely with every passing second. She could see a timer in her mind's eye, red numbers flipping by, counting the seconds from the explosion. A subconscious fail-safe, like counting the hourly bells ringing at a church. Most people did it, finding themselves at the count of six without having consciously begun at one. Alisha's clock was more refined than that, out of training and need, but the principle was the same.

Less than a minute had passed since the explosions. A few more seconds and her world would be irrevocably changed for a full minute. And then it would be two, then ten, and then minutes would turn to hours and months and years, going on without regard for the frailties of human life. Without care for emotional trauma, time inexorably healing wounds, as it was meant to do.

At sixty seconds, Alisha took a step away from her shattered life, and crumpled as her damaged foot refused to take her weight.

Strong and certain arms caught her around the waist as she fell, then scooped her up. "Let's get out of here," Frank Reichart murmured. "This one's my rescue."

A different sort of silence reigned, Alisha's ears no longer refusing to hear explosions in the midst of chaos. There was expectation in this silence, put off by efficient action. Reichart knelt at her feet, an ankle grasped firmly in his hand as he poured hydrogen peroxide over the cuts on her sole. Calluses from yoga had protected her from some damage, but not nearly enough, and Alisha twitched violently at the hiss and bubble of disinfectant burning the injuries. Reichart only tightened his grasp and lifted her foot, taking tweezers to bits of debris still lodged in the cuts. Alisha ground her teeth and clenched her fingers in the mattress, staring at Reichart so hard she thought he might light on fire from it.

He'd carried her a dozen blocks, neither of them speaking, Alisha too hurt and confused,

Reichart too intent on his burden and finding a rickshaw. He slid her rubber-soled shoes back over her feet once they were in it, and spoke awkward, tourist-level Mandarin to the driver. The boy barely even looked at them, only sped them through the streets, ringing his bicycle bell noisily when late-night traffic threatened their right-of-way. Reichart paid him, waited until he'd driven off, and carried Alisha another four blocks back the way they'd come, leaving behind a decent street for an inexpensive, hovel of a hotel hidden in the shadows of a red light district. Alisha kept her face hidden against his shoulder. Let the few viewers think she was drunk; better that than being recognized as a terrorist. He'd gone back out again for the peroxide and bandages, still without saying a word.

Silences, Alisha thought, were his best communication.

"They're alive." His deep voice was as startling as the change in his grasp, switching one ankle for the other. Alisha flinched again, staring at him with renewed intensity. "The Parkers," he said to her feet. "They got out. I think everyone did. A fire alarm went off just before I got out."

Cold swept over her, beginning in the abused soles of her feet with such a shock that Alisha cried out. Reichart's hand tightened around her ankle and he looked up for the first time. Only the bedside lamp was on, its cheap bulb casting dim shadows across the bruises on his face, but even in its light his eyes darkened, showing concern. The chill ran through Alisha, lifting hairs all over her body until she shuddered and shook her head. "I'm okay." Her voice was as rough as Reichart's. "You didn't hurt me. They're—?"

Reichart lowered his eyes again, returning to tending her feet. "Alive. I saw them."

"You blew up the factory." Alisha could hear the lack of emotion in her voice, knew it covered the hammering of her heart and the cold relief that now brought a sweat out on her body. "How?"

Reichart breathed laughter, ducking his head over her foot. "How'd you know to rescue me? I'd be dead if it weren't for you."

"And I'm not dead despite you."

Reichart's shoulders tightened, though his ministrations to her foot remained gentle. Alisha pressed her lips together and turned her face away, staring at the lamp. It colored the wall behind it a yellowed beige, as if the paint had given up its own color in a fight, and acquiesced to the superior shade offered by the light. "I saw you go in last night," Alisha said to the lamp. "I went in to set C4 and overheard them talking about you. They wanted you alive, so I couldn't exactly let you get blown to hell and back." The truth, as far as it went. As far as Alisha was going to let it go.

"I set charges myself, before they snagged me."

Alisha looked back at him incredulously. "And they didn't find them?" Reichart let out another breath of laughter.

"Not all of them. But since you were there I figured I'd try some of the CIA frequencies and see if you'd left anything to explode, too." He lifted his eyes, shadow of a grin crooking the bruises on his face. "Turns out you did."

Alisha felt an answering smile curve her lips, and bit the lower one to ward it off. "You look like hell, Reichart."

"You're not looking so hot yourself." He patted her ankle, nodding at her feet. "I'd tell you to stay off 'em, but you won't."

Alisha lifted them to study the soft wrappings of white gauze, so light it would have tickled if every heartbeat didn't send a pulse of pain through her soles. The giddiness of survival prompted her to wiggle her toes. Nausea rushed her and she clutched the edge of the bed, trying not to sway with pain, and carefully put her feet down again. "Thanks. Now all I need is a fifth of vodka to take the edge off and everything'll be all right."

"I'll look at them again in the morning," Reichart said at the same time, and for a moment silence cropped up again, potent and loud.

"Morning?" Alisha asked, as Reichart said, "Vodka?"

"No," Alisha said firmly. Reichart grinned, cocky and self-assured. *Bravado*, Alisha thought. He, too, had to be shaken by capture and the explosions that could have ended his life.

"To which?"

"Any combination that involves vodka and my feet being here in the morning."

Reichart's eyebrows went up a fraction of an inch. "You planning on walking out?"

Alisha took a deep breath and put her feet on the floor, using Reichart's shoulder to push herself into a standing position. Knives of pain rolled up through her feet, making her knees and the small of her back ache with it. Her nostrils flared and she could feel her cheeks whitening as she sat back down, stiff with pain. "Not right now." Her voice was hoarse. "Although it's probably not going to be a lot better in the morning."

"Alisha." Reichart put his hand on her ankle again, light touch. "I'll get vodka, if you want it. I'll get aspirin, which is probably better for you. And your honor," he said with only the faintest smirk, "is safe with me. You need some rest."

An entirely different sort of shiver ran through Alisha at Reichart's touch. Warmth spread after that chill, the strength of his hand a reassurance and a reminder. Years of separation hadn't reduced the sensuality of the man now kneeling at her feet. It would be so easy to let the past go for a night, and just be glad to be alive.

Reichart looked tired, the bruises on his cheek emphasizing that. Alisha reached out to brush her fingers against the air, not touching the injury. He turned his face away, avoiding even the intimation of closeness, and Alisha closed her fist loosely, thinking, for no particular reason, *Emma.*

"You should get some ice," she said quietly. "And some aspirin. For those bruises, and I'll take a look at the burns."

Reichart unfolded in one graceful motion, looking down at her without expression for long moments. Then he nodded and left Alisha alone in the hotel room.

As soon as he was gone, Alisha reached for the bud in her ear, the faintest pressure activating it. "Kremlin?" Cardinal and Kremlin. It had amused her at the time the code names had been assigned. Now laughter felt centuries away, every heartbeat sounding too far apart from the next, as she waited for a response. "Kremlin, come in." Her voice was cracked, old. She ought to have asked for water, not vodka.

"Cardinal?" Greg's voice came through the radio, full of disbelieving relief. "Cardinal, respond, is that you?"

Alisha slumped on the bed, pulling her feet up and wrapping herself around a pillow, finally allowing exhaustion to settle into her bones. She'd believed Reichart, but she hadn't *believed* him. *Trust but verify.*

"Christ, Cardinal, what happened? I told you to abort, and then there was a fire plume big enough to register on satellite!"

A peculiar memory cut through Alisha's exhaustion, one that almost made no sense: Greg didn't know she knew he was in Beijing. "I did abort." Her tongue felt thick in her mouth, as if it wasn't made to shape words. "I don't know what happened. The explosion knocked me for a loop." She listened to her own lies with detached astonishment, wondering why.

No. Not really. The why was simple: she might never get another chance to ask Frank Reichart what exactly he was doing. The fact that he almost certainly wouldn't answer was beside the point. Letting him go a third time with no resolution was more than Alisha intended to handle. Not more than she *could* handle, but more than she intended to.

"I've holed up at a hotel for the night to warm up and get clean," she went on. "I'll come in in the morning." That would give Greg time to get back to Langley. Time to—

—*to what, Leesh? Build his cover story?* A curl of dismayed laughter tightened Alisha's throat. She didn't know who to trust anymore, and that, for a spy, was deadly.

"I'll arrange for a convoy," Greg was saying, "at 6:00 a.m. local."

"God, Kremlin." Alisha groaned. "Can't it be like ten? It's already two. I'd like some sleep."

She could hear the frown that colored his voice. "Are you sure you're all right, Cardinal?"

"Just tired. A little beat up." Alisha hugged the pillow tighter to herself. "Look, I'll get a commercial flight. Don't worry about it, Kremlin. I'll see you tomorrow."

Long silence, before Greg said, "Take care." Alisha fished the bud out of her ear and deactivated it with a fingernail, then curled it in her palm.

"Leesh," Reichart said from behind her. She hadn't heard him come in, but didn't startle, only turned her head toward him without speaking. He sat down on the edge of the bed, his weight shifting her back. "They're alive?"

"Just like you said. Greg is, anyway. He doesn't know I know he's here." The shadows on the ceiling wove a dance in her vision, seeming to fall toward her and then scoop themselves back up. "Are you working for the Sicarii, Frank?"

"No," he said, so easily that Alisha turned onto her back, still clutching the pillow, to look up at him. There was no guile in his dark eyes, only a patience she didn't expect, and weariness that she did. "I brought aspirin," he said. "And water." He slid a hand under her shoulder, offering help she didn't think she needed in sitting, then handed her a travel packet of the drug and a bottle of water. "Already took mine," he said, digging a torn-open packet out of his pocket to show her. "No nagging."

"I don't nag." Alisha popped the aspirin and drank most of the bottle's content in one long chug. "Thanks. Why should I believe you?"

"Because I'm telling the truth." Reichart got up to fetch a towel, dumping ice from a bucket into it and snarling without sound as he held it to his face.

"Come here." The water had made her feel a little better; Alisha could hear the imperiousness in her tone as she pointed at the bed again. Reichart shot an eyebrow up and walked over, a saunter that would have been considerably more impressive had he not been bruised, burned and blackened from smoke on almost every visible inch of skin. Alisha reached for his hand and the hydrogen peroxide at the same time, managing not to smile as the faint light of wicked delight faded from his eyes to be replaced with resignation. "I told you I'd clean these."

"I never knew you had a Florence Nightingale streak."

"I didn't know you had one either." Alisha turned her attention to his burns, concentrating on them so she didn't have to look at his face. "Did you shoot me?"

"No." He didn't sound surprised at the question. Alisha wondered if she could ever surprise him. "Cristina did." The quality of his voice was the same as before, steady and without guile. He drew in a breath as she swabbed the round burn on his hand, but said nothing else. She could feel his gaze on her.

"Did you love Emma?"

Reichart drew in another breath, this one sharp enough to make her look up. There was pain in his brown eyes, more than just physical, and a question. But no deception, as he exhaled and answered, "Yes. But not before you."

Alisha bent over his hand again without speaking, tending to the burn and inspecting bruises.

Maybe, just maybe, Frank Reichart was finally telling her the truth.

Nineteen

"We make a fine pair, don't we," Alisha murmured a while later, the first words spoken since Reichart had answered her questions. He cast a wry grin at his swaddled hand and nodded at her equally well-wrapped feet.

"Between the two of us we might make one whole person." He lifted his arm, prodding carefully at the bruising his ribs had taken. Alisha moved his hand out of the way and put her palm against the damaged muscle, ignoring his sharp inhalation.

"I don't think anything's broken. Not displaced, anyway." She pulled her hand back, eyeing the soot and grime that she'd collected off his skin. "You need a shower."

"That an invitation?"

The look Alisha gave him wasn't as flat as she wanted it to be. She could feel the edges of a smile crinkling her eyes, and Reichart gave her a full-out grin in return. "It was worth asking. You're not exactly Ms. Clean yourself." He nodded at the pillow she'd clutched earlier. Alisha glanced at it, lifted eyebrows turning into a grimace of disgust. She'd left a fine layer of oily dirt on the pillowcases, which hadn't been the cleanest to begin with, and the bed-clothes where she sat weren't much better.

"I probably shouldn't get my feet wet." It sounded like a feeble excuse even to her, although she actually meant it.

"Probably not. Spit bath, then, while I take a shower." Reichart stood, scooping her into his arms before she had a chance to object. Alisha reached to poke him in the ribs in offense, but stopped herself.

"What are you—" The question didn't need answering; by the time she had the first words out, Reichart had carried her into the bathroom and put her down on the toilet, letting out a grunt of pain she was certain she wasn't meant to hear.

"You can't stand and there's no point in me carting you back and forth if one of us is clean and the other's filthy." Reichart pulled a towel and a washcloth off the rack and tossed them to her, nodding at the sink. "You wash, I'll shower." He turned his back with great deliberation, reaching for the tub faucet. Alisha watched the waistband of his pants loosen as he undid the button, and was caught staring as he shot a glance over his shoulder at her. She laughed and blushed, both more from surprise than guilt, and looked away.

For a moment, anyway. She slid another look over her shoulder as Reichart shucked his pants. No underwear. It was his philosophy that going commando made strip poker much more interesting. His skin paled abruptly at the hips, partly from the tan fading away, mostly from the protection from grime that pants had offered.

"You're peeking," he said without looking at her again, and stepped into the shower, pulling the curtain closed. Alisha's grin broadened and she really did turn away, stripping her hooded shirt off. Getting the pants off required more wriggling, her nostrils flaring as she put pressure on her damaged feet.

"Are you really a Tudor?" she asked to distract herself, pitching her voice to carry over the shower. She heard the pattern of water falling change as Reichart shifted.

"A what?"

"A Tudor. Like Elizabeth the First."

"How the hell should I know?" Reichart sounded so affronted that she laughed, leaning forward to turn the sink on and let the water run warm.

"I thought that's what the Sicarii were. Descendants of royalty trying to get their place back in the world."

Reichart gave an evocative snort. "What's that got to do with me?"

"The records show you're descended from Henry Tudor. Henry the Eighth."

The shower rod scraped as Reichart shoved the curtain open. Alisha felt his stare and held herself still, refusing to turn around. "Seriously?"

"Yeah." She shot a brief look over her shoulder, deliberately keeping her gaze high. "If you're not working for them, Reichart, who are you working for?"

"Did you check your own name in these records?" Reichart demanded. "You're probably descended from Charlemagne, or something. Half of Europe says they are, anyway. Did Parker tell you this crap? Did you check his name?"

"No," Alisha said, without specifying which question she answered. "You're staring, Frank."

Reichart muttered, "I do that when there are naked women around," but the hoops scraped again as he tugged the curtain shut. "I told you, Leesh. I'm working for the Russians. Nobody more esoteric than that."

"Why'd you lie to me about the Sicarii?"

"How'd you know about Emma?"

Alisha pressed her lips together, then shrugged her eyebrows, scrubbing sticky grime off her face and arms before she spoke. "I saw you in London a couple of years ago. I followed you. You and Emma and Mazie."

"Christ. Alisha…"

"Don't. It doesn't matter. Are you still with her?" Alisha pulled a hollow smile, shaking her head, but Reichart didn't ask the obvious: *if it doesn't matter, why are you asking?* Instead he only said, "No. Why didn't you say something?"

Alisha bent to the task of washing, rinsing out the washcloth more than once before she brought herself to answer. "You looked happy."

The shower shut off. Alisha straightened her spine defensively, but Reichart didn't pull the curtain open again. "You thought I shot you," he said quietly, "and you didn't have me arrested and brought in because I looked *happy*?"

Alisha wrapped her towel around herself, still sitting very straight. "Yeah."

Reichart said nothing for so long Alisha thought he might never speak again. The silence was a pressure, broken only by the burble of sink water. She could almost feel her own determined bubble of withheld explanations bumping against Reichart's, catching them together in an endless vortex of secrecy. No wonder it hadn't worked, she thought, admitting her own fault for the first time. Maybe people like them weren't supposed to be together.

"The CIA, the FSB, MI-5 and 6, all of them, they're all governmental agencies. Whether or not you agree with them, their fundamental job is to hold to an ideal, and to help that ideal be perpetuated in the world at large." Reichart spoke so suddenly that Alisha turned, watching the blur of his shape through the shower curtain. He'd braced himself beneath the shower head, arms stiff, head dropped between them. His nearer leg was cocked forward, making long clean lines of his body even through the plastic curtain.

"The Sicarii have no ideals, Leesh. They're functioning from a Dark Ages mentality, might makes right. They believe God speaks to them and through them, and that any action they take is divinely favored. It permits them to act without conscience."

"Jihad," Alisha said. "Kamikaze. Crusaders."

"Exactly." Reichart lifted his head, staring at the shower wall. "Those kinds of people don't try to protect their assets. They just discard them when they outlive their usefulness. They're insane, Alisha, and they're dangerous. And that's why I lied to you. I didn't want you to get tangled up in anything they had a hand in."

"You could have told me."

Reichart barked a sarcastic laugh. "Sure," he said, and turned a grin on Alisha that she could see even through the curtain's blur. "Because *that's* in my nature." He reached for the curtain and Alisha turned around hastily, pointing a reluctant grin at the countertop.

"So how do you know about them? The Sicarii Brotherhood."

"Brotherhood." Alisha could all but hear Reichart's eyebrows rising. "Catchy. I like it. What the hell do you think I was investigating when I showed up at your boyfriend's camp? I'm decent," he added, which was just as well, because Alisha turned on him, offended. He'd wrapped his towel around his hips, attractively low, but Alisha's focus was on his face and the challenge in his gaze.

"Boyfriend?"

"You and Parker seemed to be hitting it off pretty good."

"You've got to be kidding me." Alisha put a hand on the counter, setting her teeth in preparation for standing. "Jealousy doesn't look good on you, Reichart." A bare chest and an unfairly low towel, on the other hand....

"Maybe not. Don't squirm." He lifted her into his arms before she put more than a fraction of her weight on her feet. Alisha didn't object as he carried her back to the bedroom, his skin warm against hers. The purpling bruises on his ribs were more visible now that he was clean. "What do you mean, you were there about the Sicarii?"

Reichart sighed, backing away from the bed to sprawl heavily in a chair, towel loosening. Alisha wrinkled her face and glanced away. "Not that I don't appreciate the view, Reichart, but..."

"Shit." Reichart kicked his feet forward instead of out, crossing them, comparatively demurely, at the ankle, and adjusting his towel. "He works for the Sicarii, Leesh. He has for years."

"That's not possible. Greg got into his files, his op is CIA. It's not possible." Cold trickled over Alisha's shoulders, making her pull the towel tighter around herself. It wasn't possible.

Unless Greg was lying to her, too.

Cascading images fell through Alisha's line of vision, memories of words spoken resounding inside her mind. Greg and Brandon, cavalierly leaving Reichart behind in the building

Alisha was under orders to destroy. The strain in Greg's voice could have been because she'd broken through to a level of operations that he knew about, but she wasn't supposed to. It didn't seem impossible, just then, that she'd been set up from the beginning.

"Where'd you get the intel on the observatory? Why were you there?" Alisha asked, voice hoarse. Reichart's silence stretched taut before snapping.

"Because I knew you would be."

Alisha's gaze jerked to him, a whole new wave of shock spilling through her and making her body colder than before. Only her handler and a few people above him had known where she was going that night. Alisha's hand went to her waist as if looking for the pouch she'd carried that night. The data she'd retrieved from the observatory had led her to Brandon. Had led her to the Sicarii.

What if it had been a ploy?

To what end?

"I've got to go." Alisha shoved to her feet, clenching her teeth against the wave of sickness that swept through her as cuts and scrapes hurt more than their size seemed worth. Foot injuries usually seemed to heal quickly, but the pain that went with them made up for it.

Reichart was on his feet again too, strong hands warm against her bare shoulders. "Leesh, you might as well get some rest, unless you've got clean clothes hidden in that backpack of yours. I didn't think so," he said as her face fell. "Lie down, sleep. It'll help you heal and it'll clear your head. I'll wash the clothes. Besides," he said more gently, "what're you going to do? Waltz in and demand to know who Greg Parker's loyalties really lie with What do you think he'll say, Leesh?"

"I don't know. Why should I trust any of what you're telling me?" She did, though. His arguments felt like a searing cold line of truth that burned through her middle, but there was no reason to trust him beyond her gut instinct. She didn't know whether to trust even herself anymore. "Did Cristina really shoot me?"

Reichart sighed and put his forehead against hers, his eyes closed. "Leesh, this Sicarii thing goes back to then. To before then. The pickup you were making that night, do you know what it was about?"

Alisha pulled away, folding her arms around herself and hobbling to the end of the bed, out of Reichart's reach. Shards of agony shot up her shinbones and took up residence in her knees, making them ache like she was getting her period. "It was, um." She swallowed, then sat, putting her face in her hands tiredly. "A terrorist threat, I think. Against Rome proper, not Vatican City. It didn't pan out, though."

"No." Reichart crouched in front of her, hands dangling over his knees. His towel loosened again precariously, and Alisha lifted her gaze to his face rather than call him on it. "The Sicarii made a power play inside the Church. They needed Cardinal Nyland out of the way in order to move one of their own into a stronger position for an eventual attempt at the papal seat."

Alisha breathed laughter. "The Pope had been ailing for years, Reichart. Why then? Why Nyland?"

He shrugged a shoulder. "Nyland was popular, and maybe too smart for his own good. He thought there was more to the maneuverings than simple politics and started investigating. He came up against the Sicarii, Leesh. The intel he was passing you was regarding them."

Alisha shook her head. "But I had the papers he gave me."

"You had the papers the Sicarii replaced the originals with. I watched Cristina switch them, Leesh."

"Cristina!"

"I don't know," Reichart said harshly. "I don't know if she knew what she was doing, if she was working for the FSB or the Sicarii, Alisha. All I know is I watched the papers get changed and then I lifted them off her in the chaos while they were preparing to move you to the hospital."

"How could she have shot me? She was in the plaza. I saw her." Alisha's voice dropped. "What were you doing there, Frank?"

"The first I saw of her, she was coming from the stairs in front of you. She was high enough to have shot you. And I was *supposed* to protect the Cardinal." Reichart ghosted his hand over her cheek. Alisha closed her eyes, tempted to lean into that bare touch. "I *wanted* to protect you. Neither worked out so well."

"If you didn't shoot me, why'd you disappear?"

Reichart huffed a laugh of frustration. "I got another assignment."

"Another assignment worth leaving your fiancée bleeding to death in a Roman piazza. I hope it was a nice fat paycheck, Reichart." The venom Alisha might have spat had been watered down by time and her own growing weariness.

"Alisha..."

Alisha shook her head. "It's history, Frank. Maybe it doesn't matter anymore. And right now I don't know what to believe, so I'm just going to get some sleep. If you're still here in the morning, we'll talk then."

Twenty

A cheap cotton T-shirt lay neatly folded on the bed next to her when Alisha opened her eyes. Its presence spoke volumes that her ears would have heard anyway: there was no sound of another sleeper in the hotel room, no noise in the bathroom to indicate someone might be in there. Alisha curled her fingers into the thin fabric and sat up, pulling the shirt on at the same time.

It didn't matter: there was no need for modesty. Her ears hadn't betrayed her. Reichart was gone, the T-shirt an apology for the man not being there. Alisha said, "Bastard," without heat to the empty room and folded her feet up to examine the soles beneath their loose-wrapped bandages.

The cuts and punctures were clean, no signs of infection, but walking was going to hurt. She pressed her lips together and reached for new bandages, left by the bedside along with the bottle of hydrogen peroxide. Very thoughtful of Reichart to sneak out only after getting all the materials she'd need for a discreet exit from the hotel.

It was just barely possible that he might have still been there, had she not ended the evening on the weary snipe. Possible, but not likely. Reichart wasn't a man to be counted on.

But at least the shirt he'd brought her fell to her hips, covering the sleek fibrous material of the black stealth suit she'd worn the evening before, and he'd left her the rubber-pebbled shoes. Tugging them over the fresh bandages on her feet made her dizzy, but once on they constricted in a friendly fashion, as if the snug fit supported and cushioned her soles more efficiently than normal shoes would. She left the hotel with her expression held carefully neutral, not that anyone in the dingy lobby even looked up. She caught a glimpse of herself in front door's glass, her usual golden skin tones sallowed to yellow from the shards of pain that every step brought. The thin rubber shoes were still better than being barefoot, and after the first minutes, the pain mutated into a thick constant ache that made her joints hurt halfway up her body, but was manageable. It was wonderful, she thought with a mix of honesty and sarcasm, what the human body could adapt to.

She collected a small suitcase of belongings from a luggage locker at one of the supermarkets near the Dongzhimen train station, then hobbled to one of the station's bathrooms to change clothes.

Elisa Moon wore heels. Alisha stared at her clothing choices—really fabulous three-inch red heels, long black silken trousers that brushed the toes of those shoes, a wrap top to match the shoes, and a light bolero—and hated her past self for not anticipating cut-up feet needing to go into those shoes. At least she could keep the rubber shoes and the bandages on beneath them, but putting the heels on sent a new wave of dizziness through her, roiling her belly and making her light-headed. She left the bathroom trying to focus on anything beyond her feet: the hot air sticking against her skin, the scent of dust and fuel and bodies thick in the air as she minced across the platform to board the airport train. Humanity pressed around her, sweaty, in a hurry, careless of toes, and she bit the inside of her cheek to keep from crying out when her feet were stepped on. There were no empty seats on the train and she held a ceiling strap with a white-knuckled grip, eyes closed as she swayed with the train's motion and tried to keep her weight off her feet. After a few minutes a young man tapped her shoulder and gestured to his seat, his expression concerned. Alisha whimpered thanks in a bad accent and sat, shivering with pain. Her feet were throbbing less by the time the train reached Beijing Capital International Airport fifteen minutes later, but standing started the whole cycle over again.

At least she had fast track clearance, and could breeze through security to wait in the first class lounge before priority boarding. It was all a performance: walking lightly, like her feet weren't on fire, smiling at the security agents, greeting the flight attendants pleasantly. She took her seat in first class with a swallowed sob of relief and pushed her shoes off before the flight attendant could even offer her a drink. "Orange juice with vodka, please. It's after five o'clock somewhere."

The attendant laughed and went to get the drink while Alisha turned her gaze out the tiny window. She could suddenly breathe more easily, tension unraveling in her shoulders and releasing the feeling of being watched, as if she'd escaped Frank Reichart's intent gaze only when she'd boarded the airplane.

Alisha closed her eyes and inhaled deeply, tasting the air's manufactured quality. Even with the doors still open, it was recycled and too dry. She felt for the bottle of water provided by the airlines, cracking its top and draining most of it without opening her eyes. Its coolness hit her belly and spread through her body, as if fighting the good fight against the dryness of the air, and bringing some relief to her aching feet. Her thoughts cleared, like fine threads of watery blue were spilling through the crooks and crannies of her mind. Alisha smiled faintly at the idea, pressing her head back into the headrest.

It cradled her skull, a promise that she could drift into sleep and wake without a crick in her neck. Alisha held on to that idea, sailing out of conscious thought and into the semi-aware state that preceded sleep. The sound of the jet's engines filled her ears, white noise that disrupted any need to focus on listening to the people around her, although she heard the flight attendant say, "Your drink, ma'am," and reached for the screwdriver to drink several large sips gratefully The alcohol almost instantly numbed her thighs and worked its way down to her feet, and she said, "Yes, please," to the flight attendant's query about another drink.

She'd drunk that, too, before she felt the chair beside her shift. The faint warmth of someone else's body heat brushed her as another passenger—a woman, from the delicate scent of perfume—sat. To Alisha's relief, the woman didn't immediately speak, and she hoped they could pass the entire flight in companionable silence. She wanted time to think, not to exclaim politely over someone's grandchildren or dogs, and the combination of vodka and weariness was just enough to let her thoughts drift in useful patterns.

She needed proof. Unless Brandon and Reichart were working together, a thought which Alisha refused to contemplate, the Sicarii must have some grounding in truth. The Vatican records were too old and delicate to be forged, but even they weren't concrete evidence of a centuries-old conspiracy to lever divine right over democracy. Alisha's stomach muscles tightened with a laugh that went no further than that. Maybe it was human nature to believe in conspiracies, just as it was to believe in predestination and a reason behind everything that happened. She felt she ought to know better, but a part of her wanted to believe, anyway. *Me and Mulder.*

She pushed the wry thought away, trying to focus on the scant handful of things she felt certain of. Brandon and Greg Parker, regardless of what other affiliations they might share, had been together in Beijing at the Attengee production facility. Brandon claimed to be working undercover for the CIA as a mole within the Sicarii, an organization that Greg claimed to know nothing about.

But the assignment to investigate Brandon had come from above Greg. From higher in the CIA. From Director Boyer. Alisha reached for and drank the rest of her screwdriver, then finished her water without opening her eyes, feeling removed from her own physical actions. Assume, she thought, that Boyer was straight. Assume that his investigation was endangering a Sicarii protocol within the CIA.

Then everything she thought she'd known for the last ten years could be a lie.

And every action she took now could be a test. She was Greg Parker's protégé, a young woman he'd groomed for nearly a decade. She was quick and smart and sometimes sentimental. If someone was unsure of where her handler's loyalties lay, Alisha's would also undoubtedly be in question.

That was the problem with spy movies, of course. They were always sending people with emotional investment into situations that required objectivity. That was dangerous, likely to result in mistakes made from clouded judgment.

Mistakes like looking for ways to keep Brandon Parker out of harm's way, which could very easily be misinterpreted as her loyalties lying elsewhere. Alisha tilted her head until the crown pressed against the chair's headrest, nostrils flaring as she drew in a deep breath. Maybe she hadn't been drawn into the tangled web she was uncovering. Maybe she'd been placed in it deliberately, to see whether she was a spider or a fly.

She exhaled noisily, pressing her fingers into the seat arms. The possibility she was being played hadn't occurred to her before now.

"It's all right," the woman beside her said in lightly accented English. "Flying is safe." The words rose and fell with gentle reassurance. Alisha gave a startled half-laugh and opened her eyes.

"Thank you. I'm all right."

The woman beside her was older than she, Chinese, and as lovely as the light floral perfume she wore, with amber in her brown eyes. She smiled and nodded, breaking eye contact with Alisha almost immediately, clearly not wishing to seem rude. Alisha returned the smile briefly and relaxed back into her seat, eyes closed again.

If it was a setup, the Sicarii could be a false lead. Brandon's midnight conversation in the bunker could have been for her benefit, introducing a third player simply to confuse the issue. But—amusement lanced through Alisha, her awareness of the irony too great to ignore—Reichart had corroborated the Sicarii story, even if the ancient records in the Vatican library hadn't lent credence to at least certain aspects of it.

Of course, he could be a double agent, too.

Alisha groaned and sank down as far as her seat belt would let her. The woman beside her shifted, concern evident in her voice as she asked, "Miss?"

"Where do we go from here?" Alisha said the words very softly, thin strains of song breaking through them, as if waiting for the fuller music of the next lines. She bit them off in her mind, unwilling to pretend even the Pyrrhic victory they promised.

"Miss?" the woman beside her asked again.

Alisha shook her head. "I'm all right," she said again. "I don't mean to be rude, but I'm mostly talking to myself right now. Tired. Sorry."

The woman ducked her head in apology, pulling her elbows in toward herself, shrinking in the seat. Alisha put her teeth together, warding off her own impulse to apologize in turn until it passed and she could concentrate on her conundrum again She had to apply Occam's razor: the simplest possibility was the most likely. Reichart had his own loyalties; the odds that he was part of a scheme to set her up were remote. Not impossible, but remote. For that matter, the idea that she was even important enough to set up seemed unlikely.

She had to choose somewhere to begin trusting. Her history with Reichart made him both the first and last choice; she wanted to trust him, and didn't dare. But Greg and Brandon being together at the destroyed production facility made her stomach curdle with foreboding. Bad choices all around. Alisha tilted forward in her seat, elbows on her thighs and fingers pressed against her face in a steeple. The plane pulled back from the jetway, flight attendants beginning their safety lectures as Alisha swayed with the jet's motion.

"Assume," she whispered out loud, the words directed at her lap. *Assume you're being played, Leesh. Assume you're a pawn. And then figure out a way to get queened.* She sat back, elbow on the seat's arm as she curled her fingers against her mouth, working through possibilities until she fell asleep.

She woke a little while before landing, the combination of relentless travel, her injuries, and the alcohol making it easy to sleep through the bulk of a thirteen hour flight. She'd deplaned, grateful to find that her feet didn't hurt nearly as much, a full day after she'd injured them, and entered the airline's first class lounge to make a critical phone call. A young family were playing an energetic game of tic-tac-toe in one corner of the lounge and earning filthy looks from the other handful of people there, which suited Alisha just fine, as it drew attention away from her. She went over to the windows, leaning against them to watch the haze on the horizon as she waited for Greg Parker to pick up the phone.

He sounded relieved when he did, voice crackling as delays broke his words up. "I've been waiting for you to check in. Are you all right?"

"Fine. Long night. Long flight."

"You're back in DC? I've got a new assignment. We cracked the files you downloaded. Turns out they're hardware schematics."

"Hardware. Shit. Um, hang on a second, it's loud in here." The kids were getting noisier. Alisha didn't remember tic-tac-toe being so loud, but she'd never played a board game version of it, either. She dug around in her purse, one-handed, to find a headset that she connected to the phone before fitting the buds into her ears. The set's mouthpiece fell just below her chin, and she lifted it closer to her lips. "Okay, I can hear you better now. Hardware. Well, crap. I mean, it's useful, but if I only got the hardware specs, the software must be just about impossible to download. It must be massive."

"We need it."

"What about—" Alisha broke off, unwilling to voice the actual question in a public area, even if no one was paying attention.

"Reverse engineering will take too long," Greg answered, intuiting her meaning. "We've got techs on it already, and the remote you delivered with the drone is proving incredibly useful. It's in perfect working condition, all of it, the remote, the drone, everything. The whole program is intact. Beautifully done, Ali. Very well done."

"Thanks."

Greg went on as if she hadn't spoken. "So we've got people on it. But their best estimates suggest weeks, more likely months, before we've gone far enough back to begin moving forward again. We need the software."

"There can't be many facilities prepared to host that kind of backup," Alisha said, more to herself than to Greg. She wanted to just flat-out ask why he didn't turn to Brandon for help, but squelched the impulse until she actually knew who Greg was working for.

The thought made her mouth dry, ashy distaste filling her throat. She swallowed against it and crossed the lounge to a water cooler bearing an expensive brand name to fill a glass—real glass, but not crystal—so she could drink her fill. "Do we know if Brandon's got a copy of the software?"

"I assume not, after our acquisition and removal of the target," Greg said. Alisha drained her water glass and set it aside, retreating to the window again. The woman from the plane came into the lounge, exchanged a brief smile with Alisha, and sat closer to the laughing family than anyone else in the room did. Unlike everyone else, the woman looked pleased by their joy, and Alisha smiled again as she turned away from all of them and focused on the green horizon, and on what Greg had said.

On the surface of it, Greg was almost certainly right. Odds were that even if Brandon had had all the drone software on the Kazakhstani base computers, he hadn't had the capability to back it up onto something he could take with him. But that was on the surface, and Alisha didn't trust much of anything Greg had to say right now. He almost certainly knew for certain whether Brandon had the drone software, and could presumably get ahold of it himself any time he needed to.

But she wasn't supposed to know that, and letting even a hint of her knowledge slip could spell disaster. For whom, she didn't know, but it probably wouldn't go well for her. Trying to keep her voice neutral, or at least like she sounded determined to do the job, she said, "We need to be sure. Not many places have the kind of processing power or storage he's using."

"I've narrowed it down to five or six facilities," Greg agreed. "If he's looking for backups himself, we might catch him at one of them. The two most likely places in the States are in San Jose and Dallas. Where are you?"

Alisha lifted her gaze to the lounge windows again, looking out over the plane-littered runways and beyond them at the green haze that hid the distant Potomac River that welcomed visitors to the Washington, D.C., metropolitan area.

"Los Angeles," she said easily. "I'll go to San Jose, and call you when I've got something."

Twenty-One

Alisha was accustomed to slipping through foreign cities, avoiding their surveillance and keeping her head down. Doing the same thing in DC felt genuinely strange, but she'd purchased jeans, a t-shirt, sneakers, and an "I <3 DC" baseball cap in the airport mall and slipped out into the afternoon sun with her hair tucked into the cap like any camera-wary tourist. She called a ride-share to the airport pickup ranks instead of using a legitimate taxi service, because it was far less likely to have an in-car camera she could be tracked with. It took her to Georgetown, where she called another one, which dropped her off a dozen blocks from a CIA safe house outside of Fairfax. She went the rest of the way on foot and regretted it by the time she got there: her feet throbbed in the heat and sweat poured down her spine. After all that, she was still early, and went inside gratefully to shower, dress again, and sit with her feet in a pot of cool water until she drifted off.

She awoke to a deep male voice saying, "Well, this is unusual, Cardinal," and jolted to her feet, knocking the pot over as she did. Water spilled

everywhere while she dropped back into the
couch, white-lipped with pain from stubbing her
feet against the pot's sides.

Director Daniel Boyer let out a startled yelp
and danced backward, avoiding a deluge over
his leather shoes. Alisha, mortified, stood up
again, eyes watering with pain. "Director Boyer.
Sir. I didn't hear you come in."

"You don't say. What on earth, Cardinal."
Boyer, a big man with very dark skin and close-
cropped curls receding from his hairline, lifted
his hand. "Never mind. Sit back down while I
get this cleaned up and then you can explain.
Don't argue," he said firmly as Alisha inhaled to
do just that. "You're obviously injured. Sit."

Alisha sat, face hot as she watched the
director of the CIA clean up her mess without
staining his well-cut tan suit. After he'd tidied
up, he looked around as if assessing his efforts,
gave a satisfied nod, and sat across from his
barefoot agent, hitching up the thighs of his
slacks as he did so. *The Picard Maneuver,* Alisha
thought, and wondered if he would know
what she meant by that.

"All right, Alisha. "What's going on?"

Alisha puffed her cheeks and blew out the
breath. "This might take a while, sir."

"Really." Boyer's deep voice was as dry as a
desert. "An agent makes a personal call to the
director of the CIA to request a clandestine
meeting at one of our own safe houses, and you
think he can't figure out explaining it might

take a while? I'm insulted."

Alisha laughed despite herself. "Sorry, sir. Um, the shortest version is that Greg said I was supposed to report to you as well as to him and I'm taking advantage of that."

"Why do I get the feeling that's the tip of the iceberg?" Boyer gestured for her to continue.

"Because it is, sir. Director, I understand that it's not necessarily my job to know what the reasons behind my missions are. Most of the time that's okay."

Boyer's eyebrows, dark straight slashes, rose a little. "But not this time?"

"Not this time," she agreed. "Sir, I really need to know where we got the intel that sent us after Brandon Parker. I need to know if he's an undercover agent, and whether Greg knows about it or not."

Boyer's eyebrows shot up again, higher this time. "Would you like to know who shot JFK, too?"

"Oh, come on, sir." Alisha made a face. "This isn't that important." Cold nerves knotted in her belly, making a burp there, and she felt her expression slide toward disbelief. "Wait. First, do *you* know who shot JFK? And second, *is* it that important?"

Boyer chuckled. "No. You just looked so serious."

Alisha ducked her head, exhaling a quick laugh. "Oh. Okay. Sorry. I'm feeling the strain on this one."

"You need to be taken off this mission?"

"No, sir." She looked up again, quickly. "But I'd feel a lot better if I knew what I was dealing with. I feel like I'm being played, and I need to know who's playing me."

Boyer leaned back, considering her. He was broad-shouldered and thick through the waist, not fat, but barrel-chested, and the cut of his suit jacket made him look too large for the dim, neutral colors of the safe house living room. Reassuringly dangerous, Alisha thought. Like he could break a neck or rescue a kitten with equal ease. "I can't tell you where the intel on Parker came from," he said after a moment. "I can tell you that you were specifically recommended for this mission by someone whose judgment I trust."

"That's very flattering, sir," Alisha muttered. "Are my loyalties being tested?"

Surprise turned into a one-sided grin on Boyer's face. "What do you think?"

"I think if you deliberately sent me in to investigate an undercover agent who could identify me that you're being reckless and careless with both his and my life, and I resent it. Sir."

Boyer's eyebrow quirked again. "To the best of my knowledge, Brandon Parker has not worked for the CIA since he left nearly ten years ago."

"Is it possible that he's working undercover without your knowledge?"

"Anything is possible, Cardinal. Langley isn't

the only operations center, and while I'm kept apprised of other operations, I'm sure there are a few of my own that would come as a surprise to some of the other directors."

"Thank you," Alisha said dryly. "That fills me with confidence."

"As well it should. His story, then, is that he's working for the CIA?"

Alisha nodded. "As a double agent within the Sicarii."

That garnered a reaction from the director, a brief look of surprise flashing over his face. A knot of tension she hadn't realized existed unlocked at the base of her neck, relaxing the muscles in her shoulders. "So they are real. Jesus." Alisha lifted a hand to rub her eyes. "That's actually a relief."

"If Brandon Parker claims to be working as a double agent for the Sicarii," Boyer said, words slow and measured, "you will proceed as if he is telling God's own truth, Agent MacAleer."

"Is he?"

"I don't know." Boyer's voice dropped into a deeper growl, making Alisha straighten her spine against the chill that ran over her. "But I will find out. In the meantime," he went on, voice resuming its normal baritone, "what about Greg? You asked if he knew about Brandon's theoretical assignment. Why?"

"Because I saw them together in Beijing." Alisha spread her hands, shaking her head. "I don't know who to trust anymore, sir. Greg doesn't even know I'm in D.C. That's why I wanted to meet here instead of at the offices."

"You *have* gotten paranoid." Boyer pursed his lips, eyebrows shifting upward again. "What do you propose to do?"

Alisha took a deep breath. "Nothing." Boyer's eyebrows lifted higher and she shrugged. "I'm going to steal the software backups for the AI prototypes. I'll deliver a copy to you, but I want to give one to Greg as well. A corrupted copy, with a tracer set in it to see if the files are copied before you get them."

"And if they're not?"

"Then I'll be incredibly relieved, sir. I want this to turn out clean. I want it to turn out that Brandon Parker is working so far undercover that only six people in the world know about it."

Boyer rumbled a laugh that lifted the hairs on Alisha's arms again. "A secret known by six people isn't a secret, Cardinal."

"Heh. Yes, sir. But honestly, sir, I want this to be above your head."

"You want it to be. But you're afraid it isn't."

"I wouldn't be here if I wasn't."

Boyer nodded, then stood. "You have a go, Cardinal. Set your bait. We'll see what happens."

Alisha stood as well, wincing as she put weight on her feet again. "Thank you, sir." They shook hands and Alisha remained standing until the director left the room. Then she clenched her hand into a triumphant fist and grabbed her purse off the couch's end table, upending it over the couch cushions. Passport, loose change, lipstick, a pad of paper. Elisa Moon's life in a bag, Alisha thought, searching for a flat makeup case.

Habit made her check her hair in its mirror —it looked fine, not smashed down by sleeping on it with a wet head—as she worked the bottom loose, exposing an LCD panel that covered two-thirds of the box's bottom. Powder dusted the panel, kicking up a fine sweet-smelling spray as she puffed her cheeks and blew to clear it. She could almost hear Erika scolding her: *that's a delicate piece of equipment, Alisha! Don't spit on it!*

Pressure on the lower third of the pad activated it without so much as a telltale beep. The screen came up, so dull it was difficult to see under the bathroom's overhead lighting. Alisha cupped her hand over it, making shadows, and the monitor came into sharper relief.

Now a grid was visible, a single point—two letters, A-4—blinking silently. Alisha mouthed, "Hit," as if she played Battleship. The blip might be a dead end, but at least it was still active. She had a chance of finding Brandon Parker.

Alisha fished the eye makeup brush out of the main section of the case and left a dot of silver-brown on the screen where the point blinked. The lower half of the screen cleared, coordinates writing themselves out in dim green block letters.

Forty-seven degrees, twenty-three minutes north. Eight degrees, thirty-three minutes east. Alisha closed her eyes, visualizing the curvature of the globe, counting out bars of latitude and longitude. Europe, certainly, with the latitude line crossing so high on the line of longitude. She superimposed the European states over the lines, grade-school colors differentiating one country from another. The images centered together easily, Alisha using Greenwich as the starting point. Germany, Austria—

Switzerland. Zurich.

Alisha opened her eyes, grinning. *Hit and sink.*

She had barely been in the States six hours before she left again on another commercial flight, her CIA-issued phone stripped of its battery so she couldn't be tracked on her way to Europe. She hadn't touched the passport she was now using in years, although the brazen persona that went with it stretched back to the beginning of her career. Career consultant Doreen Green got by on abrasive charm, and Alisha MacAleer, beneath Doreen's surface, loved every minute of it. Doreen took up more space than Alisha, wore high heels and big hair, and walked with a swing to her hips that made people stare. Usually that was sheer fun, although now both the shoes and the strident walk made Alisha very aware of the ache in her feet. Approaching the target still filled her with sassy good humor, because these were her favorite moments in the spy game: bold engagement with a target when she had nothing but the most illicit of plans in mind.

A tilt of her head brought the short-cropped A-line wig, dark brown and full of waves, swinging forward to conceal the angle of her cheekbones. She wore wire-frame glasses, tinted to further alter the contact-changed color of her eyes, and penciled-in lip rouge thinned the shape of her mouth. A bulky, if well-tailored, suit added weight to her body until at a glance in the mirror, not even she saw herself. It was what she wanted: no one would see the agent beneath the brassy figure she cut.

Brandon had long since left Zurich when she deplaned there, the tracer she'd put on him indicating he'd gone back to Italy. That was fine: she would catch up with him later, after planting what she hoped would be a crippling blow. For now, she had what she needed to deliver that blow: the address of the Swiss security headquarters where the Attengee files were stored.

The modern-built headquarters, on Zurich's edge, were pleasantly unremarkable: clean-cut Swiss architecture that stood out against the summer greenery but didn't draw the eye with unusual detail. A guard came to attention and opened the door for her as she swaggered up the steps and winked at him. He pretended not to see, but the corner of his mouth twitched as she swanned by and entered the lobby. All marble and metal, it glowed with sunlight pouring in through massive windows that Alisha bet were bulletproof as well as visually appealing. Despite its brilliance, it wasn't a friendly space: there wasn't even anywhere to sit down, and only a single, unadorned reception desk broke the lobby floor. There were a couple of hallways to either side of the lobby, and one tremendous steel door off to the desk's left, like a behemoth waiting to devour the unwary. Alisha sauntered up to reception and drawled, "Doreen Green," to the pasty-skinned young man sitting there. "Ah called yesterday."

"Yes, of course, Ms. Green." She could see him sizing her up with disapproval, although he mostly kept it out of his tone. "You're late."

Alisha rolled her eyes. "Aw, only a couple of minutes. Don't tell me you're gonna be a stick in the mud about that, honey. I hate it when cutie-pies are sticks in the mud."

The faintest hint of alarm creased the corners of his eyes. Alisha fought an urge to laugh, leaning forward over the desk instead. "So have you got a little tour of the—" She raked her gaze over him and came back up to his eyes with a smile. "—the *facilities* for me?"

"I'm afraid that will be my associate's pleasure, Ms. Green." He lifted a hand, gesturing for a blond man who appeared through a heavy steel door. "You represent—"

"An expanding IT corporation," Alisha said lavishly. "Quantum computing. It's the new plastic."

"I think you'll find our facilities an excellent backup storage site, Ms. Green. We already have at least one other client storing the quantities of data capable of being run through quantum computing here."

Bingo. Alisha thrust a hand out at her guide, who shook it with the enthusiasm of a man accepting an aging dead fish. She fixed a brilliant smile in place and allowed herself to be ushered through the steel interior doors, into an elevator, and down into literal acres of data-storage warehousing.

The air was cool to the point of being frigid, the pervading sound that of air-conditioning running full-blast. It wasn't comfortable, but it kept the enormous computers from overheating. Alisha shivered, but nodded in approval, which her guide looked faintly smug about.

"Ah trust," Alisha said, laying on the drawl for all it was worth, "that each computer is independent of the others, so a failure in one won't result in a catastrophic chain reaction?"

The guide's expression changed from smugness to mild affront. "Of course."

Crap. That didn't make it easy to set a virus. Her mouth, however, smiled and said, "Fantastic. Now, without compromising the security of your other clients, might Ah see an array that could ostensibly handle our quantum chip backup needs? All Ah'm saying, you understand, is that a quantum chip is capable of processing huge amounts of data in a way standard chips can't, and we're gonna require storage for massive quantities of raw data." She leaned into her accent until her guide looked pained.

"Of course, Ms. Green."

She fought off a grin, imagining what he and the kid at the front desk would have to say about Americans when she was gone. "Tell me about your security measures," she commanded as he led her through towers of data storage units that stood twice her height. "Ah notice you've chosen a real low profile instead of makin' this place showy."

"Security is not about gleaming walls and bright lights, Ms. Green," her guide said a bit severely. "I'm sure you've noticed the chill. Among other things, our sensors are calibrated to detect body heat in the midst of this facility. We only turn it off for client arrivals and tours like this one. Otherwise the alarms would have long since sensed us and the police would be on their way."

"How efficient," Alisha said without a trace of the irritation she felt. A well-insulated cold suit could get past the cold; the alarms, she was certain, were silent, and she'd already counted dozens of security cameras covering every angle of the storage acreage. Pity she couldn't just drop several blocks of explosives

around the building, but would have un-
wanted ramifications, to say the least. "And
redundancies?"

"We *are* the redundancy, Ms. Green," the
guide said with a stern note of reprimand in
his voice. "Our clients keep their files on location. We merely provide backups, which are
updated as regularly as our clients send new
material, usually once a month. More than
monthly," he added darkly, "is of course increasingly expensive."

"Of course." Alisha had the impression he
didn't like her, and put a little extra swing in
her step as they strode around a corner into a
new set of arrays.

"These are the servers your data would be
stored in." The guide looked increasingly like
he'd sucked on a lemon, making Alisha want
to beam at him. "From the outside, I'm afraid,
they don't look terribly impressive."

"But internally, with each hard drive capable
of holding a hundred exabytes of information
and those drives being clustered together in
groups of ten or more, they start lookin' a little
more showy." Alisha gave him another bright
smile that entirely soured his expression.

"Yes. It seems you know your equipment,
Ms. Green."

"That's my job." Alisha let ice water splash
through her voice, and watched the guide's chin
come up as he reassessed her, then inclined his
head in what might have been apology.

"Of course. If you'd like to return with me, Ms. Green, we'd be pleased to begin your paperwork."

"Don't bother," Alisha said. "We'll be going with your competitors in San Jose. My company has a strict policy of never working with condescendin' assholes." She smiled brilliantly and let him lead her out.

Twenty-Two

"I love it when you call me for the illegal stuff." Erika's voice came through the line as if she sat next door, full of good humor.

"How do you know it's illegal?" Alisha turned her wrist up, glancing at the time: almost noon. It wouldn't be full dark for nearly twelve hours, not in the midst of a Swiss July. Plenty of time to do reconnaissance and preparation for invading the secure server business she'd left just long enough ago to pick up a burner phone to call Erika with. "This is legit." *Mostly.*

"Greg about popped a blood vessel in his eye when you didn't call in from San Jose and nobody can track your phone, which means you took the battery out, which means you're using a burner and are off-book. Where are you?"

"If I tell you that, you might feel obliged to tell someone else. Which means, yeah, okay, I'm guilty. I need to corrupt a whole lot of data on about a dozen unlinked high-security servers."

"Dude," Erika said with all sincerity, "you shoulda called me to set this up like last week."

Dismay coiled in Alisha's stomach. She took a deep breath, dispelling it. "So you can't do it?"

Erika's voice took on a note of offense. "'course I can. When do you need it done by?"

"Forty-eight hours. I can go in and adjust the hardware however you need."

"I'm gonna need an outside line to each of the boxes. How total do you want the destruction?"

"Totally total would rock," Alisha admitted, "but I'll take anything above, say, twenty percent."

"Greg know about this?"

"…in a manner of speaking."

"Awesome," Erika said, happy again. "How about Brandon? You bang him yet?"

"No," Alisha muttered, "but I almost blew him up." Technically, Reichart had almost blown him up, but she was almost certain Brandon wouldn't care about the details. "Look, E," she said, interrupting Erika's cheerful flow of chatter. "I won't be able to get an outside line for ten or twelve hours, and there's a lot of stuff I need to pick up. I'll call you when it's set up, all right?"

"It's a date."

Only a spy would think infiltrating security-heavy warehouses constituted a date. Alisha flashed a grin at the floor she dangled thirty feet above, upside down, a skylight above her feet. Well, she thought, spies and thieves, probably.

The cold suit she wore constricted her ribs,

making deep breaths difficult, but it did provide excellent traction for the leg she had wound around a taut line, reaching back up to the skylight. Seven or eight feet below her, the massive servers put off enough heat to be felt against the bare centimeter of skin that was exposed between the suit's mask and the rim of the infrared goggles she wore. Even those were cold, making thin chilly lines against her cheeks.

Directly beneath her lay a latticework of lasers, eighteen inches in depth. They scattered above the servers, intended to prevent exactly the assault Alisha was attempting now. For an irrational moment she was tempted to simply drop through them and move fast, testing her own skills against the speed of the warehouse's security and Zurich's police. The impulse passed almost as soon as it arrived, though it left lingering vestiges of delight in her system.

Pay attention, Alisha. The lasers weren't on a sweeping pattern, making caution the key.

Caution and luck. There was a patch big enough for her to slide through, except for one gleaming line that cut through it, just left of center. Alisha lowered herself bit by bit, approaching that problematic beam of light. A thousand movies showed a trick of using a mirror to fool a laser, but even if that worked, the thing that needed stealing was always under a glass case that could then be lifted, the laser uninterrupted. Films never addressed the problem of having to get a hundred-and-thirty-pound body through the area that the laser passed, at least not from a skyward approach.

Maybe she should have hired an actor to slink through the security network for her. They'd have gotten caught, of course, but it would have been a great distraction. Alisha, amused, reversed herself on the wire she hung from and carefully released the hook in her belt, suspending herself by one arm wrapped in the line.

Pointed toes, muscles stretched as long and thin as she could make them. Butt tucked tight, watching the traitorous laser over her shoulder, her smile gone. The pulley system that lowered her was thankfully silent: a single creak and Alisha thought she'd shatter and smash into the thin lines that would betray her presence. Hips past, so nearly brushing the line that she sucked in her belly, trying to eke another millimeter of slimness out of her body. Breathe, she reminded herself, but even with the reminder she exhaled what felt like the last of her air, making tiny modifications to her pose as she crept by the laser. Midriff. Shoulders. Head. Only the line and her right arm, trembling a little from the strain, remained to pass.

As Alisha's toes touched the ground, the dangling line lay so close to the laser that it took her over a minute to release it, afraid a single tremor would send it bumping into the thin red light. Her feet throbbed, unhappy with the rapidly changing pressure their injuries had been subjected to. Alisha promised herself a long soak in a bathtub when this was all over.

She could see the security camera lights, red dots making small arcs, but no alerts went up. The warehouse's darkness and her black, all-encompassing suit complemented one another as well as she'd hoped, making her one shadow among many. Alisha allowed herself a tiny nod of congratulations and slipped to the floor, edging forward along the servers quietly.

Quick puffs of liquid nitrogen from a small bottle opened breaches in the server casings without the heat signature a soldering iron would produce. Alisha muffled her work as best she could, clipping wires just inside each of the servers and twisting delicate tiny modems into place. She even fit the broken pieces of metal back into the breaches she'd made: not a perfect fit, but better than leaving small gaping holes in each server. The work was efficient, almost without thought. Later, she knew, she would find herself suddenly weary, adrenaline and endorphins that she wasn't really aware of leaving her system.

But that was later. For now the natural drugs made her hands quick and steady, and her heartbeat regular. Only if she focused could she feel the nervous burn of acid in her stomach. Only if she deliberately paid attention did she notice the subconscious counting of seconds that told her how long she'd been inside the server warehouse.

Long enough. She slipped the last pieces of metal back into place and pushed up from the floor, deliberately stretching her back muscles long. They released with a sigh and she resisted the urge to crack her spine. Being noisy and getting caught now would simply be embarrassing.

She curled her arm into the filament wire that she'd lowered herself into the warehouse with, letting herself stretch out entirely. It lengthened her body, making her feel more slender and as if she'd fit through the laser network better in the escape than she had in the entrance. Her stomach remained tight with nerves as she watched the pulley system braced in the skylight begin to reel her back. The wire seemed closer to the off-center laser now, and Alisha held her breath as she caved her shoulders back, trying to avoid both brushing the beam in front of her with her breasts or the ones behind her with her shoulders. Only when she'd cleared the lattice entirely did she allow herself a soft breath of relief and turn her gaze upward.

The pulley winched her in and she swung up into the skylight, closing it and crouching to rewire the perfunctory security alarm that had been attached to it. She pulled her night goggles off, dropping her chin to her chest with another, more exaggerated sigh, and sent a quick grin at the servers below.

A shadow reflected in the skylight window.

Alisha whipped around, hands lifted defensively. The lovely Chinese woman from the Beijing flight spread her hands in a mock-apologetic shrug, then kicked Alisha in the jaw, sending her staggering backward toward the skylight. An instant later the woman's hand caught in Alisha's close-fitting jacket, hauling her forward again. "Sorry, honey," she murmured without the trace accent she'd used on the plane. "No point in going to all that trouble and letting you blow it by falling right back through again. I'm sure I approve of whatever you did down there."

Alisha smashed a hand up, trying to break the woman's grip, and got a dark-eyed smirk for her troubles. "Uh-uh. Sorry, honey," she repeated. "Reichart's orders."

Surprise burned away under the white heat of rage, every shred of Alisha's impartiality disintegrating. She dug her feet into the roof, ignoring the pain in her soles, and dropped her center low so she could bring a shoulder forward and drive it into the Asian woman's stomach. She lost her grip and Alisha charged forward, temporarily willing to fling herself off the roof, just as long as she took Reichart's woman with her.

The other woman dug her hands into the back of Alisha's jacket, pulling herself forward with enough strength to squirm out of Alisha's grip. She hit the roof in a roll and Alisha turned, crouching, to face her again as she came to her feet. Neither moved, not even feinting, until Alisha bolted forward, grazing deliberately wide of the woman's torso. The woman spun out of the way and Alisha lashed out with a powerhouse kick that caught the woman in the ribs, lifting her several inches and knocking her across the roof. Alisha's hands hit the roof and she sprang back up, ignoring safety and the roof's angle to bunch her legs and pounce toward the other woman.

The other woman flipped onto her back, raising her legs. Alisha hit belly-first, like a child 'flying' on its parents' feet. The woman let momentum do most of the work for her, but added her own surge of strength to send Alisha tumbling ass-over-teakettle toward the edge of the roof.

Rage left her as she skidded to a halt, fingertips dug against the metal. The Chinese woman got to her feet, looking both breathless and pleased. "He said you were a spitfire. I'm glad this didn't turn out boring. Look, honey, all he wants is to have you out of the picture. You could make this a lot easier on yourself by just calming down."

Alisha put kicking Reichart's ass back on her list of things to do and scuttled backward, searching for the roof's edge. It didn't matter why Reichart wanted to stop—or capture—her. The only thing that mattered was that he did, and so the only thing that mattered *more* was not letting it happen.

The drop was over twenty feet onto asphalt and concrete. Too far, if she wanted to be able to walk away. Too far, especially onto already injured feet. She could see the Chinese woman's smugness, radiated in the way she sauntered across the roof toward her, in no hurry at all. She knew as well as Alisha did that the fall was too much to risk.

Alisha gave the woman a brief smile, muttered a prayer, and slid off the roof.

The pulley brought her up short six feet above the ground with a jolt hard enough to send a headache spiking through the back of her neck. The plummet had sent her stomach into her mouth; the relief of stopping before she splattered against concrete was almost enough to send the contents of her stomach *out* of her mouth. Alisha unclipped the hook from her belt and dropped the remaining few feet, going cross-eyed as the impact ricocheted through her damaged feet.

A soft curse sounded from the rooftop. Alisha bolted for the street, listening to the rattle of the line against the roof and wall as the Asian woman scrambled down after her. Sore feet or not, Alisha had enough of a head start that when she glanced back, there was no sign of pursuit. She ducked through a few alleyways anyway, finding her way back toward Zurich city center, and passed up the first few cheap hotels she saw to check in to the fourth or fifth. There, her jaw set against curses, she abandoned every article of clothing she'd worn around Reichart, and scrubbed thoroughly, in case he'd bugged *her* rather than her belongings. Barely an hour later, still damp from the shower, she rented a car and left Zurich. Not until she was in the mountains did she remember that she was supposed to call Erika. Swearing in German—the guttural tones suited her mood—she dialed the tech's number with her burner phone, leaving a terse, "Go for it," on voice mail. Then she rolled the window down and threw the phone out, the futility of the gesture going a long way to restoring her equilibrium.

Once on the road it was safe—*safe*! Alisha barked laughter at the thought, aware she was already driving much too fast for safety. She ground her teeth and slowed, putting the vehicle into cruise control to prevent her speed from climbing again.

Still, the road was a comparatively safe place to give in to the livid fury she'd had to cut through to escape Reichart's flunky. The worst of it—by far the worst—was she'd let herself trust him again, despite everything. Despite having seen Cristina in the square, in a place she couldn't possibly have shot Alisha from. Despite having given him enough information about Greg and Brandon's activities to allow him to concoct a reasonable story. Alisha banged her hand against the steering wheel and pressed her foot against the gas pedal, accelerating again, as if speed could outrun her anger.

Anger that was almost wholly directed at herself. There would be no escaping it, no matter how fast she drove, no matter how far. Well, if she couldn't escape her rage, perhaps she could use it. With a glance at the road signs, Alisha turned south, heading for Rome.

Twenty-Three

"I've been an idiot."

It was mildly gratifying, at least, to watch Brandon Parker all but startle out of his skin at the sound of her voice. Alisha saw him reach for a weapon and check the impulse all in the same brief action as he twisted toward her. She stood in the doorway of the little room across from the Vatican, the door pushed open just far enough to let herself be seen.

Proceed as if Brandon were telling God's own truth.

Boyer hadn't said anything about telling the truth herself, though.

"I hoped you'd be here." She took a breath. "I bet on it." The little room had been tidied since she'd overturned the table, and now glowed in the white light of day instead of the golden burnish of sunset. She'd interrupted him at some writing task. He now splayed his hands on the table on either side of his laptop, slumping like a man releasing surprise. "Sorry for startling you."

She wasn't, and didn't expect him to buy the perfunctory apology. Nor did he, but after a few seconds he closed the computer and tilted his head, an invitation. Alisha stepped far enough into the room to close the door behind her, gaze lowered and shoulders caved forward. The very picture of contriteness, she thought.

"Apparently I'm going to have to find a new safe house," he said after a moment.

Alisha looked up, dogged guilt coloring her expression and her words. "Only if you don't trust me."

"Alisha," he said, gentle mocking in his voice. "You blew up my factory."

"I swear I didn't." She came forward with her wrist upturned. "I know I'm trained to beat lie detectors, but you can test me anyway."

Brandon pressed his lips together, then curled warm fingers around her wrist, two of them on the pulse point. Her pulse jumped at the touch, physical betrayal of a different sort. She wanted Parker to be on the side of right; wanted the flirtatious game she played to have the chance to develop into something real. He cocked his head, smiling faintly at the change in her heart rate.

"Did you blow up my factory?" he asked. Alisha made no attempt to control her heartbeat through breathing, and felt it bump a little as he put the question to her.

"No," she repeated. "I didn't." Her pulse remained a little high, the consistency hopefully more telling than the rate itself. Brandon studied her, frowning, then let her wrist go as he exhaled a laugh.

"I don't know whether to believe you."

"It's true," Alisha said softly, but left it at that, knowing there was danger in protesting too much. "Brandon... "

"What've you been an idiot about?"

A thousand things, and most probably this. Alisha shook the thought away. "I didn't trust you," she said in a low voice. "I've been digging through your CIA files."

Nothing in his expression changed. "And?"

"And I can't find solid evidence you're still working for the CIA." Alisha sat down at the table, letting weariness show in the slowness of her movements. "Everything ends in a snarl of red tape. That's more than there was last time I looked."

"Last time?"

Alisha shrugged one shoulder. "After you left the CIA. Greg told me about you. I looked you up. Doesn't everybody?" She smiled grimly. "Your file just followed you through the tech industry then. Now there's red tape everywhere, with clearances I can't get through. So you're probably telling the truth." Or someone far enough above him was tangled in the Sicarii business, and was covering for him. Somebody above Boyer. Alisha had to believe that, had to trust that *someone*, at least, was not involved in the Sicarii affair. Because if Boyer was lying to her as well, she had nothing left, and that was more than she could handle.

"Which means I might've screwed you," she

finished with a sigh, "because I told Greg you were still an operative." Keeping to the truth. As much as she could, at least.

A flash of emotion highlighted his eyes. Anger. Frustration. Not surprise, though. "I asked you not to."

She shrugged, looking away."I told you I was an idiot. If he starts digging...look, Brandon, I'm sorry if I've screwed up your op. I just—all of a sudden I don't know which way to turn." That, at least, was true, though she'd chosen her path and had every intention of seeing it through to the end.

"Alisha..." Brandon reached for her wrist again, turning her hand up and rubbing his thumb across her palm. She groaned, letting herself relax a little at the touch, and heard his quiet chuckle. "Why are you telling me this?"

"Because I'm tired of lies. I'm tired of not knowing who to trust and if I've screwed up a long-term undercover operation the least I can do is take responsibility for it." Alisha pulled away, getting to her feet and crossing to the window, arms folded around herself. "Because I want to do the right thing." Because she'd told her boss that she'd act as though she believed in him, and the absolute bitch of the thing was she wasn't sure she didn't. Uncertainty came with the job; it was one of the prices paid. But standing in Brandon's presence in the tiny Roman apartment made it harder to question him than she expected. The lines between what should and shouldn't be had blurred. The things that were, were not the things she wanted. But Boyer had told her to act like she believed, not to fall for the guy.

Brandon stood and came up behind her, putting his hands on the round of her shoulders. Warmth shivered through her, making her tighten her arms around her ribs. "Is that why you're a spy?" he asked. "So you can do the right thing?"

Alisha made a sound in the back of her throat, an explosion of air that served as a short laugh. "You asked me that once before."

"And I said I'd ask again. I knew money wasn't the answer." He squeezed her shoulders, renewed warmth. Alisha nodded, relaxing incrementally back toward him. Pretending that everything was going to work out the way she hoped it would. She had a few moments, maybe even a few hours, in which she could pretend, before her job took its toll.

Me and Peter Pan, she thought sadly. *Believing in fairies.*

"I liked the idea," she said before silence had gone on too long. "Back in the beginning, it was romantic. A secret lifestyle, disguises and great clothes, cool Bond gadgets. It took a while for that glow to wear off. To realize there wasn't much romantic about lying to most of your friends or getting shot at." Nothing romantic about planning to seduce and rob the man whose arms she stood in. For a moment it struck her as funny: both seduction and robbery were entirely heartfelt objectives, for wildly different reasons. One was personal, the other professional.

Which was why they preached compartmentalization, she thought wryly. "It'd been all Truth, Justice and the American Way before that, you know?" she said aloud. She didn't get to be completely honest all that often, and while what she had to do would taint it in retrospect, she wanted to hold on to the moment as long as she could. She felt Brandon's nod against her hair, and sighed. "The thing is that when the romance faded, it turned out I really believed in all those things. I never thought of myself as being all that patriotic, but I honestly want to make the world a better place. A safer place. And if people won't talk to each other in a straightforward manner, then I'm willing to get my hands dirty to find out the secrets. Information is power." Which made her wonder which of them was more powerful, just then. She was offering up a lot of truth about herself, and so far Brandon had said almost nothing. Alisha shrugged. "Some days I think I'm still hopelessly idealistic. Others I think I'm just pragmatic. Either way, it gets me out of bed and on the road every day."

Bemusement filled Brandon's voice. "How the hell did you end up with somebody like Frank Reichart?"

Alisha laughed, surprised into it. "Opposites attract, I guess. What about you?" She turned her head toward him, feeling his breath stir the hair at her temple.

"I've never found Reichart attractive," Brandon said, deadpan.

Alisha laughed again and nudged an elbow back, trying to ignore the spike of frustration that made her stomach sour. It wouldn't be fair for him to avoid the question through laughter, the way Reichart might. Not after she'd been as honest as she had. "You know what I mean."

"Yeah." He went silent a moment, before shrugging against her shoulders. "I got into it because Dad was a spy, and I was so pissed that he hadn't told me. I figured that meant he didn't want me to be one. Teenage rebellion, you know?"

"Because you seem like the rebellious sort," Alisha said with a dry nod. The coil of discomfort in her belly settled, her confessions no longer seeming like such an exposure.

Brandon grinned against her hair and went on without responding to the teasing. "I left because governmental research and development was too slow for me, and because I could make so damned much more money in the private sector. But after a few years the money stopped seeming so important."

"How much did you have by then?"

"A lot," Brandon admitted, and she could hear the smile in his voice again. "Which may have had something to do with it not seeming as important. Anyway, it was then that the

CIA approached me again, and—I had to think about it, Alisha. I had to think for a long time. But it came down to building those drones. I'm not naive enough to think they'll just be used for peacekeeping, much as I wish they would be. I thought the world was probably better off with that kind of technology in American hands, and the truth is, I was going to develop them one way or another. It's what I've wanted to do my whole life."

"Look at us," Alisha murmured. "A couple of wide-eyed idealists. Look, Brandon..." She turned in his arms, tilting her chin up to study him from a few inches away. "The CIA's got one of the drones now. Can't you come in? Haven't you been outside long enough?" She was surprised at the hope in her own voice, making her sound younger and more innocent than she was. She wanted him to agree. The idea shouldn't have come as such a surprise to her, she knew, but somehow it did. Brandon, and even the situation she'd deliberately put herself in here, was more than just the job to her.

Brandon exhaled a sigh, sliding his hands down her arms and settling them at her waist. Alisha smiled at the touch, leaning into him a little more. "I could," he said reluctantly. "But the drone itself—that's a loss I can explain away to the Sicarii. As long as the CIA doesn't have the critical software, I'm still useful to the Sicarii, and that means I should stay in the game."

Genuine disappointment settled around Alisha's heart, making her next breath harder to take. *No going back, then,* she thought reluctantly, and slid her fingers into his belt loops, tugging at them in a gesture of futile frustration. "You're not making it easy," she said in a low voice, "for a girl to find a way to see you a little more often."

Brandon looked down at her. "This is probably the last time we should see each other, Alisha. Maybe for years. You being here at all is dangerous." Reluctance filled his tone. Alisha bumped her hips forward, nodding.

"For both of us," she agreed, then rocked back on her heels and crooked a smile up at him. Tugged on his belt loops again, and murmured, "Maybe we should make the most of it."

Brandon's grin was bright and quick. "That's probably a bad idea for about a million reasons."

Alisha grinned back. "Yeah." The smile faded and she stepped back, shaking her head. "Yeah, maybe you're right. Too much time spent trying to figure out who's right and who's lying in all this mess. I'm—" She broke off with a horrified choke that turned into real laughter. "God. I was about to say something like, 'I'm feeling vulnerable.' I think I have to go turn in my Tough Girl card now. 'Scuse me." Still laughing at herself, she turned away. Brandon caught her wrist and pulled her back, grinning down at her.

"C'mon, I've never had the vulnerability card played on me. You can't make me pass up the chance to take advantage."

"Oh, so now we're taking advantage." Alisha let laughter come into her voice as Brandon curled his arms around her waist again.

"Hell yeah."

Alisha laced her fingers through his hair and stood on her toes to steal a kiss. "Well, if you insist." One tryst, she thought reluctantly, and then she had to do her job.

Brandon lifted his hand to brush her jaw, and the last thing she felt was a cold needle piercing the flesh at the joining of her shoulder and neck.

Twenty-Four

Thick black fog roiled through the world, clogging Alisha's ears, her eyes, even her nostrils as she tried to gag in a breath of air. Paste filled her mouth, sickening and sticky, making her tongue swell and adhere to her teeth. Discomfort ached along her spine, as if her arms had been pulled out of alignment and her head was too heavy to lift.

"The part I liked best," Brandon's voice said from a long way away, "was finding the tranq dart in your pocket. Kind of takes away any guilt a guy might feel over drugging a pretty woman."

Alisha swallowed against the thickness in her throat, barely able to move her tongue. The strain in her upper back intensified as she tried lifting her head, muscles protesting and shuddering with the effort. A gong sounded in her ears, endless repetitive bongs much deeper than the tinniness of ringing. The idea that there was a word for those crashing sounds drifted through her mind, but she couldn't think of the word.

"You should have said you did it for the money," Brandon whispered in her ear. She forced herself to snap her head around so she could meet Brandon's gaze with her own forthright and angry one, except nothing happened. Her head just bobbled in place, making him laugh.

Rage bubbled up inside her, recognizable only because she knew that must be what she felt. The emotion itself was cut off, muted by the drug Brandon had slipped into her system.

That's what had happened. She remembered now, the feeling of a cold needle sliding into muscle. She wanted to be angry, but her sense of betrayal and irony were both too remote to care about. A ludicrous giggle escaped the thickness that gagged her mouth and throat: she was finally compartmentalizing. *Good job, Leesh.*

And that was another complete thought. Alisha swallowed again, trying to rid herself of some of the murk that filled her throat. The gonging in her ears faded, becoming recognizable as her heartbeat. She'd known there was a word for it. Heartbeat.

"What..." The word was little more than the vowel sound, croaked out through dry lips.

"It speaks!" Brandon crowed. She heard his footsteps beyond the heavy clanging in her ears, and concentrated, tightening one muscle at a time, to lift her head. An inch or two; just enough to prove that she could.

It did almost no good. Her vision was blurred, as if tar had been smeared across her eyes. She blinked, slow thick deliberate action; no tears came to clear away the darkness. She could see a shadow of movement, the only warning before Brandon put both hands alongside her face. "Speak," he encouraged her. "Try again, Alisha. We're all waiting."

"...we?" That was her training speaking, not her conscious mind. But Brandon laughed and shook her head back and forth with his hands. Dizziness swept over her, nausea building. It seemed to burn away some of the fog, so Alisha clung to it, closing her eyes so it would be harder for Brandon to see that his actions were helping her.

"You don't really expect me to answer that, do you? Of course not. Pretend I'm speaking in the royal we, Alisha. After all," the warmth fled from his voice, leaving cool aristocracy in its place, "I should be."

"Si...carii." She couldn't spare the mental space to berate herself, even as the sickness in her stomach burbled and pressed away more of the fog. She was beginning to feel her body again, the tension in her spine brought on by her shoulders being pulled as far back as they could go without dislocating. Rope, thin enough to feel like wire, bound her wrists behind the back of the chair she sat in. She didn't dare flex to test it, but through the fading drug haze she felt certain the rope that bound her ankles was the same piece that held her wrists. She could feel the chair legs pressing against her inner ankles, her whole body pulled awkwardly back toward the knot point that kept her tied. She forced her eyes open, staring down. Even gravity was set to work against her; the chair was tilted forward. No wonder lifting her head took such effort. Alisha let her eyes close again and her head hang heavy.

"Sicarii," Brandon agreed. "Someone had to be." He sounded pleased with himself. Alisha tried curling a lip, managing a twitch instead.

"Wha...d' youwan?"

"Your help," Brandon said pleasantly. Even through the black fog, Alisha barked a laugh, such a raw sound that it hurt her throat.

"Y'can..."

Brandon leaned in, close enough that Alisha could smell his clean masculine scent. Enough of her mind cleared to let her think, *I liked it better before,* as he said, "I'm sorry, what was that?"

Alisha lifted her head, muscles straining with the effort, and pried her eyes open to stare directly at Brandon. "You can," she said more clearly, then enunciated every syllable with all the concentration she had: "Go. Fuck. Yourself."

The blow across her cheekbone was surprisingly welcome. Pain and dizziness swept her again, tears forced from dry ducts. Black fog cleared from her vision, replaced with red throbbing agony that dissipated into a dull pulse within seconds. Through the spilling tears she saw someone catch Brandon's hand: a woman, fingers smaller and more delicate around Brandon's wrist than a man's would be. She said nothing, simply stayed his action, then disappeared again, moving so quietly that Alisha didn't even hear her footsteps.

"And here I'd thought," Brandon said nastily, "that fucking me had been your agenda."

"Silly me," Alisha whispered. There was nothing in Brandon's tone, nothing in his actions or his gaze that suggested that his behavior now was a show. Nothing but sheer disdain and arrogance. Alisha's taste in men was nothing short of stellar. She coughed out a little laugh, using the tiny jolt of motion to test the ropes that held her. Yes, no doubt: wrists and ankles were tied together, wrapped around the back of the chair. Getting out was going to be a bitch. And there was at least one other person in the room, the silent woman. Alisha closed her eyes again, trying to listen past the slowly reducing gonging in her ears.

"Whaddoyou need my help for?" She was getting more control over her tongue; not slurring the words took less effort now.

"What," Brandon said, disappointment clear in his voice, "you're going to roll over just like that?"

Alisha snorted, painful little sound that sent a spike of pain through her bruising cheekbone. "Curious." She took a slow, deliberate breath, relaxing as much in the ropes as she could. Her weight slid forward a little, putting more strain on her wrists and ankles, but the breath helped center her. The heavy ringing in her ears faded away, not gone, but less important. She heard her own exhalation, and Brandon's inhalation a few inches away.

The rest of the room was silent. No hint of another person, no warning that the woman she'd glimpsed was still there. Alisha drew in another slow breath, letting Brandon's answer wash over her. A third slow breath; another. Brandon was waiting for her response. Alisha lifted her head very slowly, paying more attention to listening than to answering as she echoed, "*Assassinate* someone?"

Brief amusement darkened Brandon's eyes. "Don't look so surprised, Alisha. Or do you really believe the CIA never stoops to a little politically motivated murder from time to time?"

Surprise, Alisha thought, has nothing to do with it. *There.* Two more people, their breathing just barely out of sync. Standing far enough away that their body warmth couldn't be felt; standing close enough together that there was no chance Alisha could see them, no matter how far she was able to turn her head. Almost directly behind her. One woman, if the glimpse she'd had was accurate. The other could be a man or a woman. It hardly mattered. Three was too many to fight, when she was starting out hog-tied to a chair.

"You've been sent out to do a nasty job or two yourself, in fact, haven't you? Tell me, Alisha. Which is worse, seducing the enemy or shooting a friend?"

Alisha brought her attention back to Brandon, still listening for any actions the guards might take, but focused on the man in front of her. He might be the weak point, especially if his harsh question was based in hurt rather than a deliberate attempt to rile her.

"Shooting a friend," she answered in a low voice. Her throat still felt thick and dry, though the fog had largely cleared. "I wasn't exactly under orders to seduce you, Brandon. More like making the mistake of trying to mix business with pleasure." She managed a faint smile. "I really was looking for a way to save you." Treat him as if he's telling God's own truth, she thought wearily. More fool she. "Just who is it you think I'm going to kill for you?"

Brandon smiled. "Director Boyer."

Despite herself, Alisha's shoulders tensed and she pulled at the ropes, more an action of surprise than an attempt to escape. "Are you serious?" Brandon only cocked an eyebrow, and Alisha let her head fall again, trying to stretch a little of the strain out of her shoulders. "Guess that means he really is one of the good guys, then," she muttered. "That's nice to know. What's he done to you?"

"Aside from head up this inconvenient investigation you're on?" Brandon asked. "Ask Frank Reichart sometime."

Cramps knotted Alisha's stomach, sending tension wrapping around to her spine and down through the tops of her thighs. "What's he got to do with this?" Everything, she couldn't help thinking, and nothing.

"He got you involved in this business, Alisha. You really should think more carefully about where you put your trust."

The stomach-knotting discomfort faded as amusement, badly out of place, washed through her. Alisha lifted her head to give Brandon a wry look. "No kidding. What's Greg's involvement in all of this?"

Disappointment flashed through Brandon's expression. "Do you really think I'm going to answer that?"

"You've answered a bunch of other things." Alisha tried to shrug and cramped the already-wrenched muscles between her shoulder-blades. "It was worth a shot." Actually, Brandon had answered very little, and she knew it. He wasn't a Bond villain to spill his grandiose plans in the moments while the convenient femme fatale found a way to throw Bond the bone that would allow him to escape.

Besides, Alisha thought, weariness making her sag again. She was the femme fatale and Bond all wrapped up in one, which meant any rescue had to come from within. "You know I'd rather die than assassinate Boyer."

Brandon reached forward, brushing her hair off her neck, and pressed his fingers against the top of her spine. Alisha felt a knot of pain there, a shape that didn't belong, perfectly square, digging into the muscle. "I know,"

Brandon murmured, "and that's exactly what will happen if you don't. Feel that?" He applied pressure again, a sharp flare of agony spiking through the base of her skull and down her spine. Alisha grunted, the only sound she could make that had more dignity than a whimper.

"You've been out a while, Alisha," Brandon went on, voice as low and sweet as a lover's. "While you were sleeping, you had a little surgery to make you more compliant. I know it doesn't feel like much, but it produces a remarkable boom. Rafe?" He stepped back from Alisha, who swallowed thickly and stared at the floor.

It might be a bluff, but she doubted it.. Whatever was lodged at the base of her skull didn't belong there, and Brandon had told her once already that she was expendable. She craned her head up, forced motion against the awkward position and the shard of pain that seemed more evident now. Rafe Denison stood looking down at her, lip curled in a sneer.

"I liked you," he said, the graceful accent gone flat with anger. "I even liked you after Brandon told me you were CIA."

"I take it we've had a parting of ways since then," Alisha said, voice hoarse. There was only one person behind her now, the woman. Too bad she hadn't known it was Rafe behind her. She might've tried taking on the three of them after all. "Something about a gun to your head, maybe?"

Rafe's sneer flashed to a snarl, the expression wiped away almost as soon as it came. He held up a tiny chip, barely a centimeter square. "One of my best pieces," he said. "Bit of a riff on the storage capacity gig, I like to think. A very small device with a great deal of explosive power. You won't believe idle threats."

"Occupational hazard," Alisha agreed. Her throat was dry, tasting of old copper, and her answers kept coming out snidely. Not the best survival technique, under the circumstances.

"Bring him in." There was an unexpected note of command in Rafe's voice, more confidence than she'd expected from the slender Englishman. A door behind her opened and two men entered, dragging a third between them. Alisha heard quick, light footsteps: the woman leaving, she thought. Twisting her whole body around granted her nothing more than a glimpse of pale hair before Brandon grabbed her chin and brought her gaze forward again. Pain lanced through Alisha's face, the new bruise on the cheekbone protesting the rough handling as much as the muscles of her spine did.

The man they'd brought in was drugged, she thought, looking as hazy as she'd felt a few minutes earlier. He was a stranger, pale-cheeked and confused, gaze dilated as he looked from face to face. Rafe held up the chip again, and bile flooded Alisha's stomach.

"Jesus, *no*, what are you doing? Rafe! Rafe, *Jesus*—!" Alisha slammed her shoulder down, using all the force and concentration she could muster. A sick pop sounded, the bile that'd soured her stomach rising into her throat as her right shoulder dislocated. Her vision tightened to pinpricks, blackness and the frightened prisoner's face all she could see. Her feet slipped free of the chair legs, the extra inches provided by the dislocation enough to begin working her way free.

Brandon cracked both fists, knotted together into a sledgehammer, across her face again. Alisha toppled to the side, hitting the floor hard enough that her shoulder popped back into joint. She screamed, short aborted sound, and lurched forward, flinging her body weight as she tried to move the chair. Rafe put the chip into the drugged man's mouth, then stepped back, smiling down at Alisha as she struggled.

"Don't! You don't have to—I'll do what you want!"

"One man's life for the cost of another's? A stranger's life over a friend's? What a good person you are. Should we believe her, Brandon?"

Alisha could hear the shrug in Brandon's voice. "CIA doesn't like unnecessary casualties."

"If you kill him," Alisha grated, "you might as well kill me, too."

Silence reigned a few seconds, before Brandon muttered, "Now that, I believe." He stepped forward to smack the prisoner on the back of the head. The man spat out the chip, coughing, and Rafe kicked it away. Alisha heard a faint click, and the corner of the room shattered into concrete dust and shards, more than enough explosive power to kill a man.

"You're a very brave woman," Rafe murmured. "Stupid, but brave. Get him out of here. Now, Alisha." He crouched in front of her, reaching down to tilt her chin toward him. The muscles in her neck cried out with protest at the movement, but she set her teeth together and stared up at him. "That chip is embedded against your spine," he said. "It will go off in seventy-two hours, unless one of us activates the fail-safe code that will prevent detonation and make it safe to remove. Do you understand?"

Alisha jerked her chin out of his grip and turned her head to stare at the fragments of concrete scattered over the floor. "I understand." She could hear the rage and helplessness in her voice. "What do you want me to do?"

Twenty-Five

"Erika. Tell me you're as cool as I think you are. Tell me you're cooler than that." Barely an hour later, Alisha sat on the hood of a rented car, both hands bunched in her hair as she held the phone to her ear. The chip at the back of her neck felt larger than it was, itching like it was trying to escape her skin. Alisha tugged her hair rather than let herself poke at it; she was afraid prodding might set it off early, and she was already certain it would detonate when it was supposed to. She desperately needed, to pull a new trick out of her hat. Rafe, Brandon—*the Sicarii,* she thought bitterly—had let her go with simple orders. Continue as you would have continued. Act as though nothing has changed. Draw Boyer out. His life or yours.

Alisha preferred it be neither, though when it came down to the wire she had no intention of being the weapon used to kill Director Boyer. Suicide was preferable.

"I'm at least three times cooler than you think I am," Erika said. "What do you need?"

Alisha pressed her eyes shut, fingers tight in her hair. "You know my makeup case?"

"I still think those golden-browns are good colors for you, Ali," Erika protested. "They really warm up your skin. I don't want to trade them out."

Alisha choked a laugh. "You're right. They're great colors. I shouldn't have argued with you in the first place."

One of Erika's silences filled the line. When her voice came across again, it was quiet with worry. "Something bad's going down, isn't it? Can you talk about it?"

"Not really." Despite her best efforts, Alisha's fingers drifted to the chip beneath her skin. They'd only called it an explosive device. She had no idea if it had more properties than that: capabilities to track her movements, or listen in on her conversations. Better to be cautious.

"Shit," Erika said. "All right. Makeup case, that's the GPS locator, right?"

Alisha nodded, forgetting for a moment that the other woman wouldn't be able to see her, then curled a lip. "Yeah. You'd talked about making some changes to it."

"Yeah. Yeah. Oh!" Erika's chair creaked in the background, a sharp noise that told Alisha the techie had sat up very straight. "You mean the route tracing option. Yeah, I totally enabled that months ago, it's a satellite linkup. Basically once the tracker's turned on it'll record the trackee's path for forty-eight hours. Then it starts rewriting over the old data. Whether I can backtrack it further depends on how well erased the old data is. Why, you need more time?"

Relief sagged Alisha's shoulders, making her want to curl up on the warm hood of the car and give in to a few exhausted sobs. "No." She could hear the roughness in her own voice as she moved her hand from the chip to press it against her eyes. "No, forty-eight hours is enough." She'd turned her tracker on after talking to Director Boyer in D.C.. Brandon had been in Zurich then, only thirty-six hours ago. "Can you send all the data to this phone's e-mail address?"

"I can share it," Erika said dubiously. "It's gonna be too big for email. Can you access a secure FTP server?"

"I'll find a way," Alisha promised.

"All right. Is there anything I can do to help, Ali?"

Alisha shook her head. "This is it."

Do exactly as she would have done had she not been captured. A very nice idea, if the Sicarii were willing to hand over the drone software, which was what she needed, if she wanted to carry on as if she hadn't been captured. Since they weren't going to, on the surface, nothing had changed. Nothing, except her plan to copy Brandon's hard drive so she could search it for clues about the drone software's storage had been shot to hell, and she still had to find the files.

She downloaded the files Erika sent, discarding everything since she'd met up with him in Rome. He'd traveled from Zurich to Milan before heading to Rome, lingering in the northern Italian city long enough that he'd clearly done *something* there. Alisha got a high-speed rail ticket from Rome to up Milan and fumed the whole way, unable to enjoy the countryside zooming by. The enraging thing was she'd put herself in this position by choosing—by *wanting*—to trust Brandon Parker. Everything happening now was her own fault, and unless she was damned clever, she'd pay for it with her life.

Brandon hadn't lingered in Milan. The data entries were time stamped and he'd only visited one area outside the airport for more than a few minutes. Alisha pulled her hood up and took buses until her GPS nearly matched the coordinates Brandon had stopped at. She left the bus and walked down the street, slowing as she realized which building Brandon had gone to. Hundreds of years old, imposing, with columns and stone arches, upper windows lined by wrought iron barriers and numerous front doors set above broad, shallow steps, it made a declarative statement against the intensely blue sky.

Alisha, genuinely offended, thought, *wait, other people aren't supposed to hide things in* banks! Banks were *her* purview, her own way of hiding her stories from the public eye. Somehow she had gradually settled into the idea that no one else would use a bank's security features, even though that was obviously ridiculous. But dammit, banks were *her* game, not anyone else's.

Except, of course, they weren't. Brandon, with the same training she'd received, probably had one key for a safety deposit box on him. The idea of finding him and asking to borrow it shot through Alisha's mind, and she laughed shakily. *Excuse me, honey, could I borrow that key? Thank you!* Brandon's reaction would be priceless.

But no, she didn't have to do that. If he'd followed protocol, there was probably secondary key left somewhere near the original site, able to be picked up in a moment of desperation. Not in trash bags, but often in the receptacles themselves, a magnet ensuring the key would stay in one of the hidden crevasses of the bin's lid or underside.

The bank had no outside trash cans, only streetlights with ornate casings older than Alisha herself. She glanced up and down the street, trying to imagine where she'd hide something if she were Brandon Parker. Her own first impulse would be the third streetlight to her left, if she'd been storing one of her journals in the Milan bank. Three was a lucky number and she was left-handed. Her *choice*, then, would be to do something else: use the right-hand side and the second or fourth streetlight. But Brandon was right-handed and would probably choose his own opposite. Contrariness in action, Alisha thought; that was practically a spy's job description.

And there. Across the street on the left, five lights down, there was a trash bin. Alisha jogged down the bank steps and ran across the street, snapping her hand into the inner rim of the cone-shaped can top.

Gum. She came away with a key coated in gum, the slimy, semi-dryness sticking to her fingers. It felt absurdly good to shake her hand and squeal, trying to get the sticky stuff off both her fingers and the key. Disgust was better than fear or anger, and helped lighten her mood for her as she approached the bank with its gleaming floors and tall, vaulted ceilings. She had better clothes for this kind of job, but not with her, and some days just being youthful and hopeful in a hoodie and sneakers was enough. Especially when the manager on duty was young, male, winsome.

He'd been there the day before, too, when Brandon had made his deposit, and fell completely for Alisha's story as she sparkled a smile, shrugging outrageously and leaned forward to confide, "Is a game we play, no? It is hide and seek. He give me the key, I find the bank. Someday," she whispered, "I hope there is ring in box, no? Maybe today." Another delightful shrug and a hopeful smile. The manager, bright-eyed with the idea of helping romance along, escorted her to the marble-

floored room where she was to wait for the
box, and hovered in clear anticipation when it
was brought to her. Alisha flapped her fingers
at him, tsking.

"Go. I tell you when I come out. But maybe
it is something else private, no? We do not
want to be embarrassed." Not that she could
think of anything that would embarrass an
Italian man, but the pretense worked, and the
manager, disappointed, took his leave as
Alisha keyed the box open.

Not until the lock clicked did it occur to her
that she might have been outplayed again.
Then the thought that she might find nothing
more than an empty box, or worse, a teasing
note struck her, and for a few seconds she sat
frozen, staring at the box like it might contain
Schrödinger's cat. But waiting wouldn't help,
and there was almost certainly not a cat, dead
or alive, in the strongbox, so she flipped the
top open in one swift motion.

A flash drive lay in the bottom of the box.
For a moment she was so convinced she had
been out-maneuvered that she couldn't understand what it was, but then a gasp of relief
escaped her and she scooped the drive up. It
looked like nothing at all, barely larger than a
tube of lipstick, hardly big enough to contain
the kind of information that she believed was
on it. But Rafe had been working on quantum
storage, and a small quantum drive could conceivably hold untold amounts of data. Either

way, it was hers now. Alisha curled her fingers around the drive in triumph.

Then she did her best girlish squeal, pulled a ring from her purse, and darted out of the bank's security room to sparkle the diamond-cut glass at the manager.

Alisha slung her purse crosswise across her body, digging her elbow against the compartment she'd stored the tiny stolen drive in. She had her queening piece now, and if she didn't control the board, she was at least in a much stronger position than she'd been in. Despite the chip in her neck, she thought. There would be no more reacting, she promised herself. That knowledge made her palms tingle, her heartbeat quicker than it should be as she ambled up the road, turning to stick a thumb out when vehicles whisked by.

She needed time to meditate, to stretch her muscles and push them to their limits in a hot room. It would cleanse her mind, cleanse her body, allow her to focus on the task at hand without the distracting thrums of fear and excitement jittering through her bones. Alisha wanted it settled inside her, a core of chi that she could access. She shortened her stride, wincing as doing so made her aware of her feet again, but ignored the throbs of discomfort and drew herself straighter, focusing on bringing her energy inside, rather than letting it bubble off under the Italian sun. It would be worth it later.

A Fiat convertible stopped and she climbed over the door, smiling. "*Nord?*"

"*A Como,*" the driver agreed. "*Parlate italiano?*"

"*Soltanto un piccolo,*" Alisha lied. Only a little. "Sorry," she added in English. The driver—in his fifties, graying, and cheerful—gave an elaborate shrug with his fingers and launched into a cheerful lecture on local history, unbothered by the fact that his passenger at least nominally couldn't understand him. Alisha smiled often, letting his chatter flow around her as she leaned back in the seat and thought about her plans.

The cheerful Fiat driver left her in Como, just over an hour's walk from the Swiss border, and Alisha picked up a backpack, hiking boots, and cargo pants to cross the border in. Her feet objected mildly to the hike, but the open borders between European Union countries were a blessing; even Switzerland, which didn't belong to the EU, largely allowed visitors to cross in with an EU passport and no further inspection, especially as a hiker. She caught a bus on the Swiss side of the border and reached Zurich after a few hours of watching glorious scenery slide by.

The hostel she checked into wasn't CIA sanctioned. Not a safe house, not secure in any way, and not, Alisha thought, watched. It catered to mostly-young backpackers, many of them carrying their whole lives in carefully-filled packs. Alisha twisted the front of her hair into braids and tucked the rest under a baseball cap, the better to fit in with the bohemian characters littering the lobby and hostel stairs as she went to check in. An indifferent young woman glanced at her passport, took her money, and gave her a key.

Alisha took the first steps up two at a time, then, hissing, went more sedately on her sore feet to find her small, single room. It was old-style European with a sink and mirror, but the toilets and showers were communal, down the hall where any of the hotel's denizens could access them. Alisha left the room door open as she dropped her own backpack and purse onto the bed, toeing off her shoes to sit and inspect her soles. They were reddened and tender to the touch, still swollen, but nearly healed. She winced her way to the basin, turning cool water on and dragging the room's solitary chair away from its desk to set it next to the sink. A few seconds of contortion later, she had her feet dunked in the slowly filling basin: total luxury. She found her company-issued cell phone deep in her backpack and put its battery back into place for the first time in days. She'd gone to ground as best she could. It was time to start pulling in the players.

"This is Cardinal," she said to the secretary who answered the phone. "Put me through to Director Boyer, please."

Twenty-Six

"You're playing a dangerous game, Cardinal." Even over the telephone, Boyer's voice rumbled deeply enough to make Alisha shiver. Though it wasn't just his voice, she had to admit. It was talking to a man the Sicarii wanted her to kill.

"I don't have a lot of choice, sir." She was taking a terrible risk, counting on the chip in her neck not being bugged as well as explosive. She'd done what she could to check: a sweep had found no outgoing radio signal. Even so, she was walking the fine line of not telling her superior that she'd been compromised.

If she got out of this alive, she was going to be court-martialed.

Alisha exhaled, climbing to her re-bandaged feet so she could wincingly pace her little hostel room. The door was long since closed, an ancient black-and-white television's Swiss sitcom creating white noise that conflicted with music playing from her burner phoned. She'd drawn the drapes over the windows and tossed the heavier blanket from the bed over the curtain bar to add another level of muffling fabric between the glass and herself. Short of leaving the hostel and locking herself in a soundproofed booth, it was all she could do to make certain she wasn't overheard.

"I think offering the drone software on the open market will draw everybody involved into play," she said, almost as much to herself as to Boyer. "It's worth the risk. The problem, sir—"

"*The* problem?" Boyer asked drolly. "Singular problem? Your optimism astounds me."

Alisha huffed a quiet breath of laughter and wrapped her free hand around the back of her neck. The bump there felt larger, possibly because she kept prodding at it. "I'm putting myself in a rogue position here. If Greg comes, representing the CIA..." *Hook,* she thought.

"Then we have no one we can trust absolutely as our man on the inside," Boyer finished. "I'll see what can be done."

Alisha leaned on the dresser that doubled as a TV stand, chin dropped to her chest. "Thank you, sir. I wish I knew who to trust." *Line.*

"I assume we wouldn't be having this conversation if you didn't trust me."

Alisha closed her eyes. *And sinker.* It was no guarantee that Boyer himself would come— she'd be surprised if he did—but she intended to walk the tightrope as far as she could. If there was any movement out of Boyer, the Sicarii would take it as an act of good faith on her part.

Assuming they weren't listening in on the conversation right now. Alisha pushed the thought away, answering the director quietly. "I do trust you, sir, but it's a choice. You initiated the investigation into Brandon Parker, so I have to believe you have nothing to hide with regards to him or any operation he may be involved with. And if I'm wrong, sir, then frankly I'm so completely screwed that it doesn't matter anymore." That was perhaps a little more honest than politeness would dictate, she thought, but with her lifespan turned down to a number of countable hours, she no longer cared very much whether she was playing by society's rules of conduct.

And Boyer chuckled. "Eloquently spoken. Where do you intend to run this auction from?"

"There's an unused safe house in Moscow," Alisha said. "Half the people involved in this are former CIA. They should know it."

"I know it," Boyer agreed. "It's derelict. Are you certain that's where you want to go?"

Alisha nodded against the phone. "Yes, sir. It feels like neutral territory."

"All right. Go through Berlin. I'll have a visa waiting for you there. Time frame?"

Alisha felt the bump at the back of her neck again. "Thirty-six hours."

Only half an hour later, she sat downstairs in the hostel at a computer barely able to run on the modern web, and paid almost thirty euro an hour for the privilege. Other denizens of the hostel kept giving her sympathetic, or baffled, glances, as if feeling sorry for somebody so old she couldn't even use her phone to go online. She couldn't blame them, but any phone she used would be tracked directly to her. Using the hostel's computer was risky enough, but she wanted to keep her head down, and leaving to find a more secure location to log on from also meant potential exposure. It was bad enough that part of her wanted to email Brandon and taunt him for having lost the drone software out of the Milan safety deposit box. Alisha didn't need to add any further complications or temptations, so she stuck to the hostel computer and message boards instead.

Almost since the inception of Usenet and other online bulletin board systems, the paranoid had believed clandestine agencies used the tremendous noise-to-signal—nonsense versus worthy content—ratio on the internet to send and hide messages to one another. Those less inclined toward conspiracy theories tended to mock them, *but,* Alisha thought, *just because you're paranoid doesn't mean they're not out to get you.*

It took several messages, linked to a new throwaway phone's e-mail address, to seed specific boards with a dribble of information here, a drabble there. One popular home gardening board carried a lot of messages from one agency to another, as if they were keeping the house in order. Then she linked to a financial advisor's site, and ultimately to travel boards discussing Russia. A few comments, nothing that would be noticed or understood by civilians, but to the right eyes her messages announced an auction for black market weapons technology designed by quantum chip inventor Brandon Parker. The location was to be Moscow, the time 1800 hours local, the specific place to be announced six hours prior to the auction.

Alisha turned her wrist over, glancing at her watch. There was time to nap before she left for Russia. *Enjoy it*, she whispered to herself. It might just be the last sleep she'd ever get.

Hours later she awoke with every muscle in her stomach clenched, an instinctive "freeze" response while she waited to understand what had wakened her. A second tap at the door answered the question, and she glanced at the clock. Four in the morning. No one tracking her with intent to harm would announce himself with a knock on the door at that hour.

God damn it. She should have known better than to stay in the hostel after using its computer to leave her trail of breadcrumbs. She whisked her gun from beneath the pillow and pressed herself against the wall beside the door, unwilling to risk a glance through the peephole. The tap sounded again, less patiently, and a familiar voice said, "Ms. Moon?"

Alisha curled her fingers around the door's lock and eased it open, teeth set together and bared at the impossibly loud click it gave. "Elisa," the voice said with growing impatience. Alisha slid her hand to the knob, inching it open, then yanked the door open with such force it banged against the desk and canted slightly on its hinges. Alisha whipped to face the visitor, and found herself looking down the barrel of her gun at a wholly exasperated, gum-popping Erika.

Erika blew an enormous pink bubble, put her finger on the gun's muzzle, and pointed it away from herself gingerly. "What?" she demanded, as Alisha fell back a step, staring. "You think somebody stole one of my voice modulators and was passing themselves off as me?" She closed the door behind her, unloaded a massive backpack onto the bed, and turned around in the dim room, eyebrows lifted in challenge. "Earth to Alisha. Hello? You can put the gun down now."

Alisha brought the gun up to beside her face, pointed at the ceiling as she held it in both hands, trigger finger resting on the trigger guard. "Erika?"

"In the bodacious flesh." Erika spread her arms and gave an all-over jiggle that would've worked better if she hadn't been wearing a sports bra under her jeans jacket. Even she noticed, looking down at the compressing fabric with a shrug. "So maybe not that bodacious. Turn the lights on, babe." She popped another bubble and sat down on Alisha's bed, one hiking-booted foot folded up beneath her.

"What are you doing here?" Alisha moved for the lights, putting one hand on the switch without turning it on.

"Dude." Erika lifted a dark eyebrow at her. "Boyer sent me to make backups." She unzipped the backpack's main compartment and dumped what appeared to be forty pounds of computer innards onto the bed. A flack jacket fell out after the parts and Erika tossed it to her. "Boyer sent this, too. Said it came out of Kazakhstan. Guess it's your souvenir."

Alisha caught the jacket, surprised at its weight, then peeled back a section of cloth to examine the matte black material beneath. Not Kevlar, she thought, or at least not standard issue. That phrase triggered a memory and she closed her hands on the jacket. "Thanks. I'll treasure it always."

"You should. So I hear you're lugging around the Granddaddy of all software programs. What were you gonna do, save it to a flash drive and FedEx it home?"

"I—"

"And even if you had," Erika went on blithely, "you might be good with the kicking of ass, but you need my brilliance to alter a complex program enough to make it dysfunctional without being obviously tampered with.

Face it, babe. You missed me. Are you going to turn the lights on, or what?"

Alisha, starting to smile, clicked the light on. Erika squinted against the light, then nodded in satisfaction and started rooting through her hardware. "Better. So I've been thinking. I'm considering readjusting the scorecard, kind of like they did with the Richter scale. Scoring people eights and nines is giving 'em a lot of credit, don't you think? I mean, seriously, how many sexual encounters genuinely rate a ten?"

"I thought they slid the Richter scale up, not down," Alisha said, blinking. "Why are you so awake?"

"Been up on the plane all night. Besides, it's only eleven, my time. Where's this hard drive? Dude," she added, genuinely impressed as Alisha dug the tiny drive out of her purse. "That's it? And they say size doesn't matter."

"I think it's using a new kind of storage," Alisha said. "Quantum storage."

Erika eyed her. "I've heard of quantum processing. So this is the new and improved memory stick, huh?" She lifted the card up, peering at it as if she could see the information stored on its molecules. "Anyway, so it all kind of depends on how you look at it, eh? The Good Friday quake up in Alaska was an eight point six when it occurred, got bumped up to a nine point three when they readjusted. So I'm thinking that if a nine point three is one of the worst—or best—in human memory, that a guy rating a seven point eight like I gave Brandon, that's really pretty good." She sat down on the bed, one leg folded under herself as she rooted through the pile of hardware she'd upended on the quilt.

"This is what you were thinking about on the plane?" Alisha asked, fighting back a grin.

"Doesn't everybody? So if we're working on a sliding scale, and I reevaluate at seven tenths of a percent lower, you end up with a baseline —my experience—as a six point eight, which seems generous enough for a college sophomore. Then let's say a guy improves by a whole percentage point over the next decade. That'd be something, wouldn't it?"

"Are you taking these by orders of magnitude?" Alisha asked faintly. She felt laughter bubbling inside, finding herself unwilling to let it break free for fear of ruining the beautiful absurdity of the moment. "I mean, isn't that how earthquakes work?"

Erika stopped hooking ports to one another and gave Alisha a look of dubious politeness. "If you find a guy who is that kind of order of magnitude better in bed than the others, either you've totally been sleeping with the wrong people, or he's got, like, a serious allergy to Kryptonite."

An image of Frank Reichart, bruised and wearing a towel wrapped low around his hips, flashed through Alisha's mind. She pressed her lips together, put the safety on her weapon and laid it down on the desk with careful, deliberate movements. She inhaled, deep and slow, pushing the image away, then fixed a smile on her face and spread her hands. "I hate to change the topic, but is there anything I can do to help?"

"Absolutely." Erika looked up eagerly. "There's a luscious German guy downstairs in the lobby. Go find out his room number for me."

Alisha gaped, then laughed. "Are you serious?"

"Totally. Go on, won't you? Please?"

"I, uh. Sure. I..." Alisha blinked and smiled, then turned for the door with a shrug. And stopped, her hand on the knob. "Um. Look, E, I don't mean to sound paranoid..."

"Yes you do."

"What?" Alisha looked back over her shoulder.

"You totally mean to sound paranoid. You are paranoid. It's what you do for a living. You really think you're going to understand what I'm doing any better if you sit here and watch me? Like you're going to see me make some kind of mission-critical mistake? You won't. You can't. That's why there are people like me and people like you."

Alisha leaned heavily on the doorknob, putting her forehead against the frame. "People like me?"

"Adrenaline addicts, or whatever it is that makes you tick. Hero complex. The whole, 'If I'm not right here right now doing this job the world as we know it cannot go on' thing. Don't get me wrong." Erika clacked at a keyboard, typing out functions even as she spoke. "Obviously the world needs people like you, but thank God I'm just the support structure. And since you can reap the benefits of my support without understanding what I'm doing, how about I reap the benefits of yours and you go get that guy's room number?"

"What, saving the world as we know it isn't enough?"

"Not with shoulders like he's got. Go on. I've got a file to corrupt."

Alisha, bemused, went.

There was no longer a hot German guy in the lobby, nor, in fact, any male of any ethnicity, hot or not. Two sleepily cheerful Nordic women nodded at Alisha as they passed through, one of them stopping to take her heels off and groaning in mingled agony and pleasure as she stepped on bare feet. Alisha smiled in return and poked around the lobby, resisting the impulse to go back upstairs. She rarely had to work with someone physically looking over her shoulder, and found it moderately annoying when it was necessary. Erika probably felt the same way, and besides, she was right: Alisha wouldn't be of any help.

Which left her with nothing to do. Alisha chuckled and avoided the TV, fully aware that anything on at four in the morning wouldn't be worth watching. Instead she pushed one of the lobby chairs out of the corner, inspecting the floor for accumulated dirt. It was carpeted and meant to hide filth, but there was no build-up of grime along the trim, so she turned her back to the corner and settled into a meditation pose, her feet crossed onto her calves.

Time drifted, leaving her alone with slow thoughts. As soon as Erika was done with her work, Alisha would pack up and leave. She ought to have done it earlier; that Erika was there at all was proof that the CIA had leaped on the chance to track her phone once she'd put the battery back in, and the posting she'd made to the discussion boards could be traced by IP. There were certainly factions that would be more interested in acquiring the drone's software for free rather than paying auction block prices. She heard a door open, but people came in and out of the hostel all the time, and she didn't think anything of it until Brandon Parker murmured, "I don't suppose you'd believe it was all a show?"

Alisha's stomach knotted around a sharp spike of caution as she opened her eyes. Brandon sat on the corner of a coffee table a few feet away, his hands dangling between his knees. He looked relaxed and casual: deceptively so, like a cat. There might have been regret in his voice, but if there was, she didn't trust it. Watching him, all she could think was that every minute she kept him talking was another minute for Erika to finish her work.

"No," she said, just as quietly. "I wouldn't. Is that your story?"

"It's the price of being a double, Alisha." His voice was barely pitched to carry; no one farther away than she was would have heard him. "If you don't trust me, you probably won't kill me. If they don't, they will. You saw what they wanted to do to that poor bastard."

"Did they?" Alisha asked, ice in her voice. "Once I was gone, did they kill him?"

His gaze skittered away, answer enough. Alisha curled a lip. "You could have saved him."

"At what cost?" He looked back at her, sharply. "Alisha, I'm begging you to trust me. Give me the software back."

"Like hell," she said mildly. "You're fucked, aren't you? I corrupted your backups and stole your originals. You must be pretty high on the Sicarii hit list right now. Why'd you bother stopping to talk?" She touched the back of her neck again, eyebrows rising a little. "Although I ought to say thanks, I guess. You wouldn't have if this thing was bugged."

Alarm creased Brandon's face for one brief instant, gone so fast Alisha almost laughed. "Or you didn't think about it."

Brandon curled a lip, shaking his head. "It's not. And I stopped to talk because I hoped we might resolve this thing with words. At the least, I wanted to say I'm sorry."

"Resolved it," Alisha said in disbelief. "Did you not put an explosive under my brain?"

"I can disable it."

"I," Alisha said with all the precision she could muster, "don't believe you."

Anger and tension flashed through Brandon's eyes. It was the warning Alisha needed: she could almost see the motion beginning in the clench of his jaw and speeding its way through his nervous system, bunching his muscles for action.

They bolted for the hostel stairs at the same moment, Brandon's advantage of a head start negated by Alisha's facing the right direction. He grabbed her pajama waistband as she gained a step on him, hauling her back several inches and surging ahead as they reached the stairs. Alisha tackled his ankle, bringing him down, and put her full weight in the middle of his back, hoping to knock his breath away as she scrambled over him. He grunted and she surged forward, feeling the warmth of his fingers just missing her ankle as she took the stairs two and three at a time.

She burst through her hostel room door yelling, "Go go go go go!" and was left gasping in surprise to find the room empty but for the flash drive sitting on the bed. A sticky note with a smiley face was pasted to it, lit by the sun rising through the open curtains. More time had passed in meditation than Alisha had realized, and for an instant she gave in to a breathless, grateful laugh.

Brandon slammed through the door behind her and Alisha snatched her gun from the dresser, whipping to face him with the weapon lifted and cocked. He came up short, shockingly pale in the warming gold light, and lifted his hands.

"Back up," Alisha snapped. "Other side of the hall. Now."

"Bitch," he said incredulously.

Alisha grinned and gestured with the gun. "Now."

Brandon snarled with anger as he stepped back, hands still lifted. Alisha saw it before he moved: the quick glance down the hall that promised he'd run for it. She wasn't prepared to fire a weapon inside a hostel, so there wasn't much she could do without tackling him and risking getting hurt—or worse—herself..

Not *much* she could do, maybe, but she could at least get in the last word. Her grin grew even more edged. "I'll see you in Moscow."

Brandon gave her a look of scathing fury and ran down the hall, disappearing from sight.

Twenty-Seven

Alisha took the train out to the Zurich airport, not because she couldn't be tracked on it, but because it was fast, and she wanted to leave Brandon Parker well behind. Besides, she had phone calls to make, and the train's noise masked most markers about where she might be. She put the battery back in her phone again and called Greg, putting relief in her voice when he picked up. "It's me."

"Alisha?" A combination of relief and anger made the soft edges of her name sound sharp. "Alisha, where the hell are you? I thought you were going to San Jose. I thought you were coming in."

"I know. I know." Alisha pressed her eyes closed, keeping her voice pitched low. No one else on the train even looked her way, the rumble of engines and the persistent thrum of wheels against the tracks going a long way in drowning out her quiet conversation. "I tracked Brandon to another storage facility. I got the software, Greg."

"What?" Her handler sounded dumbfounded. Alisha searched the solitary word for depth, wondering if she heard distress or merely surprise. "It's you," he said an instant later. "That software sale I saw on the boards. It's you. My God, Alisha, what are you trying to do?"

I saw you in Beijing. I'm trying to learn whose side everyone is really on. Alisha bit the words off, hunching her shoulders up and pressing her chin to her chest. "A copy is on its way to you," she answered, avoiding the question he'd really asked. "I didn't know what else to do, Greg. I couldn't compromise Brandon, but we needed that software. If I make myself look rogue, we might be able to get a lot more information about the..." she took a deep breath, exchanging that for the word *Sicarii*. Even hid-den by the noisy train, she didn't want to voice it aloud. "...than we've got now."

"And you didn't go through me." Ice filled Greg's tone.

Alisha winced, pulling her knees up toward her chest. "You wouldn't have let me, Greg. It's a bad situation—I can feel it—and you wouldn't have let me go into it."

"I want you to get off that train at the next stop and stay there," Greg said harshly. Despite the turmoil in her stomach, Alisha found a little smile. There was nothing subtle about the sounds a train made, but the fact that Greg had recognized her mode of travel still amused her. "I'll meet you in twelve hours. We'll figure this out from there."

"In twelve hours my auction time will have

passed," Alisha said with a shrug. "I can't. I'm sorry, Greg."

"Alisha." The commanding note slipped from Greg's voice, leaving concern behind. "You're going blind into what you think is a bad situation. We've got the software, we've got the prototype. You've done your job. Leave it alone. I don't want to see you get hurt."

"I haven't finished it yet, sir." Alisha pulled out the honorific deliberately, knowing it would blur the line she walked between truth and lies. "I still don't know whether he's a clear and present danger, and if he is it's my responsibility to stop him. And, sir," she added regretfully, "you told me yourself that this operation came from above you. You don't have the authority to pull me."

She heard the click of his teeth setting together, and could imagine his single short nod. "I'll talk to Director Boyer," he said after a few long seconds. "I *do* have the authority to instruct you to report in before you go charging into this hash. That's an order, Cardinal."

"Yes, sir." Alisha hung up and took the battery out of the phone again. The train seat's headrest smelled faintly of old cleaning solution and older sweat, a sting that made her nose prickle. She'd laid two lines in her dangerous, ugly game now. The careers and even lives of people she cared about would depend on what she learned and how she used that knowledge.

And the lives and well-being of hundreds, perhaps thousands or millions, of others she would never meet depended on her playing that ugly game, and making decisions she would have to live with, so that they could.

"It's not about my ego, E," she whispered, knowing her friend would never hear, and might not understand even if she could. "It's about caring for something so much bigger than yourself you can hardly see it."

A minute later, she got off the train at the airport, and began her circuitous route to Moscow.

Boyer was right. The safe house was derelict, empty for at least a decade, probably more. More, it had been badly used, in its day. Someone, most likely the KGB, had discovered it and shredded it from the inside out, searching for cameras and listening devices. The walls were raw now, pipes and electrical wires laid bare, and the floor was weak in spots, sub-flooring swollen with water under the torn-up carpet.

But it would do. No one would be there for the decor, only for the software she promised to sell. Alisha wrapped her hand around the tiny flash drive, then slid it into her purse. There was already a weight in the handbag, suggesting a larger hard drive might be carried there. Brandon would know better, but no one else would.

Alisha turned her wrist up, glancing at her

watch. Four hours. No one would be fashion-
ably late; there was no such thing in a world of
espionage and illegal sales. A few might be
early, but not this early. She slung her purse
with its heavy cargo crosswise against her
torso with her elbow pressing it to her ribs. It
was hard to pull a bag carried that way off of
someone, and the flexible steel cable in its slender strap made it almost impossible to cut
easily. She locked the door behind her, more
form than function and making a show of leaving the premises. If her bidders came early, a
locked door certainly wouldn't stop them from
accessing the old safe house, and if they were
watching now, they would think she'd left.

She called for a ride-share and a beaten-up
Kia arrived a couple of minutes later, driven by
a woman who looked like this was her only
chance to escape four screaming children. Alisha paid her to drive almost an hour south, all
the way back to Moscow's central square, but
got out of the car under a gas station canopy
less than a mile from the safe house. She
worked her way back on foot, admiring the
block of buildings the safe house was part of.
They'd been elegant homes once, swooping
roofs and tall windows that in some still had
signs of people living in them. She slipped
through alleys between those that didn't and
found her way up to the rooftops, where the architecture provided more than adequate hiding.
Alisha settled down with a pair of dully reflec-

tive binoculars held loosely in one hand, glad for the warmth of the summer afternoon. The same stakeout held in January would have been miserable, and footprints in the snow across the rooftops would have led any sky surveillance directly to her.

A sporty red Jetta came zipping around the corner, braking hard. Alisha leaned forward, watching it. It was too sexy for the neighborhood, though not too expensive: the vehicles on the street and those that had driven through that morning were more reserved, dark colors and bigger engines. She settled back again with a little smile. Decoy, she thought. Intended to get her attention while the real surveillance was done elsewhere.

There was no sound of footsteps to warn her. Just the hard roundness of a gun muzzle being pressed against the soft spot at the base of her skull, covering the chip implanted there perfectly, and Frank Reichart's regretful voice: "I can't let you sell that software, Leesh."

The afternoon turned sticky, a prickle of sickness washing down Alisha's spine and following every nerve to its end, tingling hard enough to make her barely-healed soles ache with it. For an instant, she was tempted to bravado, to toss her head and say, *You're going to have to shoot me, Frank.*

Except an inordinate percentage of shootings

were pushed over the edge by the victim saying, "Go ahead, shoot me, to people who weren't even trained to kill. Saying it to a man like Reichart would probably end with a bullet in her head. Alisha pressed her elbow harder against the weight in her purse and swallowed. Another chill swept through her, pushing warmth away and leaving cold sweat standing on her skin.

"Are you really going to shoot me again, Frank?" Her voice was surprisingly steady, given that her heart felt like it was forcing its way into her throat. Alisha took a slow breath, willing calmness into the frantic beat. Concentrating on the flow of oxygen into her muscles. She would need it.

Reichart breathed a laugh. "That won't work, Leesh. I'm not here to argue about who shot you. Come on." The gun muzzle didn't move. "Hand it over."

Damn. The word whispered through Alisha's mind as she shook her head, barely a fraction of a movement. "I can't get the purse over my head with you holding the gun to me," she said. "I'm going to have to move." He'd have clobbered her with the gun already, if he didn't mind hurting her, Alisha thought. There was a chance she could fight, if she could get the gun away from her head.

"Unzip the damned purse, Alisha," Reichart said dryly. "I don't need the whole thing. Won't go with my shoes."

Alisha set her teeth together, frustrated that he'd seen through the shallow plan. "It's locked, Frank. You really think I'd be carrying this around with the bag open?"

Reichart hesitated, no more than a breath of uncertainty. It was all she needed. Alisha twisted to the left, knowing Reichart would subconsciously expect any attack to come from the right, most people's dominant side. Her raised arm crashed into his wrists, lacking the force she needed to do damage: her seated position gave her none of the leverage or flexibility she could usually draw on. Still, it moved the weapon away from her skull and gave her an instant to get her legs under herself. She launched herself forward under the sound of Reichart's curse. He skittered back and she hit the rooftop with a grunt, rolling onto her back.

Reichart brought the gun around again and she kicked up, connecting her booted toe with the nerve in the side of his wrist. His fingers went satisfyingly numb, clear from their sudden splay and the gun loosening in his hold. Alisha kicked the weapon again, sending it flying, and jumped to her feet. The weight banged against her hip, changing her balance, but Reichart only circled her warily, not pressing the attack as he shook the numbness from his hand.

"Alisha, I need you to trust me."

"Is that why you had me followed?" Alisha demanded. "Is that why you had me attacked?

Why you just attacked me? Because you need me to trust you? News flash, Reichart. Holding a gun to my head? Not a good way to earn my trust. You're way too late." Something popped inside her chest, like a bit of cartilage had been held tight and came unexpectedly loose. Alisha inhaled, feeling like it was the first time in days she'd truly breathed deeply. There was a curious emptiness where the tightness had been, as if she'd held that knot inside her so long that she didn't know what to do without it.

Its sudden absence gave her respite from *caring,* so ceaselessly, about Frank Reichart. There was no room for doubt or for regret in her now, just weariness that had grown for so long that it could no longer be contained.

It was hideous. Alisha suppressed a shudder, hardly recognizing herself through that cool barrier. This was how he did it. This was how Reichart answered to the paycheck and not to any kind of higher ideal. She had never thought it was in her, the cold and calculating ability to judge a job for its monetary value, and then accept it without care for its moral code.

She didn't like at all to find she was wrong. It laid open questions about herself—and about Reichart—that she wasn't prepared to face, much less answer. Anger splashed through her, bouncing off that inner cool so easily that it made her hands cold again, this time with uncertainty about herself.

And Reichart's next words did nothing to alleviate that discomfort. "Alisha, that software can't be allowed on the open market. It's too dangerous."

She barked a laugh. "Like you care. Who sent you, Frank? Don't tell me you're here out of the goodness of your heart. Somebody's paying you. I want to know who."

He fell back a step, lowering his hands, palms out. Neither of them had stopped moving until then, though training kept them both crouched low, refusing to make spectacles of themselves against the Moscow skyline. "The Russians. You know that."

"I don't know anything anymore," Alisha spat. She wasn't even sure she knew herself.

Reichart moved in that instant of her own self-doubt. Launched himself forward as quickly and easily as a striking snake, the action so fluid Alisha barely thought to react. She twitched to the side, not enough to avoid him; the impact caught her in the ribs and sent her stumbling. Reichart rolled with it, coming to his feet. Alisha slid the purse off her torso, wrapping the leather-covered steel strap around her hand twice. It made for a good weapon, weighty and solid, and she and Reichart both thought of his gun at the same time.

He dove for it, making a long lean shadow across the rooftop. Alisha went after him, giving her purse, with its heavy hard drive inside, a powerful swing.

It connected just as he curled his fingers around the gun's butt, and even underhand on its upward arc, even with the padding offered by the purse's fabric, it split his temple. Reichart went down without a sound and Alisha waited for her own internal wince of sympathy.

It never came.

Cold all over, Alisha glanced at the sun, then her watch. It was nearly six: no time to get an unconscious man to the safe house. No way to do it, either, at least not without drawing attention. She could certainly carry him, but— she shook her head and simply ripped the lining from her purse, tearing the fabric into strips that she knotted around Reichart's ankles and wrists.

There was still nothing in her, as she looked down at the bound man at her feet. No regret, no anger, no pain. *I wanted it to hurt*, she remembered thinking as she faced Brandon Parker. She'd broken through the coolness then, but it seemed to fill her now, a scar over her emotions. There wasn't even the lingering glee of battle, just blank resolve.

Alisha shrugged, and went to finish the mission that had cost her soul.

Twenty-Eight

Almost nothing else could go wrong. Alisha sat in what had once been the safe house's study, watching the screen for the single surveillance camera she'd installed over the door. She'd made no attempt to hide it, nor was it attached to any kind of video recording system. Anyone who shied away from the camera wasn't a serious enough contender for the software to worry about. The rest would ignore it or smirk at it, as suited them.

With Reichart out of the picture, she promised herself again, almost nothing else could go wrong.

Almost. Boyer hadn't answered her calls when she'd tried putting them through. Erika had; she'd promised the corrupted copy of the software had gone directly into Greg's hands. Whether he'd passed it on to Boyer, copied or not, Erika didn't know. Alisha picked up her phone again, dialing Langley one last time in hopes of catching Boyer and learning whether or not they knew which side Gregory Parker was on. It was morning in Virginia; Boyer should be in. But Alisha only reached a pleasant-voiced secretary who told her the director was unavailable and offered to take a message. Alisha hung up without leaving one.

The first arrival, just minutes before six, was Greg. Even in the grainy camera feed he looked thinner and more worn than he had the last time Alisha had seen him, only a few days previously. Maybe serving two masters, if indeed he did, was wearing on him, she thought. She hoped so.

A trio of men she didn't know, not even by reputation, followed Greg. They were thick-shouldered and dapper at the same time. Mafia, Alisha thought, either Russian or Italian. It was a good sign to have them there. It meant outsiders were taking the auction notification on the boards seriously.

On the other hand, it would have been easier to lay the investigation to rest had no one beyond the Sicarii and the CIA responded. Alisha shrugged one shoulder, folding her leg up to massage the tender sole of her foot. *Easier* was not in the job description. At least the Mafia's arrival—and that of the next trio that followed, this time an Asian woman flanked by two men—couldn't be construed as something actually going wrong. Alisha leaned in, frowning at the woman.

No: she wasn't the one Reichart had sent after her, the woman Alisha had shared an airplane ride with and then fought on a building roof in Zurich. Alisha leaned back again, switching feet. The energized blood flow made her soles ache, but also warmed her whole body. She still felt removed from her own emotions, but the warmth began to energize her. She would need to be at the top of her game in just a few minutes.

Brandon and Rafe arrived separately, the latter with a sneer of confidence that she imagined would go over poorly with those already waiting. She wouldn't be lucky enough to have them decide to eliminate the competition, but Rafe's cocky stride might set someone against him enough to make the bidding interesting.

The thought jarred her, sending a spike of cold over her body. A matter of life and death—her *own* life and death—had been relegated to merely *interesting* inside her mind. The idea that accompanied it jolted her further: it wouldn't be terribly difficult to simply make the sale and disappear with the cash. Overlooking the minor detail of the explosive set into the base of her skull, Alisha reminded herself, but she'd never before been tempted to sell out.

Maybe more could go wrong than she'd anticipated.

A group of Middle Easterners arrived, clearly bickering amongst themselves even with the audio turned off on the video feed. They could have been Elisa Moon's employers, Alisha thought wryly, had Elisa really existed.

She turned her wrist up, glancing at her watch. Several minutes after six: anyone who wanted to be taken seriously in the bidding had arrived by now. She stood, pulling her shoulders back in a grounding tree pose, and drew in a few deep breaths, although she already felt calmer and more uninvolved than she was used to.

That's good, Leesh, she told herself without believing it. A glance in the mirror said her makeup was professional, her hair well-kept. The suit jacket and slacks she wore were too bulky, with Boyer's gift—the flack jacket— worn beneath them, but she wasn't willing to forgo its protection in order for a better fit. The shoes she stepped into were flats, vanity and an extra inch or two of height giving way to practicality. Her gun was tucked into her waistband already, and she wasn't fool enough to carry the drone schematics on her. That would leave her vulnerable, and with the growing number of bidders, the auction already had the possibility of turning into a blood bath, should anything go wrong.

Nothing would, she told herself again. She turned away from her video monitor, then glanced back again at a motion on the screen.

CIA Director Richard Boyer entered the safe house under the camera's watchful guard. Alisha's hands grew cold despite her breathing exercises.

Nothing would go wrong, she corrected herself. But everything might.

✝

"Good evening, and thank you for coming. Some of you may have heard that the United States government recently acquired new military technology in the form of artificially intelligent combat robots." Alisha handed out folders as she spoke, satellite pictures of the Attengee at the top of the materials inside them. Beneath that were a few pages of the drone schematics, and several of the software code printed out. It was an almost embarrassingly low-tech way to provide her buyers with the data they'd need to make a decision, but while the raw wires of the safe house still conducted electricity, Alisha had lacked both the time and the desire to rig a computer for her presentation.

"You're CIA," one of the Mafia trio said. He was a big man, no real tapering from shoulder to waist. His English was tinged with a Russian accent, and his voice unexpectedly good-natured. Alisha turned a thin smile on him.

"I've given it up in favor of being rich." The idea suddenly sounded unbelievably appealing, and got a snort of laughter out of the speaker. Brandon, standing behind him, looked increasingly sullen. Alisha felt as if she was standing in the middle of a powder keg. "I don't have a computer with the processing power to prove to you what I'm selling," she admitted freely. The shortest man of the Middle Eastern contingent sneered and took a step back.

"You expect us to make a purchase in blind

faith? You're an amateur and you insult us."

Alisha lifted her hands, slow movement of acquiescence. "No. My proposal is to accompany the winning bidder to a supercomputer of their own choice in order for the software to be loaded and proven. There are hundreds around the world and at least a dozen in Russia, most of which are here in Moscow. For combat purposes the software needs to be run on a computer with quantum processing power. Nothing else is both small and powerful enough. But a modern supercomputer's processing capabilities will at least prove to the buyer that the software can respond creatively in a real-time fashion to any military situation presented to it."

"You had one of those already," the Mafia speaker said dryly. "You called it Deep Blue, and it played chess."

"And it beat your best player," Brandon muttered.

Alisha stepped forward, raising her voice sharply as the trio as a whole rumbled dangerously and began turning toward Brandon. "Please. This is not a time for petty political sniping. If you can't behave yourself, I'm quite certain some of the other bidders would be glad to remove you on my behalf." She stared Brandon down until he thrust out his jaw and turned his head to the side, offering a gesture of submission. Alisha nodded and took a step back again. "As much detail as I have available is in the folders you've been given. Take a few minutes to look it over. Then, if my terms are acceptable, we'll begin the bidding."

"Ten million," Brandon said without hesitation.

Alisha wondered if it was the amount he had available to him from his personal accounts; it was almost impossible that he was bidding on behalf of the Sicarii. Either way, she snorted. "Don't insult me."

"Twenty. It's only specs, not the actual machines. Don't get greedy, madame." Greg swept his own folder closed and watched Alisha, not Brandon. His expression was inscrutable; not even she could tell if he believed that she'd sold out. Both the Asian and the Mafia contingents glanced back and forth between the two early bidders, then at Alisha. The short Middle Eastern man swore in Arabic and turned on his heel, stalking out of the safe house. The men with him followed silently.

"You have your believers and your skeptics," the Mafia speaker said to Alisha, voice still pleasant. "Did you plant them?"

"I'd have had them start the bidding higher if I had," Alisha muttered. She wished she had a name for the big Russian, but couldn't so much as think of one to assign him. Russian names didn't tend to connote good cheer, and a dour Dmitri or Ivan seemed wrong, even for her own convenience. The big man chuckled and nodded, making caution creep down Alisha's spine. There was too much uncontrolled in the room, and she didn't like it.

At least she knew why Boyer hadn't answered her calls in the last few hours. She wished he hadn't come, though a throb at the back of her neck reminded her that she'd set the bait for him, and he'd only taken it. Rafe, all but hidden in a corner, watched first Alisha, then Boyer, with avid interest, and turned his wrist over to ostentatiously examine his watch when Alisha caught his glance. Three hours, fifty-two minutes, she thought. She didn't need the reminder.

"You." The Mafia speaker nodded to Brandon. "Why do you believe?"

"Because he's the one she stole the software from," Rafe said lightly. Everyone, including Brandon, turned to stare at the Englishman, who shrugged his thin shoulders.

Alisha felt the tenor in the air change, the three Mafia gentlemen exchanging glances. They didn't need to speak for her to guess what they thought: why bother bidding, if they could simply take the creator away with them? "You are a bidder like the rest of us," the Mafia speaker said cautiously. "Why should I believe you any more than I believe her?"

Rafe shook his head. "I have no intention of bidding."

"Really. Then why are you here?"

"To take back that which we've already paid for."

Alisha thought, *oh hell,* and flung herself at the Russian.

Twenty-Nine

She managed to move before Rafe did, driven by instinct and suspicion rather than concrete knowledge. She hit the jovial Russian in the back of the knees, bringing him down with an outraged shout that was lost beneath the whine of weapons fire and the roar of a wall exploding inward. Alisha somersaulted over his back, coming out of the roll to lunge at Rafe, an instant too late. He dodged to the side and she turned with him, heat sizzling by her cheek as a laser bolt burned close enough to singe her hair. Too close.

Only one, she heard herself praying, and wasn't certain if she spoke the words aloud or not. She could feel the play of every muscle in her neck as she continued to turn, toward the source of weapons firing and roiling dust from the demolished wall. *Please let there be only one.*

She twitched her head to the side again, eyes closed this time against the brilliance of laser fire. Only one. Only one that she *saw*: she didn't dare trust she could see everything she needed to. A single Attengee drone, gleaming silver amidst the rubble it had created, was enough, though.

When had Rafe brought it in? Maybe while she'd been distracted by Reichart. Maybe only after all the players were in place within the safe house. Maybe the moment she'd announced the auction location. It hardly mattered.

Gunfire spattered, not her own. Alisha yelled a useless warning, the sound hollow beneath the hiss and spit of laser fire. The Attengee swept a circle, firing continuously. One of the Russian Mafia men dropped, cut in half, the wounds cauterized even as they were made. The scent of burning linen and flesh mixed with dust in the air. Alisha drew her gun from the small of her back and knelt on top of the man she'd knocked to the floor, shoving the weapon against the back of his head. "Stay," she growled, "the fuck down."

She looked up again to chaos. The drone stepped farther into the room, feet clanking against the ruined floor, smoke billowing behind it. Wires in the walls spat sparks, as if the drone was encouraging them to life. She could hear voices raised behind her: the Asian contingent, shrieking in fury and fear as they scrambled for the door. The third Russian, bellowing rage at his compatriot's death. None of the Americans. Alisha didn't dare look to see if they'd already fallen. She would be the drone's primary target; she was the one with the software. The others, assuming they chose not to be fools, might survive.

She came to her feet with a sudden absurd wish to be carrying six-shooters, so she might draw them crosswise and go out in a blaze of idiotic glory. Instead she fired one shot, low, aiming for the drone's feet, as she had in Kazakhstan. It skittered to the side with startling grace, blasting back at her even as she flung herself to the side and rolled across the floor.

She came to a stop at Brandon's feet, exchanging one frantic, furious glance with him. "How do I stop it?" She could barely hear herself over the cacophony in the room, pieces of sub-flooring breaking away, the walls creaking alarmingly as the third Russian fired again. The drone whipped its attention away from Alisha, blasting at the Russian with a volley of blasts that lit the walls beyond him on fire when he fell.

"You can't." Brandon's voice was peculiarly calm in the roaring firefight. "We're dead."

"Wrong answer." Alisha slammed her hand, wrapped around her gun butt, into Brandon's crotch. He went white and doubled, and she cracked the revolver butt against his temple. He collapsed, Alisha rolling out from under him just before he crashed on top of her.

"Alisha?" Greg asked incredulously. Alisha looked up from the crouch she'd rolled into and brought her gun up again.

"Get out of my way." She could hear every action in the room as if it were carried on thin wires implanted under her skin, making her itch and tingle. Greg started to protest and she stood in one easy motion, her gun pressed between his eyes. Confusion and injury washed over his face and he stepped back, hands lifted as she snarled, "Get down, Greg, or I swear to fucking God, I will shoot you right fucking now." *Alisha, Alisha, Alisha,* she thought. *Your language has gone to hell. Shame on you.*

She saw the warning in Greg's eyes the instant before he dropped to the floor, and collapsed with him, rolling onto her back to shoot uselessly at the drone. Bullets spanged off the silver plating, more than just hers: Greg was firing, too. Score one for the good guys, Alisha hoped. She twitched to the side, angling her next shot beneath the laser arm that protruded from the drone's smooth surface. A satisfying *clang* accompanied a brief shower of sparks. It wasn't quite indestructible. Not quite undefeatable. Laser fire shattered so near to her shoulder she lost feeling for a moment, the concussion enough to numb her. The drone whirred and then twisted to fire at her with the other laser. A surge of doomed triumph slammed through Alisha's belly: she'd knocked out one of its weapons. It was going to kill her anyway, but she'd damaged it.

Hands as big as meat hooks clamped on her shoulders and hauled her to her feet in one smooth motion, laser fire shooting between her legs to set the floor on fire. Alisha shot one astonished look over her shoulder to find the speaker for the Russians grinning down at her with an enthusiasm that bordered on violence. "I see you were telling the truth!" he bellowed. "A hundred million Euros!"

A hundred million. *Fuck. I could walk out of here rich.* If she walked out of there at all. "I hear a hundred million from the gentleman in the Armani suit," she yelled to the room at large. "Anybody wanna top that? Going once!" It was possible no one was left alive to answer. Alisha didn't wait for to see, diving forward between the drone's legs to grab the closest and pull it with her, hauling with all her strength. The drone toppled with a gratifying smash, firing erratically at the ceiling and walls as it went. Alisha heard a cry of pain, but didn't know who'd made it. Electrical sparks fell from the walls, making a brief fireworks display before fading out. There was wet on the floor, a ruptured pipe spraying the already swollen floorboards with more water.

The world finally slowed down, clarity of thought descending over Alisha like a gift from the heavens. She surged forward, losing her grip on the drone's ankle, and heard it clattering to its feet again behind her. She ignored it, rooting through the damaged walls.

There. A thick banded power line, running up the side of the house. Alisha shot through it, closing her eyes against the brilliant flare of sparks that arced out, sizzling as they hit her cheeks and arms and made tiny burns. She put a foot against the wall, bracing herself, and yanked the line with all her considerable strength. Brackets holding it in place popped and tore free, the line coming loose in her hand. Alisha whipped her other hand out, shooting at the drone without looking. "Over here, you son of a bitch."

It turned as if it understood her, laying off pursuit of the big Russian, who moved much more quickly than his bulk would suggest. Greg lay in a heap beyond the drone's feet, but even as alarm sounded faintly in Alisha's heart, she saw him draw a breath, and returned her focus to the drone.

It gathered itself and leaped toward her, suddenly fluid and catlike in its movements. Alisha jumped to meet it, clutching the power line. Fire lanced along her shoulder as a volley of laser blasts hit, the scent of burning fabric and flesh now her own. Alisha dug her fingers into the break in the drone's body where the disabled laser still protruded, letting her weight go dead. The drone's legs splayed, then locked in place, bearing Alisha's weight but unable to move without compromising itself.

Alisha kicked her shoes off, planted her feet in the water, and set her teeth together as she plunged the power line into the pooling water on the ruined sub-floor.

Voltage spasmed through her body, taking the path of least resistance through delicate flesh and into the drone's electronic network.

There was no room for thought or action in Alisha's mind, electricity shaking and vibrating her body at its own whim, as if it was as alive as she was. A dozen different kinds of agony erupted through her body, rawness in her throat as she screamed, cramps in every muscle as they knotted and re-knotted, unable to release. White-hot fire erupted at the base of her skull, as if a bullet had smashed through fragile skin and bone. She couldn't unclamp her fingers from the drone's body, the electricity that used her as a conduit keeping her locked in place. The acrid smell of burning hair made her want to cough, but her lungs had seized up and she couldn't draw enough air to cough *with*. Her heartbeat slammed erratically, pushed out of syncopation by the power coursing through her.

And then the pain lessened, unexpected and blissful relief in her traumatized muscles. The flack jacket beneath her suit coat, doing its work: absorbing much of the energy smashing through her. It was meant to take a direct hit, not leach power from a human body, but it worked. That was all that mattered.

The scent of burning wire and electrical fires pervaded through the other smells. The drone body above her sparkled and shone with destruction, electricity zapping over it in hard crackles and surges. The entire drone shifted, then collapsed, knocking Alisha aside as it fell. The voltage shooting through her smashed to a stop, power line yanked out of the water as Alisha twitched to the side. Exhausted muscles began unknotting, sending tremors through her. Alisha flung the power line away, trembling with effort as she pushed the drone's body away. Her ears rang painfully, a distant voice making its way through the tinny sound. *Rafe*, she thought.

Christ. Rafe. Alisha fumbled for her abandoned gun, unable to focus her eyes. "You shagging whore," broke through the noise in her ears, and she struggled to focus on the man suddenly standing above her. "You nasty little bitch. You thought you would win this. Not so fucking clever after all, are you? I still have the detonator." He palmed it long enough for Alisha to see it, then slammed its button down with malicious glee. Alisha inhaled, sharp and shaking, expecting it to be the last breath she took.

Nothing happened. Even with her vision swimming in and out, she could see disbelief writ large across Rafe's expression. Alisha laughed, then coughed, and fumbled her hand to the back of her neck where the chip had been. Blood and seared flesh came away and she laughed again. "Sorry." Her voice was hoarse and raw. "Blew out the chip, I guess. Lucky me."

Rafe's disbelief mutated into a snarl of rage. "Not lucky enough for Boyer." He turned away, stepping over the drone's dead body to scoop up Greg's gun. Alisha shoved herself to sitting, squinting through the sparks and black spots of her vision. Director Boyer lay in a heap against the back wall, one hand wrapped around his shoulder, head nodding as he tried to retain consciousness. Blood dripped down the side of his face.

Alisha lurched to the side, snatching her gun from beneath one of the drone's legs. She dragged in a deep breath, trying to gain enough strength to center herself from it, and pushed up to her knees, both hands cupping the gun as she pulled the trigger. "You're dead, motherfucker."

The chamber clicked.

For an instant neither of them moved, both too stunned, and then Rafe turned back to her with a harsh laugh. "Very dramatic, Ms. Moon. You couldn't have done that better if you'd meant to. Boyer first," he whispered, "then you. More satisfying for me that way."

A gunshot, loud as Gabriel's horn, shattered Rafe's last words. Alisha jerked violently, the sound completely unexpected, and watched as pure astonishment washed over Rafe's face. He began turning away from her a final time, the strength draining from his body as he did. His collapse was oddly graceful, a rose of red spreading over his back as he fell to reveal Frank Reichart standing in the room's doorway, lowering his gun.

Alisha gaped at him long enough that he cracked a wry grin, then opened his palm away from the gun to reveal the quantum flash drive nestled in his palm.

"You son of a bitch," Alisha said in amazement. Reichart shrugged, blew her a kiss, and walked out the door, leaving Alisha and a scene of carnage behind.

Thirty

She awoke in a hospital, hooked up to more monitors than she'd known could fit on one person, and watched over by Greg, who didn't look like he'd slept in days. His thin beard had come in scruffy and the bags under his eyes were deep enough to swim in, but none of that had hidden either the flash of profound relief when she'd opened her eyes, nor the tightening of his jaw as he chose his first words to her.

"You hid your location and your plans from me. From *me*, Alisha."

"You were in Beijing." Flat tone. Painful words to say, emotionally, but physically, too: speaking told Alisha she had tubes down her throat. She swallowed around them and met Greg's eyes mercilessly.

He looked away first. A coup-counting snarl contorted Alisha's face, and she waited, every bit as angry as he was, for him to offer an explanation. What he finally said, though, was, "You went into cardiac arrest after that stunt in the safe house. One of the Russians kept you alive. We flew you out of Moscow after you'd stabilized, but nobody wanted to risk an overseas flight. We're just outside of Paris now."

Alisha, memories of the safe house disaster returning, croaked, "What about Boyer?"

"Recovering. He'll have a scar to impress the ladies with."

"Reichart?"

"Got away clean." Greg spread his hands, lips compressed. "We were busy trying to save you."

"Oh, fuck you, Greg, don't put that on me. *You were in Beijing.*"

Strain showed in the cords of his neck again, and for the second time, her handler looked away. "Brandon's been trying to come in for months. I've been trying to handle it discreetly. I was at the Beijing facility to see how far his work had really gone. If he was going to come in with it, I needed to know how much bargaining power it would bring us."

"And why the hell wasn't I told?"

Greg's glance skittered back to her. "You'd been in contact with Frank Reichart three times in the past week, Ali. What did you expect us to think?"

"Three—!" The incredulous burst made Alisha's throat hurt and, angry and in pain, she clawed the tube out, gagging the whole way. Greg looked faintly ill. "He fucking broke my cover wide open two times in a row, and you think, what, I was *working* with him?"

"You met with him in Paris."

"Jesus Christ." Alisha slumped into her hospital bed, suddenly drained of energy. "He's

the one who led me to Brandon, Greg. He recognized something I hadn't."

"Or he planted that drawing himself to point
you at Brandon, so you would be in Beijing to
make sure *he* got out of that factory safely."

Alisha, out loud, said, "It's not paranoia if
they're really out to get you," and earned a
scathing look from her handler. "Cut the crap,
Greg. I've had enough of it."

"I am still your superior officer, Agent
MacAleer."

"I've had enough crap, *sir*." Alisha closed her
eyes and turned her face away, and after a
while—a long while—heard him rise and
leave. As soon as he did, she began unhooking
the other lines and tubes attached to her—
blood pressure cuff, oxygen meter, heart monitor, saline drip—and got unsteadily to her feet
in search of her clothes. Someone had brought
her hiking gear, and she changed into hiking
boots, jeans, and a t-shirt before worried doc-
tors showed up to find out why her vitals were
no longer being monitored. Alisha argued with
them all the way out the door and released
herself from the hospital's care whether they
liked it or not. No one stopped her; Greg had
disappeared from sight, and they hadn't put
any kind of guard on her.

Five minutes later she was in a ride-share,
heading south to lose herself in the European
countryside.

†

Alisha pushed the journal away from her and scooted her chair back so she could stretch, fingertips on the desk and spine extended long. Small pops and thumps came from within her spine, making her feel inches taller. She groaned, stretched a little more, and sat up again.

Her chronicle lay in a tall stack, quick handwriting sprawling across its pages. The home made paper had wonderful tooth, soaking up the ink from her fountain pen without smearing. Her left middle finger, where the pen rested, was ink-blotched from hours of ceaseless writing, but she had captured the essence of her mission, of the tumultuous emotions and exhaustive discoveries, and in doing so, released some of her frustration and fears. She could write — *type* — a neutral report now, and given Greg Parker's absolute fury with her, she would need every ounce of neutrality she could muster for the official account.

She'd called Erika from a pay phone within Parisian city limits, and verified that the software Reichart had stolen was, at least, corrupted. Alisha hadn't set him loose on the world with functional drone specs, which was something. Not much, maybe, but something. And Brandon Parker was in CIA custody, from whence he might, or might not, return. Erica didn't know and at the moment, Alisha didn't care.

Nor did she trust the story Greg had woven for her, but neither he nor Brandon were likely to tell her the truth about their connections to the Sicarii organization. Alisha would have to suss that one out herself, and—aggravatingly—she would have to go back in to do it. She had to regain Greg's trust, convince him that she *hadn't* been working with Reichart, pretend that she believed his Beijing story. The thought made her grind her teeth, and she rose from her chair to lower herself into a downward dog, stretching, clearing her mind.

She had traveled all day, hitchhiking, taking back roads through French villages and working her way into northern Italy. She'd rented another hostel room in Genoa, bought the materials she needed to work on her 'strongbox chronicle', and collapsed into exhaustion before writing a word. Relying on the kindness of strangers immediately after walking out of a cardiac unit in the hospital might have kept her off the grid, but it wasn't the *easiest* way she could have chosen to travel. On the other hand, Greg couldn't get much angrier at her than he already was—and the feeling, Alisha thought sourly, was mutual—and a day or two of delay before she turned in the mission report wouldn't make that much difference.

She'd been writing since she woke up, taking breaks to stretch and eat and use the toilet, and now she rifled through the pages she'd set aside, searching them as if they held hidden answers to all of her questions. The truth was they just contained the questions, written in frustrated longhand, and no answers at all.

The next chronicle would, she promised herself. Those answers would end up in a different strongbox in another part of the world, but the tantalizing hope that someone, someday, might find each of them and piece her whole story together was part of why she wrote them. Everyone, she supposed, wanted to be remembered, one way or another.

Weary to the bone, but satisfied with her work, Alisha bound the manuscript in brown paper and tied it with red twine, slid it into her backpack, and left the hostel to take a train up to Milan.

She really *shouldn't*, and knew it, but the temptation, and the amusement she got from it, overruled good sense. The day manager at the bank Brandon had stored his quantum drive in —the bank Alisha had stolen it from—was a young woman this time, not the man who'd fallen for Alisha's story about gifts left in safety deposit boxes. She hadn't been worried either way; a change of hair style, different clothes, British accent, diffident attitude, all made her into an entirely new person. The young male manager wouldn't have recognized even if they *had* spoken again.

She didn't go quite so far as to put the chronicle in the same safety deposit box Brandon had used. It wouldn't do to have him come back someday and find the account of her latest adventure. They were meant to be found *eventually*, not now. For now...

For now she had some making up to do, assuming Greg would forgive her. Answers to find, since she hadn't quite forgiven *him*. Secret organizations to expose, if she could.

Frank Reichart's ass to kick, for that matter.

Alisha left the bank and went out, smiling, to unearth more mysteries, and discover their answers.

Acknowledgments

The Strongbox Chronicles were originally written under a pseudonym, and languished in relative obscurity for reasons completely beyond my control. I am completely thrilled to finally republish these books as C.E. Murphy novels. Although they were never terribly well known, they were well-enough liked by those who read them that over the years people never stopped asking whether there would be more Strongbox Chronicles. I'm delighted to tell those readers that yes, there will be new books in this series. Not right away, because I've got a lot of other work to do, but there will be more someday!

In the meantime, these are the Author's Preferred Editions of the Strongbox Chronicles, which means there have been revisions since their original publication. Mostly I've added or fixed some things that I always kind of wanted to, because I'm no longer constrained by the very specific word count length that the books originally had to come in at. The truth is I'm pretty sure that unless you've read the originals dozens of times, or read the two versions side by side, you won't notice any differences, but I'm happier with them. :)

Thanks are still due, after all these years, to early readers Silkie and Jai, whose respective Google-fu and desire for more Strongbox Chronicles never failed to delight me, to Lance Henry and Marc Moskowitz for a little Latin guidance, and to my original Strongbox Chronicles editor, Mary-Theresa Hussey. I would also like to include a shout-out to editor Natashya Wilson, who called me a "dangerous writer" when this book was originally written. Remembering that compliment has gotten me through some hard moments over the years.

More lately, in terms of getting this book back out into the world, extraordinary thanks are due to my Dad, who minded my son while I worked, to Sarah Rees Brennan, who met me day after day so we would both put our noses to the grindstone and Get Stuff Done, to the Word Warriors (who have been there day after day for TEN YEARS NOW!), to Skyla Dawn Cameron for her AMAAAAAZING new cover art, and to my book designer, who will make the print edition of this look beautiful because she too is AMAAAAAAZING. :)

I also owe a *great* debt of thanks to (this round of) early readers Lisa Pegg and Mary Hargrove, who found a host of typos that had been introduced during edits. My favorite one was the bit where a coat snapped around Brandon's lips, and the most baffling one was where a chapter that used to have an ending just...didn't anymore. o.O :)

And lastly, of course, but obviously not leastly, all my love is due to Dad, and Ted, and Henry, who all did the happy dance with me for WEEKS when I got the rights back to these books!

-Catie

About the Author

C.E. Murphy is the best-selling author of urban fantasy series *The Walker Papers* as well as some thirty other works, ranging from graphic novels (Take A Chance) to short stories (the Old Races collections), as well as historical and young adult fantasy.

She was born and raised in Alaska, and now lives with her family in her ancestral homeland of Ireland, which is a magical place where it rains a lot but nothing one could seriously regard as winter ever actually arrives.

She can be found online at:

mizkit.com

@ce_murphy

fb.com/cemurphywriter &

tinyletter.com/ce_murphy (a newsletter, by far the best place to get up-to-date information on what's out next!)

Lightning Source UK Ltd.
Milton Keynes UK
UKHW011947091119
353216UK00001B/14/P

9 781613 171615